Christmas Town

Christmas Town

Christmas Town Series Book 1

by
Brian Hunter

Published by
Wizard Way
Rainbow Wisdom
Ireland

Copyright © 2024 Brian Hunter

All rights reserved.
No part of this publication may be reproduced, stored in a retrieval system, or transmitted, in any form or by any means, electronic, mechanical, photocopying, recording or otherwise. without the prior permission of *Rainbow Wisdom*

This book is sold subject to the condition that it shall not, by way of trade or otherwise, be lent, re-sold, hired out, or otherwise circulated without the publisher's prior consent in any form of binding or cover other than that in which it is published and without a similar condition including this condition being imposed on the subsequent purchaser.

With thanks to Gerd for exclusive cover image
Geralt/Gerd Altmann/pixabay.com

ISBN: 9798325680441

DEDICATION

This book is dedicated to those who BELIEVE; and those who specifically believe in the endurance of the human spirit to never give up on dreams that will be turned into reality.

CONTENTS

1	The Bully	9
2	The Painting	31
3	The Article	49
4	The Donations	62
5	The Forgiveness	73
6	The Meeting	89
7	The Mogul	106
8	The Thanksgiving	124
9	The Haircut	142
10	The Opening	155
11	The Interview	169
12	The Mayhem	183
13	The Tree	195
14	The Parade	208
15	The Hug	226
16	The Gift	237
	Acknowledgments	255
	About The Author	256
	Also by, Brian Hunter	257
	Living A Meaningful Life Series Synopsis	259

CHAPTER ONE
The Bully

IT was the first part of September, when the wind whips around in circles, giving off an inviting chill that somehow warms the soul. The sun was glistening through the trees, which were losing their leaves at a rapid rate that could be observed on a daily basis if one took the time to notice.

Change was in the air, and it was that time of year when unspoken emotions would stir within everyone who lived in our area of the world. There was no place that exemplified and magnified all of this more than Vermont.

I lived in a town, which I suppose would be called a small city. I say "city" loosely, but we had a downtown, and there were brick buildings lining our Main Street; thus, why I called our 'town' a city. But it felt like a town. This town will remain nameless for now, because the story I am about to tell could happen in any town. The name is not what matters. What matters most in any town is the spirit of its people, and how much those people choose to invest of themselves into their town.

I only mention that this story took place in Vermont because it's important to understand why Vermont was about to become the official home of Christmas. And it was all to begin in my own hometown. But any other town, city, state, or province could do the same.

Although I was only 12 years old at the time, I felt a spirit within me that was way beyond my years. My inner soul felt as if it was an ancient being with layers of hidden wisdom; but my physical body was of a boy who could easily remain invisible to almost everyone, and usually did.

I lived with my single mom in an old and simple apartment building on a beautiful working-class residential street which was lined with giant maple and oak trees. Even though I came from very meager means, I didn't feel poor. I felt "normal," because I thought that what I was living was 'normal.' Yes, I noticed many of my school mates living in larger and nicer homes; and I saw them being driven around in expensive luxury vehicles; but for some reason I never put two and two together. I accepted my circumstances as being mine, and being *my* 'normal.'

My mother always seemed busy and somewhat stressed, but I always had what I needed. However, our circumstances dictated that I never got to spend much personal time with my mother. Since she was always busy, I was expected to stay out of her way so that she could be 'busy' in an efficient manner.

Despite this, my fond memories of my mom usually involved the warm smells of her wholesome home cooking. Whether it be stew, pie, or cookies, my mom was always cooking something. The smells of what she was cooking were often a good indicator of not only what was for dinner, but also what time of year it was.

The delicious aroma of my mom's "lumberjack cookies" (molasses cookies), always indicated that Fall was upon us. Those cookies were my favorite part of Fall. I waited all year for them. I would stalk the kitchen when I knew they were in the oven so that I could be present the moment they were taken out of the oven. Although my mother hoped the cookies would be left alone to exist for a period of time, I usually interfered with that by immediately eating the first one, and then gorging myself with as many as possible before being yelled at to stop.

My homelife consisted of watching my mother cook and do house chores; and me doing my homework in my room. Although I was ordinary in every way, I was at least blessed with being a good student. I say "blessed" because I didn't have to try. I was naturally good at school. It may have been the only thing I was good at, so I felt obligated to appreciate that one talent.

I was terrible at sports, and pretty much everything else. It wasn't for lack of trying, though. My mom had put me in swimming lessons, trumpet lessons, and a baseball league. I sucked at all of it. She tried to put me into a basketball league, but I was too shy to even go out onto the court and try.

And I wasn't just allergic to sports. I was also very anti-social. I had always been a quiet kid who lacked any desire to play with other kids. I was a loner. I was the type of kid who could play outside for endless hours all by myself. This was because I loved the outdoors! I just didn't like being outdoors with others, or doing anything of great substance while outdoors. I only wanted to just "be," and that's it.

So yes, I was the classic definition of an introvert. But part of that was a lack of confidence, and the fact that I was shy. Perhaps those are the traits that make an introvert in the first place. But maybe I shouldn't have said 'lack of confidence.' I had lots of confidence in myself. I just didn't have confidence to step forward and speak up in front of others. But within myself, I had the confidence to know that I was capable of special things. What those 'special things' were, I had no idea.

All I knew was that I had my school life, and I had my home life. School consisted of navigating the other kids, and trying to keep up my high standards of good grades. My home life consisted of being alone, but I don't mean that in a bad way.

When I wasn't in my room doing homework, I was outside taking in nature; or I was riding my bike to some kind of destination of adventure. That usually meant going to the nearby park, where I could feel even more alone; or I would ride my bike downtown, where I could feel like I was part of life.

Although the downtown wasn't much, it had a donut shop, a music store, and plenty of other quirky shops that sold weird and quirky things. Because yes, this was Vermont after all, and many of our retail shops screamed offbeat Vermont cultural quirkiness loud and clear.

And although the "retail choices" I just mentioned might seem sparse to most, they were adequately plentiful for me. I was very content to buy some donuts and then spend a half hour eating them in the back parking lot. Or, I could spend an entire hour browsing through the music store looking at all of the neat stuff, for which I had no money to buy.

Another favorite pastime was to wander aimlessly through the local independent bookstore downtown. So many books! Nothing but books! Who wrote all of those books? How did they know what they needed to know in order to write those books? The diversity of material and choices fascinated me, as did my imagined images of how weird (in a good way) those authors must have been to write those books.

I would often read several pages in one book, and then pick up another and do the same. I felt I would never have the ability or inclination to write a book, but for whatever reason, I was still interested and intrigued by it.

But with all of that said, there was a major problem plaguing our downtown which I didn't think much about at my young age. The problem was that the only people in the stores were adults or kids like me who were just browsing around, but not buying anything.

Although I didn't recognize the entire situation for what it was at first, the stores were struggling, our downtown was dying, and our entire town and state were in decline. The economic environment back then was not good, and it seemed like our town and state were spiraling deeper into the abyss than most other places in the country.

And if that wasn't bad enough, I had heard on more than one occasion people referring to our town in a very derogatory way, in relation to the rest of the state. Even though this was a jab at our town and not me personally, it always made me feel bad. I took it personally.

And in my quiet moments, I wondered if it was true.

I used to pull back a few feet in my mind to try and look at the situation objectively. What I saw when I did this was an old little city with dark and decaying brick buildings, along with some rotting wooden ones. I saw old and dirty black light poles and railings. I saw lots of vacant storefronts, some of which had been vacant for years. I saw lots of cars driving *through* downtown, but nobody stopping and going into the stores.

Basically, I saw a rotting, dirty, and gritty downtown with stores that seemed to stay open even though nobody was inside. Yeah, it was depressing. Yet, I still valued and treasured those stores, and our Main Street was the only downtown street I had ever known. It was home. *MY* home.

However, being a 12-year-old kid, I still clung to the illusion that what I was seeing was 'normal.' I failed to recognize that I was living in a depressed area, which was totally lacking in any growth. No business growth, no income growth, and no development growth. A third of the population was deemed as "disadvantaged," while the next group above them would have only been deemed as "lower middle class." The tiny "upper class" in our community were the doctors, dentists, and some business owners or top executives with the banks in the area. But *our* "upper class" was likely equivalent to "financially secure middle class" in other cities.

You'll notice that I didn't include the store owners in that top group. That's because the store owners were often on the verge of shutting down, and many had been riding that edge for many years, or even decades. That is why most of the store owners worked at their own shops on a fairly full-time basis.

What I also didn't realize at that age, was that behind the dirty doors and windows within our town was a subculture of substance abuse and crime. It was the underbelly of the community, and proof that our town was dying a long and slow death. Although our city was still considered to be "safe" by most, there were still plenty of news stories of robberies and drug busts. We had our own police department, and they appeared to always be busy.

I guess if a person only looked at the ugly side of things, it was easier to see why our town had been assigned the derogatory monikers that I refuse to say, but had heard often. However, it was home, and I was proud of my home, even if some might have said there was nothing to be proud about.

As for my school, I loved my school, and I loved my teachers. I was in sixth grade, and thus, still in elementary school. My school was one of several, and although it was old, it was very "adequate."

Nobody ever said much about the elementary schools. Most of the attention was on the high school, where you would hear mixed reviews, both good and bad. The kids who went to the high school seemed to like the school, but if you did research on the school, it would be listed as an underachieving school compared to others. It was not listed as one of the best schools in the state. Were the other schools really that much better? What made them better, I wondered?

It's always hard to wrap your mind around such things when your hometown is the only place you've ever known. You consider everything surrounding you to be "normal," even if the outside objective facts indicate that what is surrounding you is "below normal."

Regardless of that, I had fully accepted my reality for what it was. And guess what? All that really mattered was that I could smell the air of Fall and my mother's lumberjack cookies. Thus, all the other stuff didn't matter. Well, it didn't matter quite yet; but it was about to matter more than I could have ever imagined.

But with all of that said, I have a confession to make. However much I loved Fall and my mother's Fall cookies, the cool September days made me think of something else deep inside. They made me think of Christmas.

For me, Fall signaled the approach of Christmas. Christmas was my favorite holiday of the year. I tried not to talk about it much because I didn't want others to pick on me. But the truth was that I was a true romantic when it came to Christmas.

I believed that Christmas was the one magical time of year. And I'm not just saying that. I really believed that to the depths of my soul. I still do.

I felt that Christmas was the one time of year when impossible things could be made possible, and come true. So for me, Fall meant the excitement of Christmas being right around the corner. We just had to get through Halloween and Thanksgiving. Who cares about those holidays, anyway? They are just appetizers for Christmas.

Halloween was when all of the other kids at school would have fun while I didn't; and Thanksgiving was just a dinner rehearsal for Christmas. If it had been up to me, I would have wiped out those other holidays and started Christmas season on September 1st. But since I wasn't in charge, I had to be patient and wait.

Fortunately, and unfortunately, I had plenty of things to distract me while I waited for Christmas season to arrive. The biggest among them was school. I sigh while saying that because although I did well academically, I struggled socially; and that fact was painfully evident to most. Unfortunately for me, another round of that painful nonsense was about to begin.

It was the first Tuesday after Labor Day, and that meant it was the first day of school. For me personally, it meant my first day of sixth grade. I was finally moving up in the world. One more year, and I would be in junior high school, or as some call it, 'middle school,' or as some call it, seventh grade. But for now, 'sixth grade in elementary school' would have to do.

After a fairly lonely and boring summer, I was eager to get back to school, despite the frequent social torture that might result. It wasn't that I liked schoolwork, but more that I was craving some social interaction, even though I wasn't social and didn't like people. And it wasn't that I didn't like people, but more that people didn't like me. And because of that, I didn't like them, even though I wished they liked me, and I didn't know why they didn't. It was complicated.

And now that I was in sixth grade, I was beginning to see endless additional complications that went along with my age. I was beginning to fully see the world around me, instead of only existing in my own tiny bubble. Not only that, but there was the added tension of boys starting to interact with girls in mischievous ways.

But that too, was complicated, because all of the kids seemed different, and on different timelines and different agendas. For some of the more confident boys, it was as if they woke up one morning and were on the hunt to see how many girls they could get to like them. But for boys like me, I was still shy and cynical of everyone, most especially girls; and my policy of avoidance would continue, even though I felt the same changes going on within me as the rest of the boys did.

However, my policy of avoidance had one exception to it. I would be remaining friends with a girl named Sally Martins. I had been friends with Sally since third grade. She was a girl, but I didn't think of her as a girl. I just thought of her as 'Sally.' We were buddies, and I was hoping that the new 'complications' wouldn't change that.

Well, as the bell rang to signify the start of the first school day, our sixth-grade teacher, who would be new to all of us, started yelling at everyone to be quiet. And he didn't stop there. He started barking out commands for us to put both of our hands on our desks. Then to sit up straight. Then to look forward. Were we in the military now? It seemed like it.

I was already having thoughts about how this year was going to suck if this is how this guy was going to be. He was known as Mr. M, because his name was too much for most kids to pronounce. He looked really young, and I guessed that he might be fresh out of college. Maybe that's why he was so strict? Because he was overly nervous?

I very quickly surmised that he was using psychological tricks to take full control of the classroom right up front on Day One. A confident and experienced teacher doesn't have to go overboard doing that. But perhaps a brand-new teacher needs to exert their authority more forcefully in order to feel that they have control over the kids?

I'll tell you what though; this school year was going to be WAY DIFFERENT than my previous school year. For fifth grade, I had the BEST TEACHER EVER. His name was Mr. Bedard, and he turned out to be my favorite teacher of all time; and that moniker still stands today. Mr. Bedard, or 'Mr. B,' was the teacher that showed me that I could be 'more;' and he did all of the right things to inspire me to rise to the level of my true potential, such as it was. If we are lucky, we all have that ONE teacher who does this for us. For me, it was Mr. Bedard.

But this Mr. M guy was going to be different, I guess. Hopefully, he would learn to chill out over time.

But that aside, the rest of the morning went smoothly, and I concluded that I would be able to follow along with Mr. M perfectly fine, and hopefully keep up my top standard of grades which I was able to establish the previous year.

Before I knew it, it was time for recess. All of the kids rushed outside, while screaming loudly in excitement. I silently and calmly followed them out. I was not a 'screamer' nor was I a 'yeller,' nor did I even speak loudly, or speak much at all. It was sort of like being a 98-year-old child. It made me different, made me feel different; and feeling different made me feel more isolated.

If I am to be completely honest, I would have preferred to enjoy my recess with the teachers, instead of the other kids. But that would have been weird, so I usually spent recesses alone, or with Sally. Sally was the same as me. She didn't get caught up in all of the "reindeer games" and drama in which the other kids engaged.

Sally was a bit of an outsider like me, and she also tended to be on the quieter side, which was a primary reason why I liked her.

Well anyway, once outside on the playground, I started taking in the fresh air by looking up into the sky, and then all around me. I spotted my ever-familiar bench that I liked sitting on during recess in years past. I made a beeline right for it.

As I was walking there, I noticed Sally watching me from a distance. I think she was deciding whether or not she should follow me over, or to talk to me at all. Like me, she sensed the new complications involved with being in sixth grade.

I tried to answer her inner questions by looking over at her and motioning for her to follow me over to the bench. She immediately accepted my invitation and strolled over.

Once I reached the bench, I took a seat. Sally quickly joined me, and she sat down a couple of feet from me. That was a safe enough distance to not ignite random thoughts from the other kids, yet close enough for us to talk.

Like me with her, I didn't think that Sally found me very interesting from a romantic point of view. We were just friends.

After we had taken our seats, there was an awkward silence, and then I said, "Well here we are. Another year and another grade higher."

She quipped, "Yep."

I replied, "What do you think of our military-drill-instructor teacher?"

She quipped, "He's mean."

I laughed. This was why I liked Sally. She always said it like it was, and always in an authentic way.

I replied, "I don't know if he's mean. I think he's just nervous. He seems inexperienced, and I bet he's more scared than we are. I bet he settles down after a few weeks in the job."

She responded, "You're usually right, so hopefully you will be right about this, also."

After a pause, she added, "It's like you can read people's minds. How do you do that?"

I chuckled, and replied, "Probably because I've spent my entire life only watching people. I have no life of my own, so I focus on everyone else."

She laughed and smiled. I think it was remarks like that which made Sally like me.

After some silence, I said, "Was your summer good?"

She responded, "It was okay, but I think bad things are coming."

I replied, "What do you mean?"

She responded, "I spent all summer listening to my parents talk about what they are going to do about our store. I guess it's not doing well. I've heard them talking about how it might have to close, and we would have to move."

I should mention that Sally's parents owned a gift shop called Martins Gifts. It was a little shop located downtown on Main Street. They sold cards, candles, magazines, books, home decorations, and all kinds of little gift items. It was the kind of store that had interesting stuff in it, but nothing anyone really needed. Even so, the store had been a permanent institution in our town for as long as anyone could remember.

My stomach sank in response to Sally's news. If Sally moved away, I would literally have nobody. Yeah, I was friends with some of the other kids, but nobody that I actually had substantial conversations with like I did with Sally.

I replied, "I was downtown quite a bit this last summer. I don't think I saw many people going into your dad's store."

She responded, "Yeah, I heard him telling my mom that traffic has been way down. When he says that, he means the number of people walking into the store. And I guess sales are down even more than that. My mom is trying to get another job, but that hasn't worked out yet. I know they're behind on their bills because I heard them talking about it when they didn't think I was listening. I'm scared."

After she said those last two words, I looked over and made direct eye contact with her.

I didn't know what to say, but I replied, "Don't be scared, Sally. Something will work out. Your family's store has always been there. Something needs to work out so that it stays."

Sally looked down, and I wondered if she might cry. I felt stupid, and I felt like what I said was stupid and weak.

I reached over and touched her knee as a way of reengaging with her while also comforting her.

She looked over at me, and I said, "Maybe there is something I can do to help."

That response of mine was much stronger, and it got her attention. She seemed surprised that I might be able to offer any help at all. She wasn't alone in that assessment. I ALSO wondered what help I could possibly offer. What in the world was I saying, and why in the world did I say it? Did this mean that whenever I gave a weak response to someone, I would then follow it up with a lie?

After a pause, she responded, "What can *YOU* do?"

And that right there was an excellent question which had no good answer. Fortunately, and unfortunately, I didn't have to answer it.

All of a sudden, a group of four boys came over, and one of them said, "HEY, LOOK AT MR. MATURE OVER HERE WITH HIS GIRLFRIEND!!"

The boys laughed. I obviously knew the four kids well. The ringleader, Jeremy, was somewhat of a bully. But he wasn't a big mean stupid bully. He was one of the 'cool kids' who was a bully because he could be. There was nothing about him that a person could pick on. He was good looking, smart, rich, and had lots of friends. He was also an a-hole. But he got away with it because of everything I previously mentioned. He was considered to be really popular; and therefore, other kids followed him around because they wanted to be popular also. The other kids were not significant to the situation or the conversation. They were only there because Jeremy was.

While they were all laughing at me and Sally was hiding in her turtle shell, I quipped, "She's not my girlfriend!"

I noticed Sally flinch, and I realized that even though she was not my girlfriend, I had likely hurt her feelings by my reaction.

I corrected myself, and exclaimed, "SHE'S MY FRIEND!"

Jeremy responded, "We saw you put your hand on her knee; and I bet you put your hand on something else when we weren't watching. So, she's your girlfriend!"

I replied, "No, she's not! We're just friends!"

He responded, "Not from what we saw. But then again, I'm not sure why she would want YOU. I see you're wearing last year's clothes and that you're expecting a flood any minute now."

All of the boys busted out laughing while pointing at my pants, which I guess were slightly too short, although not by much. It was like if your pants were a half inch too short, everyone noticed. I guess this is why some kids wore jeans that went down past their shoes and touched the ground.

Then, as a way of ensuring that his friends would never stop laughing at me, Jeremy said, "And I bet your mother cut your hair. It shows."

They all kept laughing. I looked down and was turning red. The truth was that my mother DID cut my hair. I knew that my mom did a crappy job, but I didn't think it was that noticeable or such a big deal.

Sally remained in her turtle shell.

Once Jeremy saw that I was completely embarrassed and humiliated, he knew that he had won and could leave. He started backing away while still laughing at me, and his friends followed suit.

Just then, the recess bell rang, signifying that it was time to go back inside. I stood up from the bench and looked over at Sally. She stood up, but didn't make direct eye contact with me.

I said, "Sorry."

I wasn't sure why I said that. What was I sorry for? Was I sorry for her family's struggles? Was I sorry for her having to sit through the humiliation that we (I) had just endured? Or was I sorry for so bluntly exclaiming that she wasn't my girlfriend, even though she wasn't my girlfriend?

Perhaps I was sorry for all of the above. Her reaction was to give me a nod without looking at me.

Crappy start to the school year, for sure.

We all rushed back inside the school building and resumed classes for the day. There were no more incidents that day, and Sally didn't look at me again for the rest of the day, either.

Time passed, and it was a new day in a different month, but the same old crap. We had dipped into October; the crisp air was getting sharper, and so was the B.S. I had to put up with at school.

I want to make it clear that academically, I was doing great. Our teacher, Mr. M, had lightened up a bit, and he had come to realize that I personally was not one of the bad guys. He saw that I was a good student, and he seemed to leave me alone for the most part.

But someone who wasn't leaving me alone was Jeremy, along with his friend group of stooges, who I don't think truly believed in all of the crap they were dishing out against other kids, but they went along with whatever Jeremy wanted them to do or say.

I was sitting outside alone on the bench during recess one day, and

Jeremy with his little group of sycophants came walking over to me while laughing about something (me).

Sally had learned that it was safer to avoid being seen with me too often. She started hanging out with her own friends, which I totally understood and was fine with. I knew that Sally liked me and would be there for me if I asked her to be. But I never asked her to be because I didn't want to pull her into the dark abyss with me. I liked her too much to do that to her.

I braced myself for the impending clash with Jeremy. Once he got to me at the bench, he said, "It must be lonely for you this year. You are no longer the teacher's pet like last year."

He continued, "So, tell us. What's it like to be the loser-kid now? You seem like you are doing a great job at it."

His friends all laughed in response to his comment, even though it wasn't very funny. And I mean that literally. It simply wasn't funny. I actually made a point of looking at the other kids and rolling my eyes at them as a way of signaling to them that I recognized how stupid his comment was. I was hoping that some of them might start to see reality, and realize that Jeremy wasn't all that he thought he was cracked up to be.

I looked at Jeremy, and replied, "I still get better grades than you."

That's all I said. I probably shouldn't have said that, because it made me sound just as arrogant and obnoxious as Jeremy, but I wasn't going to sit there and not defend myself in some way.

Jeremy knew I was right, and that made him mad. I could see him turn a slight shade of red.

He responded, "At least I'm not a dork like you riding around on an old bicycle wearing clothes made for a fourth grader."

His friends laughed, and Jeremy turned from red back to white again. He knew that his torpedo had hit successfully. I guess what he said was true. And that's the problem with being poor, or short, or having glasses, or whatever. There comes a point when the truth can't be denied, and that's when it hurts the most. There is nothing we can do about the truth. It is what it is.

I just shrugged and started turning red. What else was I supposed to say or do? Yes, I was poor. I had an old bike. I didn't have nice clothes. That's just how it was for me.

Once again, Jeremy saw that I was sufficiently humiliated, and he knew his work was done.

He said, "Get used to being the loser, Loser."

He then walked away while he and his friends were laughing at me.

After Jeremy and his friends had left the scene, I noticed that Sally had been watching from afar. As soon as she saw me looking at her, she glanced away as a way of pretending that she didn't see what happened.

As I said, I didn't blame her for keeping her distance. I didn't want her to be dragged into my humiliation, anyway. I knew that she had her own problems to deal with. And in fact, that reminded me of something. It reminded me of what I had said to her about her family's store. I had offered to help in some way, even though there was literally nothing I could do to help. Or was there?

That following weekend, I decided to ride my bike downtown. My mission was to first go to the donut shop and have a jelly-cream-filled donut. But then I was going to go to Martins Gifts, and take a look around. I didn't have money to buy anything, but I wanted to see what I could see.

After I enjoyed my donut, I rode my bike to the front entrance of the gift shop, and parked my bike near the door. Like all other store entrances downtown, everything was dirty, dusty, grimy, and had old, worn paint on the doors and storefront window sills and frames. It was the type of thing that nobody noticed because everyone had become used to it. All of the stores looked old, gross, and like crap. That was downtown.

I walked into the store, and reminded myself to keep my hands to myself. It was the kind of store that if your hand swept around the wrong way, you might end up pushing something onto the floor and breaking it. I didn't have any money to buy anything I broke. And yes, back then the policy was, "If you break it, you buy it."

I carefully looked around at all of the items in the store. They were mostly little decorative things sitting on glass shelving. The glass was clean, and all of the items looked nicely displayed. Other than the fact that everything in there was useless, I couldn't find anything wrong with the store. Thus, I still couldn't think of anything which I could help with.

However, I couldn't help but notice an absolutely stunning, beautiful, ornate, and most certainly insanely expensive glass looking model of a sleigh with Santa inside it, with two reindeer pulling the sleigh. And yeah, I know there are more than two reindeer, but I guess this was meant as a decoration of manageable size to display, so it only had two reindeer, side by side.

I was fascinated by it for some reason, and I started staring at it. I couldn't get a close look at it because it was displayed on a high shelf out of reach.

While I was in a hypnotic trance admiring the glass Santa-sleigh-with-reindeer decorative piece, Sally's dad walked up from behind me and said, "May I help you find something, young man?"

I knew who *he* was, but he didn't know who *I* was.

I replied, "How much is that glass Santa sled and reindeer thing up there?"

He gave me a fake smile that someone would give an idiot asking about something which they knew absolutely nothing about.

He responded, "That's not glass. That is crystal with real gold plating on the edges of the sleigh. And it's priceless, and therefore not for sale. I just have it up there for display as a decoration. But can I interest you in something else?"

I replied, "No, Sir. I was just looking around. I'm friends with Sally."

Sally's dad, Mr. Martins, got an intrigued look on his face, and responded, "Oh yeah? What's your name?"

I told him.

He got an immediate smile, and responded, "OH YES! I've heard your name plenty of times. Indeed. Well, it's nice to meet you, young man."

He then extended his hand for a handshake. I could tell that he was being genuine; and all of a sudden after knowing who I was, he really did like me. It was no longer a fake sales act.

Thus, he tried again, but this time he meant it. He said, "Well, how can I help you? If you need something specific, I might be able to give you a discount depending upon what it is."

I replied, "No, Sir; I don't have any money."

I could see disappointment in his eyes. I knew that my reply to him was dumb, even if it was the truth.

I quickly added, "Sir, I promised Sally that I would try to help somehow. So, I'm here just looking to see."

He looked at me in confusion, and responded, "To see what? Help how?"

I sighed in frustration because I knew that I wasn't being clear, but I was also digging a hole for myself, as far as having to say that I knew their store was struggling.

I replied, "I promised Sally that I would try to help your store somehow."

Mr. Martins smiled in amusement, but in a good way. He obviously knew I was useless, but I think he felt it was cute that I was making the gesture.

After a moment, he responded, "That's nice of you, young man, but I don't think there is anything you can do for us, and I'm afraid I don't have any money to hire you for anything. I'm sorry."

I replied, "No, Sir; I'm not looking for a job. I was just looking to help."

He looked at me in more confusion, but this time with some intrigue mixed in. He just shook his head in the negative.

I was getting embarrassed. I was listening and watching myself from a third-person point of view, and I knew that I was sounding like an idiot. I decided that I had better give it up.

I said, "Okay, Sir; I'm sorry. I will try to think of something. Sorry to bother you."

I could tell that Mr. Martins felt bad for making me feel bad, even though he had done nothing wrong to make me feel bad. I made myself feel bad by being an idiot with no plan.

I waved, turned around, and walked toward the door.

He quipped, "Nice meeting you, young man!"

I replied, "Thank you, Sir; me as well. I mean, same to you. Or I mean, nice meeting you also, Sir."

I shook my head at myself as I walked out the door. What an awkward moron! I was hoping that with age I would stop being so weird and stupid. I guessed that everyone probably thought I was awkward and weird; but they didn't realize that nobody knew this more than myself. I may not have been very smooth with my social skills, but I had a heightened sense of self-awareness that couldn't be beat.

After I exited the store, I grabbed my bike and was about to get on it and ride away. However, something made me stop and hesitate. I looked at the entrance area of the store, and then I looked up and down Main Street at all of the other stores.

It was then that I got an idea. And for those who have wondered "how it all began," *THIS* is how it began. It was that moment when I got *THE* idea.

I set my bike back up against the building, and walked back into the store. Mr. Martins had gone back over to stand behind the cash register, even though there was nobody else in the store.

I walked over to him, and he said, "Did you forget something?"

I replied, "No. I mean, yeah. Well, no, I didn't forget anything, but I wanted to ask you something."

He smiled in amusement at my ridiculousness, and responded, "What's that?"

In that moment, my mind-reading skills were telling me that he thought I was going to ask him about Sally. I sighed within myself.

I then said, "I wanted to ask your permission to try something, or do something."

Still likely thinking that I was going to ask him something about his daughter, he smiled, and responded, "It's okay, you can just tell me."

I sighed within myself again, because I knew what he was thinking; and of course, my query had nothing to do with what he was thinking.

I replied, "I think it would help your store if your entrance looked better and different than all of the others. I am wondering if you would let me clean up your entrance and paint your door and window frame. I promise that I'll do a good job, and if you don't like it, I can do it over differently."

He was surprised with what I said, obviously; but smiled, and responded, "That's a very generous offer, but as I mentioned before, I really don't have any extra money to hire you. I'm really sorry. I wish I could."

I replied, "You don't have to pay me. I want to do it for Sally. I'm not asking you for anything. I'm only asking for your permission if you will allow me to do it. That's all."

He seemed very uncomfortable with my offer, but in a good way. I could tell that he was itching inside his skin, and his mind was wrestling with the concept.

After some awkward moments, he nodded, and responded, "Okay. Your offer is interesting and generous. I won't do anything to discourage that kind of behavior."

I smiled with relief that he was agreeing to my plan.

He then said, "I'll tell you what. If you are serious about doing this, I will buy the paint and brushes. But I seriously don't have any extra money to pay you."

I replied, "THAT WOULD BE GREAT! If you would buy the paint, that would help me a lot. I have a little extra money for donuts and things from my allowance, but not much money for paint. THANK YOU, SIR!"

Mr. Martins was flummoxed by the notion that I was seriously intending on buying the paint with my own money.

After a moment, he said, "Okay, when do you want to do this?"

I replied, "I can start tomorrow if you have the paint."

He responded, "I'll go down the street to the hardware store and get it before end-of-business today."

I replied, "Great!"

I had a thought, and said, "Oh! Can we do a different color than black?"

He looked at me weird, and responded, "Like what?"

I replied, "All of the doors downtown are black. We need to do something different. And something bright."

After a pause, I said, "How about either green or red? That's not ugly, but it's bright and will attract attention."

And yes, I realize that green is not that bright. But in my mind, a vibrant and fresh forest green, or 'Christmas green,' was bright. My mind was weird. Still is.

Mr. Martins thought for a moment, and responded, "How about green for the door, and red for around the front window?"

I replied, "PERFECT! That will attract attention. That will work. I think this might help entice customers into your store, Sir. It's worth a try."

He smiled, and responded, "I think you might be right! I like it! Thank you! And I really mean that."

And I knew that he really did mean it.

I told him that I would come back the next day. We waved at each other, and I left. "The Painting" was about to begin.

CHAPTER TWO
The Painting

The next morning, I woke up early, and went into the kitchen for breakfast. My mother was in the kitchen doing her 'kitchen stuff,' and she said, "Where are *you* off to today?"

I replied, "I'm going downtown. I have some painting to do."

She responded, "Oh? Like what?"

I replied, "I'm painting the door and window frame for Martins Gifts."

She seemed pleasantly surprised, and responded, "OH WOW! So you got a job! Good for you!"

My mom seemed so pleased, that I didn't feel like ruining the moment by telling her that I wasn't being paid. I just remained silent.

When I was done with my bowl of oatmeal and toast, I waved to my mom and left without further words. I got on my bike and rode the short distance into the center of town. Once I arrived at the gift store, I parked my bike out of the way and went into the store.

Mr. Martins had just opened for the day and appeared to still be getting things "opened up" inside the store. He was turning on display lights and things like that.

He didn't hear me come in, and he seemed startled and surprised to see me. How could he forget that I was coming to paint when we just spoke the previous day?

After a couple of moments, he said, "WOW, YOUNG MAN! I wasn't sure you would show up, let alone so early."

I replied, "I told you I would, Sir. I hope you got the paint."

He responded, "I DID! It's in the back. Let me get it for you."

He went into that dark and mysterious backroom that all stores have which customers never get to see, and then he came out with some paint and brushes. He explained to me which was the green and which was the red.

He then said, "What are you going to do to prep the door and frame?"

I got an error message in my head because I didn't know what he meant by that. While I was trying to figure out how to answer his question without making myself look stupid, he said, "I've got a scrub brush and some rags. Let me get you a bucket of water. Just brush everything down, and then wipe it down with water before you paint it, okay? We can't have you painting over dirt."

I replied, "Yes of course, Sir."

I said it with strong authority, as if I already knew all of everything he said and was going to do it anyway, even though the truth was that I was just going to paint over the dirt. Good thing he said something. I guess this simple and quick paint job was going to be an all-consuming strenuous task. Why is everything always like that?

Mr. Martins helped get me set up outside. We put plastic down on the sidewalk so that I wouldn't drip paint on it, and he reminded me to watch out for customers who wanted to get inside the store. I was instructed to open the door for them.

I brushed the door down, and then wiped it down with a damp cloth. It dried quickly in the sun, so I was able to start painting almost immediately.

I began brushing the 'Christmas green' paint onto the door, and I was loving how it looked. I ended up putting two coats of paint on the door.

While I waited for the first coat to dry, I cleaned and painted the framing around the big window in front of the store. I painted that red, and it looked great. In addition to that, I asked Mr. Martins for some glass cleaner, and I cleaned the large front window.

All of this took me longer than I anticipated, but the final result was worth it. When I began cleaning up my mess, Mr. Martins came outside to inspect my job. I could tell that he was very pleased. Both of us noticed a few people taking notice of the new paint job as they walked by the store on the sidewalk.

As we were standing outside admiring the fresher and brighter image for the store, a man who I didn't know stopped and started chatting with Mr. Martins. Come to find out, he was one of the store owners on the other end of Main Street.

Mr. Martins explained to him that I had done the job, and that the whole thing was my idea to begin with. The man seemed impressed, and he offered to hire me to paint *his* store entrance as well.

I glanced at Mr. Martins, and he smiled and nodded in approval. Not only that, but he offered his leftover paint to be used for the next job. The other man suggested that for *his* store, I paint the door red and the window framing green, since I had a ton of leftover red paint, and less leftover green paint.

I accepted the job without even asking what the pay rate was. Mr. Martins thanked me for the job well done, and I walked with the other man down to his store, while carrying the paint and brushes. The man agreed to walk my bike down for me since my hands were already full.

Once we reached his store, I quickly started the same process as before, as far as cleaning the door and window frame in preparation for painting it. Then I applied two coats of paint as before, except red for the door and green for the window frame.

I was able to finish that job much more quickly because I was more experienced and efficient. The man was pleased with the job I did, and he paid me generously for my work.

It was getting late by that point, so I rode my bike back home. My mom asked how my first day of work went, and I just laughed and told her it was fine. What was funny about it was that I actually did earn money that day, so I guess I really did have a job, even though I didn't.

The next day, I had school. But after school, I rode my bike downtown to check on Mr. Martins. I wanted to see if what I had done resulted in any increased business yet. Yes, I know that was ridiculous thinking, but I was young.

Mr. Martins was kind in his response to me, and said that he felt people were noticing the fine job I did, and that he hoped to have more customers soon. But then he said something else.

He told me that two other store owners asked him who painted his entrance, because they wanted the same thing done for *their* stores. Mr. Martins gave me a piece of paper with the names of the stores on it.

I left his store and went over to the two other stores. When I inquired inside and explained who I was, I was promptly offered a job painting their doors and window frames. I accepted. But this time, they didn't offer to provide the paint, and I didn't have any leftover paint from the previous job.

Thus, I went down the street to the hardware store where I knew Mr. Martins had bought the paint for his store. I explained who I was and what I was doing. To keep things simple, I asked for the same red and green paint that they had sold Mr. Martins. I then used the money I made from the second job I did to buy the paint and supplies for the next two jobs.

It was silly for me to have to bring the paint all the way to my house and then back downtown again, so I asked the hardware store if I could just leave everything there, and they agreed. That was one good thing about living in a small town. You could actually do things like that.

The next day after school, I went straight to the hardware store, got my paint, and went to the store where I was doing the next paint job. I asked them if they wanted a green door or a red door. They indicated they wanted a red door.

I went to work cleaning, then painting their door red, and then painting their window framing green. They were very pleased with the job I did, and they paid me for my work, plus extra for the paint and supplies.

It was getting dark, so I had to quit for the day and go home. I had dinner, did my homework, and then went to bed. The next day after school, I went downtown and started on the next job. I asked (suggested) that I do their door green and their window frame red. Thankfully, they agreed. This meant that I could use all of the leftover paint from the previous job.

I completed that job, and they paid me for my work plus the paint, even though I had used leftover paint. I could see how contractors made extra money, if they could somehow find leftover supplies from previous jobs. I was learning about the business trade without realizing it.

Anyway, when I had finished that job, a lady came up to me and complimented the job I had done. She then went on to explain how she owned the store two doors down. She told me that she would love to get her store painted as well, but she didn't have any extra money. I guess her situation was similar to Mr. Martins's.

For whatever reason, I felt compelled to say that I would paint her entrance for free if she paid for the paint. She gleefully accepted my offer.

The next day after school, I went to the hardware store to buy more paint and supplies. I had plenty of working capital by this time. I explained to the owner of the hardware store that I was doing another job, but I had to do it for free.

After hesitating in thought, the man offered to sell me all of the paint and supplies I needed at a big discount. I gratefully accepted his offer. Not only that, but he said if I ever ran short of funds, I could buy what I needed "on account," and just pay him after I got reimbursed or paid for doing my paid jobs (as opposed to the free ones). I still preferred to pay for everything as I went because it was simpler, but I thanked the man for his offer of that flexibility.

I painted the entrance for the lady's store, and I ended up doing many other store entrances as well. It was as if one thing led to the next, which led to the next. I was working a full shift after school every day, and then working full-time shifts every weekend.

But I wasn't the only person painting store entrances. I soon noticed other stores were painting their doors and windows on their own. I'm not sure if the store owners were doing it themselves, or if they were hiring other painting contractors. But stores up and down Main Street were all painting their entrances. And guess what? They were all using the alternating green/red color scheme.

People have often asked me if I chose green and red in the beginning because I had a full vision of what our town would eventually turn into. My answer is 'no.' My choice of green and red was somewhat random at that time. I wasn't thinking about Christmas when I chose those colors. But I guess one has to wonder if something from above or within was whispering those colors to me, for the reasons which we are all familiar with today.

I don't know the answer to that, but I know it was meant to be. And guess what? The doors and windows were only the beginning. I had started 'something,' and what I started was about to expand outward in ways which nobody could have imagined.

After I was somewhat caught up on painting the doors and window frames for a good number of stores on Main Street, I had an epiphany that made me feel bad.

One day after school, I rode my bike downtown, as had become my routine, and I looked up Main Street. What I saw were many red and green doors, with windows of alternating colors.

Yes, I know this is not a news flash. But as I was taking in this sight, I remembered suggesting that I paint Mr. Martins's store entrance as a way of attracting customers to HIS store. The whole point was to make *his* store STAND OUT from the rest.

But in all of my eagerness and zest for success in making a difference for everyone, I had caused Mr. Martins's store to no longer stand out from the crowd. His store looked the same as all of the others. So, how was that helpful to him and his family, I asked myself. It wasn't that helpful was the answer.

Yeah, Main Street was starting to look really cool, and certainly much cleaner, but this whole thing had started because I wanted to help Sally and her family's store, by increasing business for them.

I know this might sound weird to some, but I felt ashamed of myself in that moment. I felt that I had offered to help, but ended up not helping. I felt so bad about it, that I decided to go see Mr. Martins and apologize to him.

I rode my bike up Main Street, near the top of the sloping hill where Martins Gifts was located. I set my bike against the building, and went inside. There was nobody inside the store, but I heard Mr. Martins talking on the phone. It sounded like he was asking for more time to pay something he owed. That made me feel even worse than I already did. Perhaps his continuing struggle was even my fault.

I obviously didn't interrupt or invade his space during the phone call. I went to the back wall where that Santa-sleigh-reindeer crystal and gold figurine-curio-decoration-model thing was. And seriously, what is the proper name for something like that? I had no idea then, and I still have no idea now.

But at any rate, I stood there staring up at it and admiring it. Something about it really fascinated me.

I heard Mr. Martins end his phone call, but I didn't break my trance of looking up at the sleigh thing until Mr. Martins came up from behind me, and said, "It's beautiful, isn't it?"

I replied, "Yes it is, Sir."

After a moment, I looked over at him and asked, "May I ask where you got it?"

He smiled, as if delighted by my question, and responded, "My wife and I got it many years ago while in Switzerland on our honeymoon, of all things."

I gave him a look of surprise. His answer was so, umm, meaningful.

After a moment, I replied, "That's a wonderful wedding present to buy yourselves."

He responded, "Oh, we didn't buy it. There was no way we could afford such a thing, either then or now."

I was puzzled by his answer, and I replied, "Then how did you get it?"

I was really hoping he wasn't about to tell me that he stole it, but I guess I had to brace myself for that potential answer?"

He responded, "We were browsing through a gift shop in a little Swiss village that looked like a permanent Christmas town, and I spotted it on display up on the wall of the store. I was mesmerized by it, and stood staring at it for several minutes. I guess the store owner noticed this, and he came over to me, at which point he said, 'It's quite a piece isn't it?' I agreed with him and then asked him how much it was. He replied to me that it was priceless and not for sale. I was disappointed, even though I knew I would not have been able to buy it anyway."

Mr. Martins continued, "I kept staring and admiring it anyway, and the store owner asked me what I liked most about it. Rather than commenting on the fine crystal and gold-plate edging, I told him that I thought it was magical. I guess my answer touched the right button deep within the store owner. He then confided to me that he was retiring soon and would be closing his store. He said that everything needed to go. I looked at him with intrigue, like maybe he might agree to sell me the piece after all, even though he said it wasn't for sale. But that's not what happened."

Mr. Martins stopped speaking, and I felt as if he might be getting emotional. I looked away from him so that it wouldn't get uncomfortable.

After some awkward silence, Mr. Martins continued, "The store owner asked me if I wanted it. I told him that I did, but that I couldn't afford it. I explained to him that my wife and I were on our honeymoon, and we had a dream of opening up our own gift store back home."

He went on, "After I said that, I could see something click within the mind of the store owner. He looked at me square in the eyes and told me that he wanted me to have it. He told me that it was important to him that someone who saw the magic within the piece, receive it and have it after he was gone. He then whispered to me that everyone in his village considered him to be the embodiment and spirit of Santa Claus. I should also add that he looked like Santa Claus, but that's not important."

Mr. Martin's continued, "I was obviously shocked and without words regarding his gesture and offer. My wife was barely breathing and without words. The man then made me promise him something. He made me promise that I would continue the magic. Although I wasn't certain what he meant by that, I promised him that I would. With that said, I quickly figured out soon enough what he meant by that, and I have always kept my word on that promise. But anyway, the man had it shipped to us so that it wouldn't get broken during our travels. When my wife and I received it at home, we knew that it would be the centerpiece decoration for our gift store, which it always has been."

Mr. Martins looked at me with great satisfaction from his own story.

I said, "That's amazing, Sir. I can see why you have to keep it."

He responded, "That's right, young man."

That was followed by an awkward silence, as if he was wondering what I was doing there, or what I wanted from him.

I said, "Sir, I just wanted to apologize to you."

He looked at me puzzled, and responded, "I wasn't aware that you had anything to apologize for."

I replied, "I told you that painting your door and window would make you stand out from all of the other stores, and that it would bring you additional business. I've obviously ruined that by painting all of the other stores the same as yours. Plus, I don't see any additional customers in your store. I'm sorry I failed you. I didn't mean to. I thought my idea would help."

And I really was sorry. Under the right circumstances, I might have even started crying at that moment. But I remain composed, although solemn. He didn't immediately respond, and I hung my head in shame.

But then he said, "You didn't fail me. To the contrary. You've probably been the best thing to happen to all of Main Street in years. You have upgraded the entire downtown area. Sometimes these things take time to yield results. Do not feel discouraged, or that you failed ANYBODY. You, young man, are a blessing to anyone who is lucky enough to encounter you."

His words were of great comfort to me. I raised my head, and replied, "Thank you, Sir. But I will try to think of something else to help you."

He politely thanked me, and I turned around and walked out of his store. And it was then that I got my next idea.

As I was grabbing for my bike, I noticed something that had always been there, but I hadn't noticed it much before, even though I had always known it was there. I noticed the lamp post that was right in front of Martins Gifts.

There were street lamp poles all up and down Main Street on both sides of the street. They were somewhat ornamental in style, but they were all painted black; and all of them were very dirty from years and years of dirt and zero maintenance.

I wondered if maybe I could paint the lamp post in front of Mr. Martins's store. THAT would make *HIS* store stand out from the rest, for sure!

I stared at the pole and thought that I could paint it green like his door. I didn't dare paint it red because I was afraid that some people might think it was "too much," and would complain. I knew that people would like the green, though. Vermont is the "Green Mountain State," so everyone there likes green. But I should add that Vermont is more famous for its Fall foliage than it is for its green mountains. It's complicated, and I digress.

Also, I should say that normally a person can't go around painting city lamp posts any color they want without permission from the city. But we were a small town, I was a young kid, and I wasn't about to ask for permission, nor did it ever enter my mind to do so.

I rode my bike down the street to the hardware store and told the guy that I was going to need more paint. However, I was smart enough to tell him that this was going to be for metal, instead of wood. I told him exactly what I was going to do. So, for anyone who wondered if I told an adult prior to doing this, the answer is yes. The owner of the hardware store knew of my plans.

He told me that I would need to clean off the metal pole really well, and perhaps even brush it with a metal brush to prep it for the paint. He agreed with me that the 'Christmas green' paint should go on sufficiently well over the old and faded black paint. The poles hadn't been painted in so long that the black had turned a shade of slate gray; so it wasn't like I was trying to paint over a strong black.

The next day, I went downtown, picked up my supplies at the hardware store, and dragged everything I needed up to Martins Gifts. I ended up leaving my bike at the hardware store in a safe place where it wouldn't get stolen, even though nobody stole bikes back then; and if they *were* going to steal a bike, they wouldn't want *my* old bike.

I needed a ladder for this job, so I had to make two trips. The hardware store let me borrow a ladder for free with the request that I didn't get paint all over it. I did my best.

When I was all set up, I started cleaning the light pole in front of Martins Gifts. It wasn't long before Mr. Martins came outside to greet me.

He said, "What are you up to this time, young man?"

I replied, "Since your entrance looks the same as all of the others now, I am going to paint your light pole so that you stand out again."

He smiled, chuckled, and responded, "I won't try to stop you. And thank you."

He walked back into his store, while shaking his head in amusement.

I got busy with my task, but I wasn't working on that pole for more than fifteen minutes before one of the other store owners came walking up to me.

He said, "Are you just cleaning that pole, or are you going to paint it, also?"

I replied, "I'm going to paint it."

He responded, "I'll pay you to paint the light post in front of my store, also."

I sighed within myself. I actually wanted to tell him 'no.' I needed Mr. Martins's light post to be different. But I also felt that I couldn't turn down this other request.

After sighing in defeat, I replied, "Yes, Sir."

The man responded, "Are you doing green and red again, or what?"

I thought for a moment, and replied, "I think we better stick to 'Christmas green' for the posts, but I'm thinking of painting the ornamental sections in the middle red. What do you think?"

Because yes, there was a contrasting square part of the post about halfway up. I thought maybe it would be cool to have that small section of the post red.

The man responded, "YES, GREAT IDEA! I LOVE IT! Start on mine anytime you want, and I will pay you ahead of time if you need the money for supplies or something."

I replied, "Okay, will do."

After the man walked away, I thought to myself how I had screwed everything up again.

Okay, I know some people might wonder why I didn't simply decline to paint the man's light pole. You have to understand that in our rural culture at that time, a child didn't turn down a reasonable request by an adult. The man was trying to pay me for a job. He was trying to be nice. Thus, there was no way I could turn down his request.

After I got most of the lamp post (somewhat) cleaned up, I began painting it. I started down at the sidewalk and worked my way up. I realized that I was going to have an issue painting it all the way to the top. Even with the ladder, it was going to be a sketchy deal and maybe not safe; but I figured I would cross that bridge when I got to it.

After I had the pole almost painted as high as I could reach, I had some unexpected and unwanted visitors. Jeremy with one of his friends came walking up the sidewalk with shopping bags. It looked like they had been doing some clothes shopping. Lucky them.

Once they got to me, I could see they had big obnoxious smiles on their faces.

Jeremy said, "Hey Loser, looks like you're working to make things nicer for the rest of us to enjoy. On behalf of myself and everyone else with real lives, we thank you for cleaning up our dirt. We need little people like you to do the cleaning and painting. Get used to it, because it's probably how you will spend the rest of your life."

He and his friend laughed at me. They resumed walking by me, so I decided not to say anything. What was I going to say, anyway? There was nothing to say. They were buying themselves new clothes while I was painting a light post, so maybe they were right. Except they weren't, but whatever.

I decided to take a break and walk down to the hardware store to see if I could get some red paint to do the middle ornamental section in red. When I got to the hardware store, I explained to the guy what I was thinking, and he agreed it was a neat idea. He made up some red paint for the metal, and sent me off with it. I didn't pay for it right then. I guess it was being put on my account? Who knows. The whole thing was starting to take on a life of its own and become a blur to me.

And in case anyone was wondering; yes, we had our own police department as I previously mentioned, and yes, I had police officers drive by AND walk by me numerous times while I was doing all of this. None of them questioned what I was doing, and a few of them waved at me.

Once I returned to the lamp post, I had another visitor waiting for me, but this time it was a welcomed visitor. It was Sally. I guess she had come by the store to see her father?

She had a bag in her hand, and I recognized the bag.

We said hi to each other, and then she said, "I know you like donuts. So, I bought you a donut. Do you want it?"

She handed me the bag, and I took it. I looked inside and saw that it was a jelly-cream-filled donut.

I said, "Thank you. That's my favorite kind. How did you know?"

She responded, "I saw you eating one a long time ago and I remembered."

I replied, "Well thanks. This is awesome."

I started eating the donut right away while Sally just stood there, watching me eat it, as if not wanting to miss seeing a single bite. Was I supposed to offer her some? Oops.

After I had eaten most of the donut, Sally said, "My dad has talked about you at home."

I replied, "Yeah? What did he say?"

She replied, "He said that you are more of a man than most adults he knows."

I didn't know what to think of that, so I replied, "I hope that's a good thing?"

She shrugged, and responded, "I think so."

I then started opening up the red paint so that I could paint the red section of the pole. Right about then, Sally's mother pulled up to the side of the road to pick up Sally. Sally and I waved goodbye to each other, and I saw her mom wave to me from inside the vehicle, so I waved back.

After they drove off, I painted the red section on the pole. After I was finished, I looked at it closely and admired it, making sure that the green pole with the red section in the middle looked okay. It did.

But doing this also caused me to think about how I was going to paint the top of the pole. I wasn't that comfortable trying to get all of the way up there with the ladder. It was really high and I was afraid of heights. Plus, there were cars driving by on one side, and people walking by on the other. What could possibly go wrong, right? I really didn't know what to do.

But my question was answered, as if God himself was answering it.

A moment later, a construction vehicle pulled alongside the sidewalk. I was familiar with this particular construction company because they had been in our town for longer than I had been alive.

A man got out and said, "Are you the young man who painted all of the doors and windows?"

I replied, "Yes."

He responded, "And now it looks like you're painting the light poles?"

I replied, "I guess so."

The man looked up to the top of the pole, as if seeing for himself my predicament.

After a moment, he said, "I'll tell you what. What if our company pressure washes all of these light poles, and then we bring our equipment up through Main Street and spray-paint all of these poles for you? We can pressure wash them in one night, and then we should be able to spray all of them green the next night. The only thing you would have to do is paint the red bits in the middle after that. What would you think of that?"

I was surprised, thrilled, and relieved by his offer.

I replied, "THAT WOULD BE AWESOME!"

But then I had a thought and said, "But I don't have the money to pay you to do that."

The man started laughing almost hysterically. When he calmed down, he responded, "You don't need to pay for it. We'll work it out on our end. Everyone in town has seen what you have been doing, and it's time that our company step up to do our part."

I replied, "Okay, great."

The man responded, "I don't know exactly which night we will get to it, but it will be soon."

I replied, "Okay. But that store down there is paying me to do *their* pole, so I have to do theirs next."

The man chuckled and responded, "Yeah, okay. But stop there. Let us come through here and do all of these for you. You should rest up, because it's still going to be a lot of work for you to do all of the red parts on all of these poles up and down Main Street."

I replied, "Yeah, okay."

After a pause, I said, "You are going to paint them all the same 'Christmas green,' right?"

He laughed again, and responded, "Yeah. We'll get the paint down the street from where you get *your* paint, and we'll have them give us the exact same mixture."

I replied, "Awesome. Thank you."

He responded, "YES, SIR!"

He then walked away, got back into his truck, and drove off. It was one of the first times that anyone had treated me with that much respect, for a stranger like that to call me "Sir" under those circumstances.

A few moments later, I was kicking myself for not specifically asking him to paint the top part of the poles for me on the two I was working on. All I could do was hope that they would do that when they did the rest of the poles.

The next day after school, I returned downtown to work on the second light pole. I cleaned it, prepped it, and then painted it as high up as I could reach. When I was done, I called it a day.

The next day after that, when I returned, I saw that ALL of the light poles on Main Street had been pressure washed. They must have done it in the middle of the night since that is the only time something like that could be done without creating a problem. I spent my time painting the red part on the second pole.

The next day after that, I saw that ALL of the light poles had been painted the correct green from the bottom all the way up to the tippy top. This included the tops of my two poles that I had already done. I was relieved to see that they had finished *my* poles.

All of the freshly painted 'Christmas green' poles made Main Street look 100% better. That, along with the alternating green and red doors (and windows), caused all of downtown to look transformed. That was the first time when I felt proud of what I had started. Downtown was definitely changing for the better.

At the same time, I knew that I still had my work cut out for me, though. I was responsible for painting the middle red parts on ALL of the light poles on Main Street, on both sides of the street. YIKES!

But I got busy doing it every day after school, and all weekend long. However, I very quickly altered my plan. After seeing a few of the poles completely finished, I decided to change my color scheme a tiny bit.

Instead of painting all of the poles red on the ornamental middle part, I decided to alternate them between red and white. One pole would have red, and then the next pole would have white. Doing that created a neat looking candy cane appearance, sort of, kind of, maybe. But even if it didn't, it still looked cool. I soon heard compliments from people indicating that they liked my color scheme.

However, I had a lot of poles to finish painting, and it was turning cold as we headed into November. I knew I had to hustle it up. But while I was fixated on doing that, I had something happen to me that would change my life.

CHAPTER THREE
The Article

On one chilly and crisp late afternoon after school, I was downtown, painting the ornamental parts of the light poles. I had developed a routine of painting red on one day, and then white the next day. This way, I only had to deal with one can of paint. To do the red, I would just skip every other pole; and then on the next day, I would paint the ones I skipped with white paint. I was making good progress and was over three-quarters of the way done. And then it happened.

I remember it well. I was painting with red that day. I was losing light quickly, and I knew I had to hurry up and then get home. However, I was interrupted.

A man and a woman walked up the sidewalk toward me with a purpose. They were fixated on me, and I kind of knew they were going to say something to me. For this reason, I put my brush down.

Sure enough, when they reached me, the man introduced himself, and then he introduced the woman who was with him. He introduced himself as a reporter for our local newspaper, and the woman as a 'junior reporter,' whatever that meant. She had a really expensive looking camera hanging from her neck.

The man who told me he was a reporter said, "Would it be alright if I asked you a few questions? You are the young man who did all of the painting here on Main Street, right?"

I replied, "Yeah, I did a lot of it, but some of it was done by the store owners themselves, and I had a ton of help from one of the construction companies in town (I gave him their name)."

The reporter responded, "Well regardless of all of that, we are aware that you instigated this movement to spruce up our downtown, and that you've done much of the work as an unpaid volunteer. Is that true?"

I replied, "Yeah, I've done some for free, and I've been paid for others. The jobs I got paid for, I've used that money to buy paint and supplies for the jobs that I've done for free. I don't have any extra money. The hardware store right down there lets me pay for the paint when I have money. They've been very nice to me."

The woman was taking notes while the man had whipped out a recorder, as if he was a ninja producing a switchblade out of nowhere.

The reporter responded, "So, just to be clear, you haven't been making much or any money from doing this?"

I replied, "No. In fact, I'm afraid I might owe the hardware store money after I'm done. But I don't care. I'm all-in on this now, and I will work another job to pay off the hardware store later if I have to. But if I can make a little money somehow, I'm going to use it to buy my mother a Christmas gift."

The reporter responded, "You mentioned your mother. Do you live with your dad, or have any siblings?"

I replied, "No, it's just me and my mom. My father vanished when I was very young, and I don't have a brother or sister."

He responded, "Does your mom stay home, or does she have to work."

I replied, "Oh, she works. We don't have much money, so she has to do what's needed to get us by. And in fact, she was excited that I was doing all of this painting because she thinks I've got a job as a painter. She's probably going to be really mad at me when she finds out I'm not earning any money from this. That's why I'm hoping to get her a nice Christmas present so that I'll be in less trouble."

The reporter and the lady started laughing. I'm not sure they realized that I was being serious, but maybe they did.

The reporter said, "I won't put this in the newspaper article, but what were you hoping to get your mother for Christmas?"

I replied, "My mother loves to cook, but all of her cooking stuff is old. I was hoping to buy her at least one really nice new pan or something."

The reporter and the lady were smiling and nodding.

The reporter seemed to look me over, as far as what I was wearing, and then he glanced over at my bike, which was leaning against the nearby building.

He said, "So, I assume you live in an apartment, or what's your living situation?"

I replied, "Yeah, we live in an apartment. My mom says that if she loses her job, we'll have to move, but I like where we are living."

He responded, "And is that your old bike over there?"

I replied, "Yeah. I know it's old, but it's okay."

I was beginning to get uncomfortable with his questions, like he was maybe going to pick on me for being poor. I think I was extra sensitive due to all of the bullying from Jeremy and his friends.

I think the man sensed that I was getting anxious.

He said, "I won't ask where you live, but may I ask which school you attend?"

I told him the name of my school.

He said, "I know you're busy and I've probably asked you too many questions already, but would it be okay if we got some photos of you that we can use with any article we might decide to publish?"

I thought for a moment, and replied, "Yeah, I guess so. Just tell me what you want me to do."

He responded, "Let's get one of you painting the pole, then another with you standing in front of the pole, and then another standing in front of that freshly painted door over there."

And that is when I had an idea.

I replied, "Actually, can you do me a favor?"

The reporter responded, "Yeah, what's that?"

I replied, "Can we do these photos up the street in front of Martins

Gifts? That's where all of this started, and Mr. Martins has been really kind to me. I want his store in the photos, if that's okay."

The reporter responded, "Yeah sure; we can do that."

I closed up the paint, and set it in a nearby alley. I knew it would be fine there overnight. I grabbed my bike, and the three of us walked up Main Street to Martins Gifts.

It was pretty much dark by this time, but that didn't seem to faze the reporters. It turned out that they had a flash on the camera, and the street lamps lit everything up really well.

Once we got to Martins Gifts, I realized that I needed my paint and brush for the photos. I felt stupid for leaving that stuff down the street. I knew I had some extra supplies inside Mr. Martins's store, so I told the reporters to hold on, and then I ran into the store. Mr. Martins was starting to close up for the day. I quickly explained that there were newspaper reporters asking me questions, and that I needed a paintbrush and bucket of paint for the photos.

Mr. Martins jumped into action and ran into his back room. He came out with a paintbrush and an empty bucket of paint.

He said, "It's empty, but nobody else will know. Just hold the paint can and the brush."

I replied, "Okay, thanks."

I scooted back outside, and Mr. Martins wasn't far behind. The lady asked me to stand in front of the green painted door, while holding the bucket of empty paint and the brush. She took a few photos. Then she asked me to stand next to the light pole in front of the store.

I said to her, "See if you can get the sign for the store in the picture with me."

The lady nodded, and took more pictures. When she seemed satisfied, she told me that she was done.

The reporter then immediately addressed Mr. Martins by saying, "We are working on a story about this exceptional young man here.

Could I ask you a few questions, Sir?"

Mr. Martins replied, "Yes, absolutely."

The reporter went on to ask him a bunch of questions. They were mostly about how all of this came about. Mr. Martins told the story about how I had offered to help increase business for his store, and that I painted his door, window, and light pole for free.

When the reporter was done with Mr. Martins, he looked over at me, and said, "Do you have any final words for us, young man?"

I thought for a moment, and replied, "Just that I am trying to make downtown nice so that more people shop at all of the stores on Main Street, and ESPECIALLY Martins Gifts."

Mr. Martins got a smile so big, it barely fit on his face.

The reporter and the lady thanked me, and took off. Mr. Martins thanked me also, but then I told him I had to get home because it was dark. My mother didn't like me riding my bike after dark because it didn't have any lights on it.

I quickly rode my bike home, and managed to get there safely. I didn't say anything to my mom about what happened because I wasn't sure what was going to happen next, or if I had somehow gotten myself into trouble with everything that I was doing.

A couple of days went by, and nothing happened. I started to assume that the story about me was too boring to go into the newspaper. It was still fun doing the interview, anyway.

That following Saturday, my plan was to finish the poles. I was excited. The painting would be DONE! Not only that, but it was too cold to paint now, anyway.

And believe it or not, I already had a couple of additional ideas up my sleeve of what I was going to do next. So no, I didn't think I was finished with working downtown. Far from it.

However, Saturday did not go as planned. Apparently, I was wrong about the story regarding me being too boring to make it into the newspaper. Not only did it make it into the newspaper, but the story was on the front page of the newspaper's weekend edition.

I found this out because my mother received several phone calls from people she knew, informing her that her son was on the front page of the newspaper. When she confronted me about this, I told her that someone from the newspaper talked to me a few days ago, but I didn't think much of it. I then told my mom that I had to leave and get to work downtown. That was me escaping what was most certainly going to be an intricate circus-maze of revelations and questions from my mother.

We didn't have enough money to get the newspaper every day, but my mom was readying herself to go to the store and a buy a copy, or two, or three, of this particular weekend issue.

To be completely honest, I truly thought that I was in big trouble. I had visions of being lectured, and then grounded for who knows how long. The reason being, that I had not told my mother everything that had been going on. She really thought that I was working for a painting company or something like that.

And no, my first inclination was not to find a newspaper for myself and read it. I think I sensed the situation to be overwhelming, and my mind pretended to ignore it, even though there was no ignoring it.

I rode my bike downtown to finish the light poles. I went to the hardware store for the last of my paint supplies, and the guy gave me what I asked for, and then informed me that my account balance was being wiped clean to a 0 balance. He also told me to come see him if I needed anything else. I was confused, surprised, and I thanked him.

I took my supplies and went to the area of the last three poles to be completed with the red and white. In this case, I was finishing with red.

That morning while painting the remaining poles, there were numerous people who walked by me smiling, waving, and thanking me. I even had a couple of people give me money for no reason at all.

Once I unceremoniously had finished painting the light poles, I decided to leave my leftover supplies at Mr. Martins's store. I had established two bases of operations. At the bottom of Main Street, I had the hardware store, which let me leave my supplies, my bike, and anything else I wanted, at their store for safekeeping. And near the top of Main Street, I had the same arrangement with Mr. Martins. I decided to leave the last can of red paint with Mr. Martins.

I went up to Martins Gifts and went inside. Mr. Martins was standing behind the customer counter with a big grin on his face, and a newspaper sitting out in the open.

I said, "I'm done with the painting. I thought I would leave the leftover paint here. Is that okay?"

He chuckled, and responded, "Yeah. Just put it down by the backroom door."

I did as he instructed. My intention was to then leave the store without bothering him further. But when I turned around to walk out of the store, he said, "You're a celebrity now, young man."

I replied, "What do you mean?"

He responded, "Did you see the newspaper?"

I replied, "I heard they printed the story, but I haven't seen it."

He responded, "Come take a look."

I went over to the customer counter, and he said, "You don't even need to open up the newspaper to find it because it's on the front page."

The first thing I saw was a large photo of me standing outside Martins Gifts, holding the empty paint can and a paintbrush. I was smiling in the photo, which was weird because I usually didn't smile for photos. But I guess I was pleased that they were getting the Martins Gifts sign in the photo, and that was the reason I was smiling. And I suppose they used that photo since it was the only one in which I was smiling.

I glanced up reluctantly at Mr. Martins, and he said, "Go ahead and read it."

I began reading the article, and it started by giving Mr. Martins's accounting of how it all started. Then it moved onto my comments about what I was doing, and why I was doing it. But after that, it began talking about my personal circumstances at home, how I came from a "disadvantaged household," how I was riding downtown every day on an old bicycle, and how I was trying to earn enough money to buy my mother a Christmas gift; but instead, was using all of my earnings to pay for paint supplies.

The last paragraph of the article included something that I was not expecting. It said that if anyone wanted to make a donation of some sort to me or my mission of beautifying downtown, that they should leave such donations at my school (and they named my school).

I had never asked for anything, and I had never even considered my situation from that angle. I was just grateful for the store owners who were able to pay me for my work, and the hardware store that seemed to always give me whatever I needed without asking for immediate payment.

When I was finished reading the article, I looked up at Mr. Martins and said, "Wow, I wasn't expecting it to be like that."

I think Mr. Martins was amused by my reaction. After a moment, he responded, "You deserve any attention and credit you get for what you have done for downtown and all of us who make a living here."

I felt he was being overly dramatic, and I replied, "Well, my goal was to increase the number of customers for your store. If that hasn't happened, then everything I did was a failure."

It looked like he wasn't sure what to say about that, and before he could respond, a pair of customers came walking into the store, and they were followed by another pair of customers.

That caused Mr. Martins to focus all of his attention on *them*. One of the customers made eye contact with Mr. Martins and said, "Is this the same store that was in the newspaper with that boy who is cleaning up downtown?"

Mr. Martins said, "It is. And that is the boy standing right over there."

All of the customers looked over at me at the same time.

The customer who had been speaking with Mr. Martins said, "WOW! How about that! Well let me just say to you, young man, that I think what you are doing is extraordinary. It's great for not only all of the stores on Main Street, but it's great for our entire town. I know in the article you said you wanted the public to support all of the stores, especially Martins Gifts, so we thought we would come down here and do just that."

I replied, "Thank you, Ma'am."

She responded, "You are a credit to our town, and you make us all proud. I wish more of our kids in this area were like you."

I was getting a bit uncomfortable and shy with her remarks and adoration. I wasn't used to people saying nice things to me. I looked down in embarrassment, and replied, "Thank you."

After a moment, Mr. Martins said, "Let me know if there is anything I can help you with, or if you find something to your liking."

The nice customer-lady nodded in acknowledgment, as did the other three customers.

Once they started looking around, I said to Mr. Martins, "I better get going."

He responded, "Okay, but let's just be clear that what you did is obviously working, and I don't think you are capable of failing. You are already a winner in my book and always will be."

What he said made me feel good. It was one thing to receive praise from strangers, or in the newspaper, but it seemed to mean so much more coming from Mr. Martins. Even though he wasn't my dad, and I didn't have a dad, the feeling I got from his words was sort of like what it must feel like to be complimented by your dad. I don't know, but that was just how it felt to me at the moment.

I smiled warmly at him, waved, and left the store. I walked out feeling very different from how I did when I walked in. I walked out feeling like there was at least one person who was truly proud of me and felt that I had value to the world. Perhaps that was my payment for everything I had done. If so, all of my work was worth it.

It caused me to take pride in what I had done. And that caused me to want to do more. It only took me ten seconds to decide what that would be.

I went back down to the hardware store, and looked for the man I usually dealt with. When I found him, he smiled at me with amusement, and said, "Well, Mr. Big Shot, what can I do for you?"

I smirked at his remark, and replied, "I need to buy a broom."

He looked at me in a puzzled way, and responded, "What kind of broom? What do you plan to use it for?"

I replied, "I need to sweep the sidewalks."

He chuckled and started nodding.

He motioned for me to follow him, and he led us over to the "broom section." Because yes, such a section existed. He glanced at the large push brooms, and then selected the one he felt was the best fit for me and the job.

He handed me the broom. I looked at the price and it was WAY MORE EXPENSIVE than I had expected. I had no idea that a broom could cost that much.

I said, "I don't have all of the money for this today, but I have some. Can we put half of it on my account, or do I no longer have that account because we closed it out from the painting?"

He laughed, and responded, "You still have your account. But just take the broom. Go do what you do. Don't worry about buying the broom."

I thanked him, and left the store with the broom. As a way of thanking him, I swept the sidewalk in front of the hardware store first. When I was finished, I walked up to Martins Gifts and swept the sidewalk up there.

While I was doing that, I noticed several customers come and go from the store. It appeared that Mr. Martins was having a good sales day because people were leaving his store with bags in-hand.

When I was finished sweeping in front of Martins Gifts, I called it a day and went home. My mom wasn't there because she was taking advantage of a rare opportunity to work extra hours at work.

The next morning, Sunday, I got on my bike and headed downtown to resume my sweeping project. I swept the sidewalk on the Martins Gifts side of Main Street for quite a while. I was careful not to get dust near anyone walking by. In case you were wondering, I was sweeping the dirt and debris into the street. I'm not sure if this was okay or not, but I thought nothing of it until a police car drove by, saw me doing it, and then stopped.

I obviously wondered if maybe I wasn't supposed to be sweeping dirt into the street, and I wondered if I was in trouble. Perhaps all of this was going to end with me going to jail? Quite frankly, I wouldn't have been surprised if it did. You have to remember that I was used to lots of grief, struggle, and hard breaks in my life.

When the police stopped, they got out of the car, and walked over to me. I naturally stopped sweeping, and started trembling nervously.

The lady cop asked me my name and I told her. She and her partner glanced at each other, smiled, and nodded at each other.

Instead of keeping my mouth shut like you should always do when confronted by the police, I blurted out, "I'm sorry, am I doing something wrong?"

It was a rhetorical question, because by that point I was fairly certain that I was not supposed to be sweeping into the street.

The lady officer responded, "Yes and no."

I didn't know what to think of that.

Then she said, "Technically, you are not supposed to be sweeping debris into a public street, but we can take care of this for you. I assume you are doing the rest of this side of Main Street?"

I replied, "Yes, unless you tell me I can't."

She chuckled and responded, "It's fine. And what about the other side of the street?"

I replied, "Yes, but I can't get to it today."

I was answering them honestly, but both officers started laughing because I guess they already knew that there would be no way for me to sweep the other side that day, also.

The lady responded, "Do you know about when you might be done?"

I replied, "I have to go back to school tomorrow, but I can finish it all in a few days."

The lady said, "Okay. What we are going to do is inform Public Works to run the street sweeper up and down Main Street when you are finished in a few days. That should take care of it."

I replied, "That would be perfect, thank you. I'll do my best to finish it quickly."

She responded, "Let me also say that on behalf of a grateful town, we thank you, Sir."

I was surprised by her words, and I had no reply.

A few moments later, she said, "My partner and I, on behalf of the entire police department, would like to award you with our citizen's law enforcement badge. Will you accept this honor, young man?"

Even though I had no idea what in the world she was talking about, I nodded, and replied, "Yes, Ma'am."

She nodded in return, walked over to the police car, got something from inside it, and then walked back over to me.

She showed me that she had a badge in her hand. I guess it was something they gave to kids sometimes. She asked me if she could put it on me, and I nodded in agreement.

She pinned the "police badge" on my jacket, and then stepped back.

She gave me a little salute, and I looked down at my new badge. It was kind of neat.

I thanked the officers, they waved, and then got back inside their police cruiser and drove off. I resumed sweeping, but now I had a police badge on my jacket. Pretty cool.

CHAPTER FOUR
The Donations

After a weekend of sweeping, I started back into school on Monday morning. All of the kids were looking at me, and there were lots of whispers. I tried to act normal; and our teacher, Mr. M, tried to keep the classroom chatter about me subdued for my sake, I guess.

When it was time for recess, we all went outside, and I made a beeline directly for my bench which I always sat on. Some people might think that my new-found "fame" might have made me the most popular kid in class; but it didn't. If anything, it made me feel more detached and isolated. I felt older than my classmates, like I didn't fit in. I don't think I ever fit in, but now it was even more pronounced.

However, feeling isolated doesn't always mean that you are alone. It wasn't long before I had visitors. Unfortunately, these were unwanted visitors. It was Jeremy and his friends. Except, I should no longer use the word "friends." These kids really were his sycophants. Meaning, I don't think they had a genuine healthy friendship with Jeremy. They were more like his "yes men," who said what Jeremy wanted to hear. If I wanted to be even more cynical and blunt, they were hanging off of him because of money and popularity. They wanted to be close to the kid who was viewed as rich and popular. I bet lots of other kids in school know exactly what I am talking about.

Anyway, I braced myself for incoming missiles. Once Jeremy and his friends reached me, Jeremy said, "Hey, Mr. Hero. I see you are grabbing your fifteen minutes of fame. I bet you think you're not a loser now."

I didn't make direct eye contact, and I just shrugged while remaining silent. Jeremy laughed at me, which caused his friends to laugh also.

After I didn't reply, Jeremy said, "Well, enjoy your fifteen minutes because the reality is that you're just a glorified maintenance worker and janitor who is working for free. WHAT A LOSER! You were nothing before all of this stuff started, and you'll be nothing after everyone has forgotten about it, which they will soon enough. Pathetic losers like you always remain pathetic losers. You were born into it, so you will stay in it. DORK!"

He then started laughing, which I guess meant that he was done speaking. That prompted his friends to laugh as well, even though *their* laughs sounded more fake.

When Jeremy saw that I wasn't going to speak, he turned around and walked away. His 'friends' followed.

Unbeknownst to me, there was someone who had been watching from a distance. They would have likely heard some of the exchange, which only consisted of Jeremy speaking. It was Sally.

She came over to me on the bench and sat down next to me.

After an awkward moment, she said, "Don't believe anything they say. It's all lies."

I didn't reply, but I thought it was a nice thing for her to say.

After more silence, she said, "I don't understand why they act that way. It's weird."

I replied, "It's just Jeremy. The others are brainless followers."

She responded, "But why is Jeremy so mean?"

I thought for a moment, and replied, "People who are mean and lash out for no reason do so because they are in pain about something."

Sally looked at me trying to grasp what I had said.

She responded, "But by being mean, they are putting others in pain."

I replied, "Exactly. And that's why they do it. They are in so much pain that they express it by trying to put others in pain with them. It's their way of trying to get others to feel what they are feeling. If they are miserable, they want others to be miserable with them."

63

She responded, "But why would Jeremy be in pain? It makes no sense. He's popular, rich, and has lots of friends."

I replied, "He doesn't have any *real* friends. Those other kids only follow him around for his money and to use him. I bet deep down Jeremy knows this. But beyond that, I'll bet you anything that there are things going on in his life that we don't know about. I can almost guarantee it."

Sally seemed to accept my explanations and didn't have any further comments about it.

But after a few moments, she said, "Do you believe in magic?"

Her question was unexpected and odd. I looked over at her, and replied, "Yeah. But why do you ask?"

She responded, "Because my dad believes in magic. He always has. And he said at dinner over the weekend that he senses magic within you."

I quipped, "Oh."

That's all I said because I didn't know what else to say. On one hand it felt good to hear that Mr. Martins had said that about me, but on the other hand, it was awkward. How is a person supposed to respond to something like that?

After Sally saw that I wasn't going to give a real reply, she said, "What do you think that means?"

I replied, "I don't know; but I will tell you this. I don't think magic is some mystical force that only a few people hold. I think magic is within all of us; but only some of us choose to use it."

She looked at me in an intrigued way, and responded, "How can someone use their magic?"

I replied, "Magic is when you do things for others that change their lives in ways which they didn't think was possible under their current circumstances."

She was taking that in, and after a couple of moments, responded, "I think I understand now why my dad said that about you."

I quipped, "Why?"

She responded, "Because my dad said that business at our store has gone way up, and it was only because of you that it's happened. So, you did something that my dad thought was impossible."

I smiled and nodded, because regardless of whether I deserved credit for that or not, Sally was showing that she definitely understood my definition of magic. That made me happy. It gave me comfort that she truly understood me. She may have been the only one.

Right then, the bell rang, and we got up from the bench and went inside the school. I didn't have any more run-ins with Jeremy for the next few days.

Each day after school, I went downtown to work. I finished up my sweeping project, and then moved onto the next. For me, the next logical project was to wash windows. I went into the hardware store and told the man that I needed to buy some window cleaner and rags. He asked me some questions, and then informed me that I needed to clean large store windows a different way.

He showed me that I needed a squeegee and window cleaner, otherwise just cleaner and rags would leave a weird film on the glass and it wouldn't look good.

He gathered up all of the equipment and supplies I would need, and then he showed me how to do it by cleaning the window at the hardware store. After we were done, I felt that I understood how to do it. Thank God he showed me, otherwise it might have been a disaster.

I asked the man how much I owed, and he told me not to worry about it. I thanked him and left the store. I decided to begin the window washing project up at Martins Gifts. I had to do the windows twice before the final result was what I wanted it to be. It was getting late, so I left my supplies in Mr. Martins's store because it was time to go home.

On Friday morning, I went to school as usual. However, halfway through the day, the school secretary walked into our classroom and handed the teacher a note. Mr. M read the note, looked up at ME, and said, "You're being called down to the principal's office. You can leave your things at your desk, but I need you to go down to the office now."

The entire class reacted with very loud 'OOOs' and 'AHHHs.' I heard kids saying that I was in trouble, and I heard Jeremy say, "Mr. Hero's luck has finally run out. Now he's Mr. Troublemaker."

Some of the kids laughed. The teacher told Jeremy to be quiet, but he didn't get into any real trouble, because kids like him seemed to always avoid getting into real trouble. It's almost like they're too cool to be punished or something.

As for me, I was terrified and started trembling. I tried to remain calm and cool on the outside because I knew the entire class was looking at me. I was trying to figure out in my mind what in the world I had done. I couldn't think of anything. It was the first time I had EVER been sent to the principal's office. That is partly why it was so shocking to everyone in the class that I was being called down there. I looked at Mr. M, and he seemed mystified. I think he was trying to withhold judgment, because he too could not imagine what in the world I could have done that was so terrible.

I left all of my things on my desk as Mr. M instructed, and I left the classroom. I walked directly to the principal's office. When I got down there, I could see that she was sitting at her desk, but I wasn't sure if I was supposed to just walk in there, or what. I was never in trouble before, so I didn't know the proper protocol for being in trouble.

I looked at the secretary, and said, "I guess I was supposed to come down here?"

She responded, "Yeah, you can go right in."

I walked into the principal's office and immediately felt out of breath; plus, I was sweating, felt light-headed, and wondered if I was going to accidentally pee my pants.

She was looking down at some papers on her desk, so I said, "Ma'am? I'm sorry. I guess I have to be here. I mean, I was supposed to be here. Or come down here. Or you wanted to see me. Or something. I don't know. What should I do? Do I sit over there, or stand here, or..."

She started chuckling and seemed very amused, but in a very friendly way. It was very strange. She didn't seem mad or stern.

I had heard horrible rumors and legends about kids nearly being devoured by her, as if she was a dragon. But she seemed really, umm, "normal" to me. Maybe even "kind?" It was confusing.

She said, "You can take a seat in front of my desk."

I immediately complied with her demand, hoping that my immediate compliance might lighten the harshness of what was about to befall me.

I remained perfectly quiet and perfectly still, although I think I was breathing too loudly, and I was most definitely going to leave sweat marks on her chair.

She took a few moments just to look at me. I guess she was sizing me up? Or was she figuring out how she was going to execute me?

Finally, she said, "You've turned into quite the celebrity. I don't think we've ever had a student like you in this school; at least not since I've been here."

I looked down at the floor. I wasn't sure if she was picking on me, complimenting me, or laying out her case as to why I was in trouble. I remained silent.

After she saw that I was a dead fish, she said, "Well anyway, I've called you down here because we have a big pile of stuff in the front lobby that you need to somehow get home so that we can have our lobby back again, although I'm sure more stuff for you will keep coming in."

I was really confused. It was one of those moments when you wonder if you're having a stroke, or if you've slid into another dimension. I really didn't understand most of what she had said. But at the same time, I was afraid to ask her because I didn't want to seem stupid.

After I once again didn't reply, she stood up from her desk, and said, "Why don't you follow me out to the lobby."

I stood up, waited for her to lead the way, and then followed her out to the front lobby, which I had only seen like twice in my life. All of us kids always entered and exited through a different entrance to arrive and leave school. The lobby was for the teachers, parents, and 'outside people.'

Once we got to the lobby, I saw an area that had been roped off and was full of 'STUFF.' What caught my eye first were three brand-new, shiny, and expensive looking bicycles. But I could also see some nice winter coats, sports jackets, work jackets, gloves, electronic gadgets, school supplies, backpacks, books, notepads, basic carpentry tools, and the list goes on and on. There was a ton of stuff, and there were things piled on top of other things.

I was still confused, and I didn't know what it had to do with me. I looked over at the principal and said, "What is all of this stuff for?"

She smiled with amusement and responded, "It's all for you."

I did a double take at all of the stuff, then back at her, and replied, "FOR ME?"

She responded, "Yeah. The newspaper article you were in last weekend suggested that people could drop things off here at the school for you, if they were so moved to do so. And that's exactly what people have been doing. This stuff has been piling up all week. You didn't know?"

I was really taken aback and in shock.

I quipped, "NO! I HAD NO IDEA!"

She seemed surprised that I didn't know.

After a few moments of me just staring at all of the stuff with my mouth open, she said, "Do you have a way of getting all of this home?"

After a moment, I replied, "Yeah, I guess my mom can come and pick it up with her car, but it's going to take her a few trips."

The principal nodded with satisfaction at my answer.

But then I said, "Are all of those bikes for *me*? What am I going to do with three new bikes?"

She responded, "Ride them, I guess."

I replied, "They won't fit in my mother's car. I will have to ride them home, but it will take me a few trips, obviously."

The principal responded, "That's fine. I'm more concerned about all of the other stuff. It's all piled up where we usually set up our Christmas tree, and it's almost that time. So, if you can get your mom to come down here and get most of the stuff, you can keep the bikes off to the side and take them home when you are able."

I replied, "Yes, Ma'am."

She seemed to remember something, and said, "OH! I have an envelope for you, but I kept it in my office so that it wouldn't get taken. Come with me and I'll give it to you."

I replied, "Okay," and followed her back to her office.

She went behind her desk, pulled something out from one of the drawers, and then came over and handed it to me.

She said, "I know what it is, but go ahead and open it."

I carefully opened the envelope. Inside was a gift certificate from a clothing store downtown that I recognized. They sold all of the cool stuff that the kids with money wore. In fact, it seemed to be Jeremy's favorite local clothing store, and most of his school outfits came from there. The place was not cheap, and therefore I had never bought anything from there. My mom and I always had to go to the factory outlet store outside of town when they were having a sale, and we usually only went there once a year so that I could pick out one or two good outfits for the year.

I looked carefully at the details on the gift voucher, and it was for a huge amount of money. I looked up at the principal in shock.

She said, "The store owner brought that down here himself and handed it to me. He wanted to make it clear that if the amount of money on the voucher was not enough, they will extend it for you. They want you to pick out five complete outfits for school that you really like."

I quipped, "WOW!"

And that really did blow my mind. I think I was thinking that maybe I would be allowed to choose one good outfit; and I would have been thrilled with that. How awesome to have at least ONE cool outfit like what some of the other kids got to wear. It would have been incredible for me. But I was going to be allowed to pick out FIVE outfits?? Holy crap!

I was stunned and was unable to fully grasp everything. The three new bikes and the clothing gift voucher had blown my mind. And then there was the rest of the stuff, too! But yeah, the idea of having new bikes and awesome new clothes had really touched me deep inside.

As I was standing there staring at the gift voucher, the principal seemed to get antsy as if she was busy, and she said, "Why don't you go back to your classroom now. I just had to take care of this before the day got away from me and I missed you again before you left school."

I replied, "Yes, Ma'am."

After a thought, I added, "Do I just walk back into class, or do I need a note?"

She laughed, and responded, "I think Mr. M will let you back in. Go ahead down there. He can check with me later if he has an issue."

I replied, "Okay. Thank you, Ma'am."

She responded, "No problem. And let me just say to you personally, that I am delighted with what you have been doing for our downtown. You are a credit to our school. I thank you for that."

I replied, "Yes, Ma'am. Thank you."

I could tell by then that she was waiting for me to leave so that she could get back to work. I immediately turned away and scooted out of her office. The secretary, who had been listening in on everything from her desk, gave me a little smile and a wave as I walked away down the hallway.

When I got to my classroom, I peeked through the window and saw Mr. M writing something on the board. I used that as my chance to quickly open the door and slide into the room, and zip over to my desk and sit down.

Mr. M noticed me coming in, but didn't say anything, or interrupt what he was doing. All of the kids were looking at me, but I didn't make eye contact with any of them. I focused on Mr. M, and remained still and silent.

When school was over, a few kids asked me what I got into trouble for, or what happened. I just told them it was nothing. I made something up about a paperwork issue that my mother had to deal with. I didn't tell anyone about all of the stuff piled up in the lobby.

When nobody was looking, I went down to the lobby. I decided that I would take one of the bikes home with me. I chose the bike that I thought I liked the best, and took it outside with me. I then went over to where my old bike was on the school bike rack, and I ended up walking both bikes home.

Even though my old bike was old and I didn't need it anymore, it meant a lot to me, and I wanted to keep it for sentimental reasons. Thus, I didn't want to just leave it at the school overnight. So, that is why I walked both a new one and my old one home that day, instead of just riding the new one home.

That evening at dinner, I told my mom what had happened. She didn't seem surprised at all. Maybe someone had told her that people had been dropping things off at the school for me all week.

She agreed to stop at the school and load up the car with as much stuff as she could, and that she would keep doing that each day until she got it all, except for the bikes.

And just like me, she seemed most excited over the gift voucher to the clothing store. The bikes were a close second for her, but the clothes shopping spree seemed to please her to no end. It made me happy to see that she was happy and relieved over that.

I realize that some people might think that all of the donations, gifts, or whatever you want to call them, might have made me feel like I had been amply rewarded for my good deeds, and that maybe it was time for me to be "done" and just be a normal kid again.

But nope. It did the opposite. All of those gifts pushed me further into what I had started, and it caused me to remain all-in regarding this new weird passion I had developed.

Believe it or not, I had only just begun, and the best was yet to come.

CHAPTER FIVE
The Forgiveness

My mission continued, and I kept cleaning windows up and down Main Street. But in my mind, I was crafting my next move already. So far, there were a few different points at which I could have exited all of this self-imposed work and gone back to being a regular kid. But for whatever reason, I didn't want to stop. In fact, I began to wonder if I ever wanted it to end. Perhaps I would just work downtown for free for the rest of my life. Ridiculous, I know. Logically, I knew this. But in my heart, I really wanted to keep going. It obviously wasn't for the money, so what was it?

Well anyway, it wasn't long before I had another stranger walk up to me for a discussion. But this stranger was someone I knew. Yes, that's right. They were both a stranger AND someone I knew, both at the same time. Life is full of things like that, by the way; where two conflicting things can be true at the same time.

This man walked up to me while I was washing a window, and he introduced himself by name, and added that he was the president of the bank that was located up the street. I obviously knew the bank he was referring to, but more than that, I recognized his last name. His last name was the same as a certain rich, spoiled, and privileged kid in my class.

Yes, he had the same last name as Jeremy. And guess what else? Jeremy sort of looked like him. Plus, I thought I once heard Jeremy bragging about how his dad was in charge of an entire bank. So, yeah.

I was standing face to face with Jeremy's father. And yes, it crossed my mind that I could tell this man that his son was a rotting butthole; but I decided to keep my mouth shut instead. Did I do the right thing? What would you have done?

So anyway, I waited to see what the man might have to say to me. If he was anything like his son, he would probably call me a loser and throw dirt in my face.

But he didn't. Instead, he launched into an almost political speech about how I was the pride of the community, and as president of the bank, he wanted to show support for my efforts.

He said, "So tell me young man. If the bank were to make a substantial contribution to your cause, how would you utilize those funds?"

This was clearly a man who spent all of his time in the boardroom, and was speaking to me as if I was 12 going on 32.

And believe it or not, I knew EXACTLY what to say. I had been thinking and scheming all during my time washing windows. I knew what my next move was, and I suppose this was God once again stepping in to facilitate my plans.

I replied, "Sir, I was thinking of installing Christmas lights all up and down Main Street. I want to do other Christmas decorations also. So, any money I get will go to that. And since it will probably take me a long time to get it all done myself, I should probably start right away, even though it's not Thanksgiving yet. Is that okay?"

When I asked him if it was okay, I was not asking his permission to install Christmas lights. I was going to do that anyway. I didn't give a crap if he liked it or didn't like it. I was more asking him if putting Christmas lights up before Thanksgiving would be okay.

But he didn't really answer that.

Instead, he responded, "SPLENDID! I LOVE IT! The bank will absolutely support you in this."

He added, "Would it be okay if the bank disclosed publicly that we provided funding to you for your purposes?"

I replied, "Yeah, sure. That's fine."

I had already been in the newspaper, and I didn't care if people wanted to take some credit for helping me. In my mind, the hardware store and the painting contractor already deserved huge credit for helping me.

The bank president thought for a moment, and responded, "Okay, great. So, look. Let me take care of the technicalities regarding this donation, and then I will get back to you on how to get you the funds. Will that be okay?"

I quipped, "Yeah, that's fine, Sir. Thank you."

He responded, "How can I get a hold of you?"

I replied, "I'll be somewhere downtown on the sidewalk every day after school and on weekends."

He laughed at the simplicity and accuracy of my answer. Even though my reply was ridiculous, he absolutely knew that he would definitely be able to find me with that information.

Two days later, I was getting close to finishing the windows when I had an unwelcome visitor. It was Jeremy with one of his friends. By coincidence, I was washing the windows of the clothing store that had given me the gift voucher (which I hadn't used yet). This store was also Jeremy's favorite store to shop at when he was downtown.

He saw me cleaning the windows as he was walking up to go into the store to buy more clothes for himself, even though he didn't need more clothes.

He looked at me in a condescending way, and said, "Oh look who it is. It's the town loser."

His friend laughed. I remained silent.

Jeremy continued, "Yo, idiot. You do realize that the only reason people in this town are cheering you on is because you are dumb enough to do all of this work for free. You do know that, right? Or, maybe not. Someone as stupid as you who would do all of this work for free wouldn't be smart enough to realize anything at all."

He laughed at me, and thus, so did his friend.

But I wasn't looking at Jeremy. And I wasn't looking at his friend.

I wasn't even looking at the ground. Do you know what or WHO I was looking at? I was looking at Jeremy's father, the bank president, who was standing right behind Jeremy and had heard everything Jeremy just said to me.

I guess his dad, the bank president, had come down to look for me about the bank's donation. His timing was impeccable.

I knew not to say anything, flinch, or blink.

When Jeremy was done, his father yelled, "JEREMY JAMES!"

I guess James was his middle name. Learn something new every day.

Jeremy and his friend lurched, as if being shocked by an electric fence. They both turned around to see Jeremy's dad standing there looking VERY unhappy. Stern, scary, and I would add embarrassed.

Jeremy's father continued, "I am appalled and disgusted by you! You are a disgrace to our family! Shame on you, you little brat!"

(*Yikes!*)

His father's words were so harsh that even I felt a bit scared and very uncomfortable.

Jeremy was quite literally quaking in his shoes, and I wouldn't have been surprised if he peed himself. This was the ultimate example of being caught doing something you shouldn't be doing, and caught by the one person who you would never want catching you.

His father went on, "Your grand life of leisure is OVER! You are DONE, Mister!"

He continued, "First of all, I will take your bank card right now. HAND IT OVER!"

Jeremy sheepishly handed his father his bank card.

His father said, "Now you can get your rear-end back home right this instant! Go up to your room, and stay there. We will then discuss the rest of your punishment when I get home."

Jeremy and his dad just looked at each other, and then Jeremy's father exclaimed, "GO! NOW!"

Jeremy, with red eyes and being close to a full emotional breakdown, started walking away. At no point did he ever make eye contact with me.

Once Jeremy and his friend were out of ear-shot, his father looked at me in a horrified and embarrassed way, and said, "I am so sorry. I cannot even express to you how sorry I am, young man. I hope this is the first and only time my son has ever spoken to you in that way before. I hope you will forgive me and my family."

I looked down at the ground in a very docile way. I was not celebrating any of this, nor was I happy about it. It had been way over the top, and I was very uncomfortable with everything. And no, I didn't want to tell him that Jeremy had been torturing me for as long as I could remember. I guess I felt that Jeremy was in enough trouble as it was, and I was uncomfortable adding to it. Imagine if his father knew the full extent of how Jeremy had been treating me? Would Jeremy be executed?

I know some people out there might wonder why I wouldn't have wanted that, or even enjoyed it. I don't have a satisfying answer for you other than to say that I wasn't interested in that. Although I didn't enjoy other people making my life miserable, I also had no desire to make other people's lives miserable, even if maybe they deserved it. It just wasn't me.

Well anyway, after his father saw that I wasn't going to reply or react in any way, he said, "Let me not forget why I came looking for you. I wanted to ask if you currently have an established bank account at any financial institution? I know you don't have an account with our bank, because I checked."

I replied, "No, Sir. I don't have any money, so I don't have a bank account."

He responded, "Well, that's about to change. What I would like to do is have you open up an account at my bank. Because of your age it will just be a savings account for now, but I will get you an ATM card and waive all of the fees involved with your account. This way, I can transfer funds directly into your account. Will that meet with your approval?"

I honestly didn't know, but I nodded, and replied, "Yes, Sir. But I don't know how to do all of that."

He responded, "I'll take care of everything. All I need you to do is come into the bank with your birth certificate and social security card. Your mother should have that stuff, and she can come with you if she prefers."

I replied, "Yeah, I know my mother has those things. I will get them from her and go to the bank. My mom works, so it's hard for her to do things like that. It'll probably just be me."

He responded, "Well, just make sure you bring those two things, and then explain to someone in the bank lobby who you are and that you are working directly with *me*. They will take care of you. Then after your account is open, you should see a deposit into your account within the week. Just go into the bank and ask them for your balance. You can then withdraw money as you need it."

I nodded in acknowledgment.

He continued, "Let's see how it goes. If it works out for all concerned, we might contribute more into your account if you need it for your plans here on Main Street."

I nodded, and replied, "Yes, Sir. Thank you very much."

He responded, "It's my pleasure. I only wish I had a son like you instead of the one I have."

When he said that, I cringed and looked down. It made me feel bad. I know he was trying to compliment me, but I felt bad for Jeremy.

It seemed we were done, but then I had a question.

I said, "Sir, I know the money you are donating is for Christmas lights and decorations, but am I allowed to buy a donut or something to drink if I really need it and don't have any other money?"

He started laughing, and responded, "You can buy whatever you want and whatever you need. I was just hoping you wouldn't use our donation to go out and buy new bicycles or electronics for yourself. But of course you can buy food or supplies that you need for yourself."

I replied, "Sir, I don't need to buy new bicycles with it because people already gave me three new bikes. I'm good with bikes."

He chuckled and nodded.

After a thought, he reached into his pocket and pulled out a $20 bill and handed it to me.

He said, "You can get yourself something right now. I should get back to the bank. Come into the bank soon and we'll be in touch."

I replied, "I will. Thank you."

He waved and walked away back up toward the bank.

I decided that I had my fill of drama for the day, and I went home. I wanted to make sure that I got everything I needed from my mother so that I could go to the bank and open up my account. I felt that time was of the essence. Christmas season was closing in on us, and I needed enough time to go big on what I wanted to do downtown.

I explained to my mother everything the bank president had said, and although she seemed confused and skeptical, she provided me with what I needed, and told me not to lose it.

I went to school the next day, and Jeremy seemed very subdued. He was quiet the entire day, and I could sense that he was in deep trouble, and pretty much in mourning over that. He wasn't joking around with his friends, and he kept his head down for most of the day. He never looked at me or said a word to me, and he never got near me.

After school, I rode my bike downtown with the documents I had brought to school with me. I went directly to the bank. I went inside with my documents and asked a lady about who I needed to speak with in order to open my account that the bank president told me to open up. Me using the term "bank president" seemed to result in a flurry of activity. I guess they knew who I was and why I was there at that point.

They took my documents and opened up my account. The lady said I would receive a card in the mail, but in the meantime, she gave me something with my account number on it and told me that I could withdraw money using the number.

She made me wait a few minutes, because she said that they were processing a deposit for me. Usually when you open a new account, you need to have some money to deposit into it. It's a good thing I didn't need that for mine, because I only had $5 on me, and that was for a snack.

I guess due to my situation, they didn't need any money from me, and they were depositing the bank's donation into my account. Once that was done, the lady gave me a deposit slip which showed the deposit and my account balance.

After I looked at it, I said, "This can't be right. Are you sure this is mine?"

The reason I said that was because the deposit and balance seemed HUGE to me. It was more money than I had ever seen before in my life; and I knew that even my mother would consider it to be a lot of money.

The lady took my deposit slip back, looked at it closely, and then handed it back to me, and said, "This is correct, and this is yours. That is the donation amount approved by the bank president. I guess you are using it for Christmas lights. They won't be cheap. You are welcome to come back if you exhaust this balance."

I was still shocked, but I shrugged, thanked her, and left.

As soon as I had walked out the doors of the bank, I saw a familiar face. It was Jeremy. And guess what? He was washing the windows to the bank, and he had a big push broom nearby as well.

I looked over at him and stared because I couldn't believe my eyes. He was seriously sweeping the walkway and washing the bank windows?

He saw me looking at him, and I was afraid he was going to start hurling insults at me. But he didn't. In fact, he looked very dejected, sad, and defeated. He remained completely silent.

Something about his demeanor compelled me to walk over to him. Once I got to him, he stopped working and just looked at me.

After a moment, he said, "Go ahead and laugh at me if you want."

I replied, "I don't want to."

He looked down at the ground.

I said, "Are you okay?"

He looked up and responded, "Why do you care?"

I replied, "Because I know what happened was kind of scary and harsh. I didn't mean for you to get into that much trouble. I didn't know that your dad was coming right at that moment. I couldn't say anything to you because before I knew it, he was standing there, and I couldn't tell you because he was right there. I'm sorry."

He responded, "Why are you saying 'sorry' to *me*? I'm the one who was mean to *you*."

I replied, "Yeah, but why? I've always wondered."

He responded, "My dad asked me that same question. And I don't know why. You are a nice kid at school, and everyone likes you. The WHOLE TOWN loves you. So, I don't know."

After a pause, he said, "And maybe that's why."

I replied, "What do you mean?"

He responded, "Everyone loves *you*, and they hate *me*."

I was confused by his statement, and replied, "No they don't. You are the most popular kid in class and you have tons of friends. Plus, your dad seems cool and he gives you money for shopping. How can you say nobody likes you?"

He responded, "I am only popular because of my dad and our money. And I only have friends because they want me to buy them things. And the truth is that my dad doesn't like me. He just puts up with me because he has to. So yeah, nobody likes me. And I guess it makes me feel like crap sometimes. I'm sorry I took it out on you."

I looked down at the ground. It was humbling. I felt that his apology was genuine so it was a bit uncomfortable.

I looked back up at him and said, "Why are you here washing windows?"

He responded, "Because I'm grounded, and my dad says I have to do a bunch of chores out in public like what you have been doing. Except I am doing them in shame, and you are doing them out of admiration or whatever. You know what I mean."

I thought for a moment, and replied, "Why don't you get all of your friends to help you? You could finish all of this in less than a day."

He responded, "Like I said, I don't have any real friends. My so-called friends only want to go shopping with me so that I buy them something. After I told them that I had to wash all of these windows and sweep everything, they told me that they were busy and couldn't help me."

I put my head down again. I felt bad for him. I also felt that it must have been very humiliating for him to be so honest and transparent with me. THAT caused me to have empathy for him, which was weird. This was a kid who literally tortured me and took great delight in it. But there was something about him feeling so abandoned, unliked, and isolated that made me identify with him. I knew how he was feeling, because I had felt that way most of my life. It was weird, but all of a sudden, I felt like Jeremy and I had a lot in common.

That is when I decided to do something that was illogical, strange, and probably nobody else would be able to understand it.

I decided to help him.

I said, "I'm actually an expert at washing windows now. I'll tell you what. Why don't you start sweeping. Start in the far corner, and work your way all the way to the other side. Then I will go behind you and clean all of the windows. This way, the dust from the sweeping doesn't get onto the clean windows. That's why you should always sweep first.

I've screwed it up before, and that's why I know better now."

Jeremy smiled, and responded, "*Oh, yeah*, hmmm."

After a moment, he added, "You're really going to help me? Even after everything I've said to you?"

I replied, "Yeah. You don't need to do this yourself. It's smarter if we do it together. I don't mind. I'm used to this."

He smiled again, went to get the broom, and started sweeping. I had to wait until he was finished with the first area before starting the windows.

After a minute or so, he said, "You know, I can't pay you back for this. I can't buy you anything or give you money. My dad took away my bank card and my allowance."

I replied, "I don't expect you to give me anything; and I don't need your money. I have my own now."

He looked at me in stunned confusion, but didn't respond.

We worked in silence the rest of the time, but when it came time for me to go home, I said, "Hey Jeremy, I need to go home for dinner, but I can help you tomorrow also, if you want."

He seemed uncomfortable with my kindness, but the difficult reality of the job facing him was enough to cause him to nod in acceptance of my offer.

He said, "I will understand if you change your mind and don't want to, but I would like that if you can do it. I know you're busy."

I replied, "Then I'll see you at school tomorrow, and then again here after school."

He responded, "Okay, see you then."

I left the bank and headed down Main Street. I needed to make one stop before going home. I needed to go to the hardware store.

Once I arrived, I looked around the store for the owner. When I found him, I said, "Sir, I'm wondering if you can help me with something. I need more stuff, but this time I have money to pay for it, so don't worry."

He smiled in amusement, and responded, "What can I get for you?"

I replied, "I'm going to need lots of Christmas lights. Probably tons of them."

He got a huge grin on his face, and I wasn't sure if it was because he was amused by what I was up to next, or if it was because he had already figured it out, and he was pleased that his guess was correct.

He responded, "Well, I've already got an order of Christmas lights coming in, but I will order more. Should I assume that we need lights for all of downtown?"

I replied, "Yes, Sir."

He responded, "That's going to be expensive, young man."

I replied, "Yeah, I figured. But the bank up the street donated a bunch of money for it."

I then told him how much money I had to work with. He seemed quite impressed.

I added, "They also said that I could go back for more money, if needed. They want to see how it goes first."

The man responded, "Okay, who are you dealing with over at the bank?"

I replied, "The bank president."

He got a priceless expression on his face, and responded, "You don't mess around, do you boy?"

I quipped, "Nope."

After a thought, he responded, "I've been trying to get a meeting with the president of that bank for months, and can't seem to do it."

I replied, "I can probably make that happen for you, Sir."

He quipped, "I'LL BET YOU CAN!"

He started laughing, but he wasn't laughing *at* me. He was laughing because he knew it was true.

After a couple of moments, he said, "Yeah, alright. So, are you going with inside or outside lights? And colored or white?"

I wasn't expecting those questions. He had me stumped.

He saw this, and said, "I'll get lights that can be used outside as well as inside. But do you want white or colored?"

I thought about it, and replied, "White looks really nice, but I want everything to look extra Christmasy, so let's go with colored."

He quipped, "YES, SIR!"

I replied, "Thank you."

He responded, "I'll have enough in a day or two to get you started, and the rest should be in within a week."

I replied, "Okay, thanks."

I waved and left. I then rode my bike home.

The next day at school during recess, I immediately went to sit alone on my bench as usual.

I sat there for about two minutes, and then I had a visitor. It was Jeremy. But he didn't have any of his friends with him.

He said, "Hey, I just wanted to make sure that you are doing okay. I saw you sitting alone, so I just wanted to make sure you weren't lonely or something."

I replied, "No, I'm fine. I just like to sit and think."

He responded, "I'm just letting you know that I saw Sally staring at you. She's with her friends way over there, but I think she wants to talk to you. I'll leave so that she'll come over. See you after school?"

I quipped, "For sure."

He gave me a friendly wave and walked away.

Sure enough, a minute later, Sally came over and sat down on the bench with me.

She said, "Hey, I saw Jeremy over here. Are you okay? Was he saying mean things again?"

I replied, "No, Jeremy's fine. We're good."

She couldn't believe her ears. She responded, "What do you mean? He's awful! He's been nothing but mean to you."

I replied, "I know; but we talked it out, and I forgave him. He and

I are friends now."

Sally didn't know what to think of that.

After a few moments, she responded, "How can you forgive someone like that?"

I replied, "Remember when I told you that people like that are mean because they are in pain?"

She quipped, "Yeah?"

I replied, "Well, I figured out why he is in pain."

I added, "Sally, there is no point in me resenting him because he is in pain. That just makes things worse. He was honest with me, and in return I gave him a chance to try and be better. That's what friends do, and that's what *everyone* should do. There's magic in it."

She was just looking at me.

It was getting awkward, so I quipped, "WHAT?"

She responded, "You're the weirdest boy I've ever known."

I laughed, and replied, "GEE, THANKS!"

She responded, "No, that's not what I meant. I don't mean it in a bad way. It's just that you're so different. But in a good way. I meant it in a good way."

I was smiling and shaking my head.

I replied, "Yeah, I get it. It's fine."

There was another awkward silence, and then she said, "I think I'm going to be downtown once or twice this week. Do you want me to bring you more donuts?"

I replied, "You don't have to. But if you bring them, I'll eat them."

She looked down at the ground while shaking her head; and after replaying what I said to her in my head, I realized that it sounded rude. So, I said, "I mean, yes, that would be really nice. Thank you."

She seemed to like that response better, and she nodded.

Just then, the bell rang signifying that recess was over. We went inside and resumed classes.

After school when I was getting my bike to ride downtown, I saw Jeremy getting onto one of the school buses. You have to understand that during that period of time at my school, it wasn't that cool to ride the bus. I always rode my bike, and Jeremy usually got picked up by his mom in her fancy car.

As it turned out, Jeremy and I both arrived at the bank around the same time, probably because the bus had to keep stopping and took a slightly longer route.

I said to him, "Hey, I thought you didn't take the bus?"

He responded, "I never did. But as part of my punishment, my mom no longer picks me up at school, and they took away my bike."

I felt bad. I knew that he deserved it, but the fact that his punishment was BECAUSE OF ME made me feel bad.

After a few moments, I said, "You can use one of my bikes if you want. And I'm not talking about my old bike. I have two other new ones that I don't even use. You can borrow one of those if you want."

He looked genuinely stunned by my offer.

He responded, "You would seriously let ME use one of your new bikes?"

I replied, "Yeah, it's fine. I keep them at the school in the lobby. I can tell them that I gave you permission to use one. You'll just need to hide it from your parents. You can keep it at the hardware store in the backroom. Just tell them that we are working together and they'll let you. Then you just need a place to hide it at your house."

He was silent.

After a while, he responded, "Who would have guessed that it would be *you* letting me use *your* bike?"

We both laughed, and I said, "Why? Because you're rotten?"

Then I splashed him with a little bit of the water in my bucket I had. We laughed some more.

Jeremy and I finished our work at the bank that day, and more than that, we had the best time doing it. We talked freely with each other about all kinds of things that boys our age usually talk about. I decided that I wasn't just being nice by forgiving him. I decided that I actually liked him, and I think we became friends for real that day.

CHAPTER SIX
The Meeting

Thanksgiving was bearing down on us, and therefore so was Christmas season. I knew that I really needed to hurry and get as many lights up on Main Street as possible. I knew that the Christmas holiday officially started on the day after Thanksgiving, and I wanted as much of downtown decorated as possible by then.

I fully realize that most people only BEGIN decorating for Christmas on the day after Thanksgiving. But I was facing the task of decorating all of downtown, and I didn't want to be finishing it the day after Christmas. I wanted downtown to look Christmasy for the entire Christmas season. So, for me this meant that I needed to get most of the decorating done before Thanksgiving, if possible; or at least by the beginning of December.

After school one day, I rode my bike downtown and went directly to the hardware store. I asked the man if he had any lights I could use to get me started. He said that he did. In fact, he pointed to an area that was sort of out of the way, and I saw a huge pile of small boxes with Christmas lights in them.

The man said, "Just take them as you need them. All I ask is that you keep track of how many boxes you take."

I replied, "Okay. I will withdraw some money from my account and bring it down to you in the next couple of days. Is that okay?"

He responded, "Yeah, that's fine."

You'll notice that there was no exact or formal procedure for me to receive and pay for the goods. It was as if he didn't really care, even though he had expressed before that the lights were a lot of money. That was my hint that he DID need to be paid for them; but he didn't seem very uptight about me paying before taking them out the door; nor did he even require that they be rung up at the register and put on my account. This was the 'honor system' at its finest, and I will admit that it made me even MORE honest than I already was, because I didn't want to violate the very high level of trust that he and others had in me.

Because of that, my next stop was the bank. I went in and asked for a substantial withdraw. After I had that business taken care of, I went to Martins Gifts, where I had left the lights before continuing onto the bank.

I went inside, and Mr. Martins said, "I guess it's pretty obvious what you are here to do, given all of the boxes of Christmas lights."

I replied, "Is that okay, Sir?"

He responded, "What did you have in mind?"

I replied, "Well for sure, I want to try and have lights on all of the store windows. But I am open to doing extra wherever you want it."

He nodded, and responded, "Why don't you just go ahead and do what you want, and then we'll see how it looks."

I replied, "Okay."

After a moment, he responded, "How do you plan on installing them? Inside or outside, and with what are you using to attach the lights to the framing?"

I thought about what he said and my mind froze. I literally had no idea. Mr. Martins was looking at me carefully, and I think he could see all of this playing out in my mind. He started laughing. This caused me to start laughing.

After we calmed down, he said, "Most of these stores don't have exterior electrical outlets, so it might be easier to install them inside. Just make sure you do it so that the lights can be seen from outside."

I nodded.

He continued, "You are going to need some nails, or tacks, or something to do it. Do you have anything?"

I replied, "No, but I will go get that stuff now."

He chuckled and nodded.

I scooted outside and took off on my bike to the hardware store. Once I arrived, I went inside, and the owner was behind the customer counter.

He said, "Let me guess. You figured out that you need a way to install the lights."

I smiled, and replied, "Yes, Sir."

He responded, "I had already gotten that together for you, but I forgot to give it to you. Sorry."

I replied, "That's okay. I needed to come back here anyway."

He responded, "Why is that?"

I replied, "I have some money for you."

I took the money I got from the bank and dropped it all on the counter.

The man counted it, and said, "That's quite a substantial prepayment, young man."

I replied, "Yeah, but I have a bad feeling that I'll still be owing you money before this is all over."

He started laughing while nodding his head in agreement.

He responded, "Don't worry about that. We'll work it out."

The man gave me a big bag of supplies. It had a couple of hammers plus a variety of tacking clips used for installing the lights.

Then he said, "Do you know how to do this? Have you done it before?"

I replied, "No, Sir."

He responded, "Here, let's do one window together. I guess you are starting at this store."

I quipped, "Okay."

We went over to his front window, and he proceeded to affix a string of lights up, and then across his window. After I watched him do it, he had me do the other half. He corrected me a couple of times and showed me how to do it more efficiently. He was very patient and attentive with me, and I really liked that. I wasn't used to that from people.

By the time we were done, I felt that I knew how to do it. I thanked him and left.

I went back up to Martins Gifts.

Mr. Martins said, "What took you so long?"

I replied, "I was learning how to do this from the hardware store man. I had no idea."

He started laughing and shaking his head in amusement.

After a few moments, he said, "Okay, well let's see what you learned."

I then proceeded to install some lights on the front window of Martins Gifts. It didn't go that smoothly, but it was the first window I ever did myself, so I guess that was to be expected.

I eventually finished, and it looked really good. We plugged in the lights to be sure they worked. They did.

So, officially, the hardware store, and then Martins Gifts, were the first two stores to get Christmas lights. I say this because many people have wondered or assumed that it was Martins Gifts. And although that was the first store I did myself, it was really the hardware store that was the first; and that was because the owner was teaching me how to install the lights properly.

For the next couple of days, I installed more lights within more stores. But early that evening when I was about to go home, I had another visitor whom I recognized. It was the lady-junior-reporter/photographer from the newspaper.

She asked if she could speak with me, and I said she could. She told me that the newspaper office had heard that I was going from store to store installing Christmas lights, and she wanted to verify if that was true. I told her it was. She then asked me what my intentions were regarding all of this. I told her that I wanted every store, and the entire downtown, to be decorated for Christmas. She asked me how I was going to accomplish that, and I told her that the bank had donated a lot of money for the lights, and the hardware store was providing me with everything I needed. She seemed skeptical that I could do all of it myself, and I just told her that I would finish as much of it as I could before Christmas.

After that, she asked me to pose for another photo like before. I once again agreed on the condition that it was in front of Martins Gifts. Thus, we went up to the store, and with the Christmas lights shining through the front window, I stood for a few pictures. The lady thanked me and left. Because it was getting late, I then went home.

The next day was rinse and repeat. More lights installed in more windows. It was starting to look really nice, if I do say so myself. Things were definitely taking shape. But I didn't do all of the work myself on that day. I had help. Jeremy found me, and he came into the store in which I was working.

I said, "Hey, how are you? What are you doing here?"

He responded, "I'm grounded and not allowed to leave my bedroom, but my mom had something she needed to do, and she let me come with her. I think she feels sorry for me, even though she won't admit it."

I replied, "How long are you grounded for?"

He responded, "My dad says until Christmas. He also said that I shouldn't expect much for Christmas this year. I'm fine with that, but what sucks is that I'm going to miss life until after Christmas."

I didn't say anything. I once again felt bad.

After a moment, Jeremy said, "I have about an hour before I have to be back to the car. Do you want me to help you?"

I replied, "Sure, that would be great."

Jeremy helped me finish the window I was working on, and then we both did the next one together. It was nice having his company, and his help.

When it was time for him to leave, I thanked him, and he went back to his mom's car so that he wouldn't get into trouble.

Regarding my run-in with the junior reporter lady from the newspaper, a second article ran in the newspaper. It had a picture of me standing in front of Martins Gifts with the Christmas lights on. The story talked about how I was going from store to store installing lights, and how I was trying to do all of downtown.

The only part of the story I didn't like was that it intimated that there was no way I would be able to complete the job on my own. But other than that, it was favorable, and it didn't say anything embarrassing about me like last time when they said I was poor. But with that said, I would have never received the new bikes and all of the great donations if they hadn't disclosed that.

With all of that said above, that second newspaper article was the catalyst for one of the miracles which occurred that Christmas season.

On Saturday morning, downtown started filling with people. But they weren't shoppers. They were volunteers who wanted to help me decorate downtown. And there were a lot of them. Not only that, but they brought their own decorations, such as wreaths, ribbons, bells, and things like that. It was like being invaded by an army of Christmas decorators.

Additionally, some of the store owners came to me and offered to install their own lights if I provided them with the lights. They wanted to remain consistent with the type of lights I had been using for all of the other stores.

I quickly realized that I would not be getting any work done that day. I ran over to the bank before they closed early, since it was Saturday, and I withdrew most of the remaining money in my account. I then scooted down to the hardware store.

I explained to the man that I needed to take a ton of the lights, and distribute them to some of the volunteers helping, in addition to the store owners who asked for some. I dropped all of the money I had onto the counter, and asked him to let me know how much more I owed, and that we would need to order more lights.

After counting out the money, he informed me that I still had a balance owed, but not to worry about it. I thanked him, but I was still going to worry about it, obviously. I knew I had to do something about the balance I owed, and I knew I would owe even more than that before it was all said and done.

But with that said, I focused on getting through the weekend. I quickly started going up and down Main Street giving out lights to the store owners who asked for them, and giving some to volunteers who appeared to be actively ready to install some.

As I walked up and down Main Street, volunteers were asking me a ton of questions about how I wanted things decorated. I guess I was in charge? I wasn't expecting any of this, although I was grateful for the help.

I suggested that the light poles be wrapped with ribbons, and wreaths be hung on the doors of the stores. Then I asked for red bows to be put on the wreaths, and for other red bows to be installed on top of the store windows.

To be honest, I was just making it all up as I went along, and saying whatever automatically came out of my mouth. Fortunately, everything I said seemed to make sense and nobody questioned any of it.

All of this continued through Sunday as well. Even though I didn't install a single string of lights myself that weekend, I was exhausted after putting in two long days of "supervising," if you want to call it that.

And I'll tell you what. Downtown looked AMAZING by Sunday evening. It looked like a Christmas town. For real.

There was still more that needed to be done, but what we had for decorations on Main Street that weekend before Thanksgiving was nothing short of magical and beautiful.

On Monday, life returned back to normal, even though there was nothing normal about my life by that point. I went to school, and then after school, I rode my bike downtown. However, I wasn't going to be installing lights. Instead, I had some serious business to attend to.

I went directly to the bank. I went inside and up to one of the ladies who worked there. They all knew who I was by then, and they always smiled at me and greeted me warmly.

The lady asked me how she could help me, and I replied, "Can I please see the bank president? I have some things I need to discuss with him."

She looked at me a bit cynically, as if she wasn't sure if she should block me from seeing him or not.

She motioned for me to stay put while she went to a nearby phone and made a call. I couldn't hear what she said except that I heard her give my name.

When she finished the call, she came back over to me, and said, "He will see you. Come with me, and I will bring you up to the executive offices."

I followed her upstairs, and found myself in a different world. The executive office area was much nicer and more formal than the public customer area downstairs.

I saw some fancy portraits on the wall, and one of them was of Jeremy's dad, the bank president. I was beginning to understand why everyone in town thought he was such a big deal, even though I just considered him to be "the bank president" and "Jeremy's dad."

The lady led me down a long hallway all the way to the end. She motioned for me to wait, and I did. She poked her head into the doorway of the office, and whispered something that I couldn't hear. But then I heard Jeremy's dad say, "YES!"

The lady turned around and motioned for me to go inside. So, I did.

Jeremy's dad looked up from his desk, and yelled my name, as if he was really pleased to see me. He then motioned for me to take a seat in front of his desk.

I sat down, and then looked all around me. It was a large corner office with lots of photos on the walls and very fancy furniture.

He interrupted my gazing all over his office by saying, "Downtown looks great! You've done an amazing job!"

I replied, "Thank you, Sir; but I've had a lot of help. I may have started this myself, but since then, I've had you, the hardware store, the big construction company in town, and lots of people I don't even know help out."

He responded, "I know! It's turned into a 'thing,' and I think it's going to get even bigger. It's good for downtown, it's good for all of the business owners, and it's good for our city. We all owe you a large debt of gratitude. What can I do for you, young man?"

I gathered my thoughts for a moment, and replied, "Well, you asked me to come see you if I ran out of money for the lights. So, I'm here to say that I've run out of money for the lights."

He started laughing. It must have been the way I said it, or who knows. I was hoping I hadn't said or done anything stupid. I decided to break that moment by speaking again.

I said, "The truth is that I overspent, and the hardware store says I owe them money on my account. If you can't help me, it's okay, though. The owner said he will work it out with me somehow."

He started laughing again, and said, "You're the same age as Jeremy, right? So, you are 12 or 13?"

I quipped, "Yes, Sir. I'm 12, but I'll be 13 in January; so almost 13, really."

He responded, "And at that age you have a large commercial credit account at the hardware store?"

I hesitated, and replied, "I guess so, Sir."

He started laughing to himself again and shaking his head.

After a couple of moments, he responded, "Well, we have to keep your good credit intact, so we'll have to make sure you can clear your account balance with them."

I replied, "Okay, thank you."

He looked at me while in thought, and said, "We were already prepared to donate more money. Plus, all of us are highly pleased and impressed with how things are looking around here."

He continued, "Here's what we're going to do. I'm going to transfer more funds into your personal account. But that money is for you, or for odds and ends that might be needed. Don't give that money to the hardware store. If it's acceptable to you, young man, the bank will settle up your account directly with the hardware store. Will that work okay?"

I replied, "Yes, Sir. But will I be allowed to keep using my account at the hardware store if I need to?"

He responded, "Yes, of course. It's just that it might be easier and more transparent for us to pay them directly. This way there will be no questions from the Board of Directors as to what I am doing. It will also allow me to give you additional contributions as you need them."

I replied, "Okay, Sir, thank you."

He responded, "GREAT! GLAD WE CAN HELP!"

Jeremy's dad was acting as if the meeting was over and I should leave. But I wasn't done. I wasn't even close to being done.

When I didn't immediately get up, he said, "Was there anything else I can do for you today?"

I replied, "Yes, Sir. I was wondering if you could do me a favor."

He responded, "What's that?"

I replied, "The owner of the hardware store has been very helpful, friendly, and generous toward me during all of this from the very beginning. He mentioned to me that he had been trying to get a meeting with you for a really long time about something."

Jeremy's dad interjected, "OH YES! I know he has. I haven't been avoiding him; it's just that something always comes up and distracts me."

I replied, "Well, I was hoping that maybe you would agree to meet with him. I don't know what it's about, but just having a meeting with him would mean a lot to me."

Jeremy's dad seemed surprised that I was pushing hard for the benefit of the hardware store owner.

He responded, "Yeah, yeah, definitely. What I will do is have my secretary call him into a meeting regarding payment on your commercial credit account, and then he can discuss with me whatever else he wants."

I quipped, "Thank you, that's great."

He then quipped, "GREAT! TERRIFIC!"

I guess that was him once again hoping that I would get up and leave. But I didn't.

Thus, he said, "Anything else?"

I replied, "Yes, Sir."

He responded, "What else you got?"

I replied, "This next one is a stretch, and it's okay if you say no, but I have an idea."

He responded, "I'm listening."

After a pause, I replied, "Do you know that stretch of vacant space on Main Street where the sporting goods store used to be?"

He responded, "Yeah. That vacant block is like a huge black eye for all of downtown."

I replied, "Well, I want to do one of those pop-up stores in that space. That vacancy is ugly and it's ruining what we are trying to do. We need to fix that, and I thought we could get things rolling by turning it into a pop-up Christmas store. It would fill the space at least temporarily, but if it did well, maybe we can keep it open and transition it to a seasonal store that changes their merchandise depending upon the time of year."

He was staring at me while his hamster wheels were grinding away.

Just then, his secretary came in and said that he had a phone call, and that his next meeting was soon.

He replied to her, "Hold all of my calls, and push the meeting out a half hour. I'm busy with this young man on some very important business matters."

The secretary nodded and walked away.

Jeremy's dad reengaged his hamster wheels. He stared into space a few more moments, and said, "Interesting. However, don't take this the wrong way, but running a big business like that is a very serious challenge, and a full-time job. I think we need to keep you in school a bit longer, don't you think?"

I smirked and replied, "I wouldn't be running it, Sir. Well, I COULD RUN IT. I'm sure of it. But I was thinking more about someone else who could run it."

He responded, "And who might that be?"

I replied, "Mr. Martins of Martins Gifts. He's very experienced, and he already knows how to run a store like that."

Jeremy's dad responded, "Yes. Yes, indeed. But I think he is struggling as it is."

I replied, "Yeah, he's struggling because nobody comes to our downtown to shop, and his store carries a very narrow line of merchandise."

I continued, "Sir, we are changing downtown. We can get more people to shop here with everything we've been doing. Plus, filling the vacant space on Main Street helps us do that, also."

Jeremy's dad just stared at me, but grew a large amused and mischievous grin on his face.

He said, "Good gracious, boy; how can you be in sixth grade? I feel like I'm talking to a 50-year-old business entrepreneur."

I remained silent with a smirky grin on my face.

There was a long silence while he moved around in his chair thinking.

Eventually, he said, "So what are you asking for? What do you need from me?"

I replied, "I was hoping that you might know who owns that vacant space, and talk to them about letting us try this. And then I was hoping you would open up an account, or loan, or whatever for Mr. Martins, so that he would be able to buy merchandise for the new store and get it all up and running."

Jeremy's father quipped, "You mean like a business line of credit?"

I quipped, "YEAH, like that. You know, so that Mr. Martins can buy what he needs for the store. He will only use the money to set up that store and buy the merchandise. We can pay it all off as we sell merchandise."

Jeremy's dad was tapping his fingers on the arm of his chair, and then his desk. He was moving around and looking up in the air, and all around. I could tell that he was intrigued, but not expecting ANY of this.

After several moments, he responded, "Out of curiosity, what would you call this new store?"

I actually had not even thought of that. But without thinking, and without hesitation, I blurted out, "Christmas Town!"

I added, "But I'm not sure. I'm open to suggestions."

He was nodding, and responded, "No, I like that. That's good. Very good. Interesting."

He did more tapping and moving around in his chair, and then he said, "Here's what I want to do. I want to meet with Mr. Martins about this. I want to make sure we have a firm understanding of what he needs from us, and what we expect from him. So, is it alright with you if I call him into a meeting?"

I replied, "Yeah, but can you give me a chance to tell him about all of this first?"

Jeremy's dad made a weird face, and responded, "Tell him about it? You mean Mr. Martins doesn't know about any of this yet?"

I replied, "No, not yet; but he will after I tell him."

Jeremy's dad started laughing hysterically. I thought he might even fall out of his chair.

After he calmed down a bit and could breathe again, he exclaimed, "GOOD LORD, BOY! YOU ARE GOING TO BE IMPOSSIBLE TO KEEP UP WITH! BY THE TIME YOU GRADUATE HIGH SCHOOL, YOU'LL BE RUNNING THE ENTIRE TOWN!"

I was smirking while looking down at the floor in embarrassment.

After a few moments, I looked up and said, "I know Mr. Martins will do it, Sir. I just didn't want to get him all excited about the idea until I could see if it was possible or not."

Jeremy's dad nodded, and responded, "Yeah, I understand. Well, it's possible. So, why don't you do *your* thing, and then I'll do *my* thing. We need to move fast because Christmas season is upon us."

I replied, "Yes, exactly."

I could tell that he was getting really itchy for me to leave again, but I had one more thing to discuss.

I said, "I know you need me to leave, Sir. But I have one more thing, and it's the most important thing of all."

He looked at me intently because of how I had phrased it.

He responded, "Well, I don't know if I can handle much more, but go ahead."

I replied, "It's about your son, Jeremy."

As soon as I said that, his face turned grim, and he looked down at his desk, almost in shame, or as if he was embarrassed.

After a moment, he looked up, and responded, "Yeah, I'm really sorry about what Jeremy said to you. He's being punished for that, and he will continue to be punished for quite some time to come."

I replied, "That's what I wanted to talk to you about, Sir. I was going to ask you for another favor."

He was intrigued and confused by my statement, and responded, "How do you mean?"

I replied, "I would like to ask you to unground Jeremy. To forgive him and let it go."

Jeremy's dad seemed to be astounded and flummoxed by what I had just requested.

After a moment of being at a loss for words, he responded, "I heard what Jeremy said to you. What he said was unforgivable. I don't understand how you could suggest letting it go."

(Imagine what Jeremy's dad would have thought if he knew about EVERYTHING Jeremy had said to me.)

I replied, "Sir, Jeremy and I talked it out, and I have forgiven him. We're actually friends now."

Jeremy's dad was looking at me in puzzled amazement, and I could tell that his hamster wheels were once again spinning into overdrive.

After a long silence, he said, "Would you happen to be part of the reason as to why Jeremy was able to magically complete all of the window washing and sweeping here at the bank so quickly?"

I smirked, and replied, "Maybe."

Jeremy's dad smiled wide, but remained silent.

After a few moments, I said, "Sir, it doesn't accomplish anything to continue punishing him. He's different now, and he needs another chance. As his friend, I want him to have that chance. I think because I forgave him, you should consider forgiving him also."

I had another thought, and added, "Plus, I want Jeremy to help with the new store. He's already helped me with some of the lights. I was going to ask him to help with the store, if you will allow it all to happen."

I could tell that Jeremy's dad was very interested in what I was saying. I had definitely hit the right button.

He started nodding, and said, "It seems that you are a better influence on my son than I am. I don't even think he likes me, if I am to be honest."

I replied, "That's not true, Sir. I happen to know that he idolizes you, and it kills him that you're not proud of him. All he wants is your attention and pride, but I don't think he knows how to accomplish that."

Jeremy's dad looked down at his desk. I had hit very deep with my comment. I hoped that I didn't cross any lines.

After a few moments, he looked up at me, and with great strength and determination, he responded, "This new store is happening. And I want Jeremy to work with you on it as you see fit. I will allow this. But don't say anything to him. Let me speak with him first. And I thank you. Truly. I owe you."

I was very humbled by his words, and kind of embarrassed. I sheepishly replied, "No problem."

To break the awkward moment, I said, "That's it, Sir. I can leave now and let you be."

He started laughing.

I stood up from my chair. But when I did, he said, "Hey. I am going to deposit some extra money in your account, and it's going to be a separate transfer from me personally. I would like you to go buy some nice outfits for yourself."

I replied, "Oh, I already have a gift voucher to Jeremy's favorite store. I just haven't had time to go yet. I've been a little busy."

Jeremy's dad laughed, and responded, "Yes, you have. But why don't you use that gift voucher for some nice school clothes. Use my money to buy some really nice outfits, like some slacks, formal jacket, dress shirts, nice shoes, and that kind of thing. I need you to start looking sharp like the business mogul you are. Okay?"

I smirked and replied, "Okay, Sir. I can do that."

He nodded, and responded, "Alright, we'll talk soon. Have Mr.

Martins call and make an appointment to see me after you speak with him."

I quipped, "Alright."

I waved and walked out of his office. I made my way downstairs, and then I left the bank. I was kind of exhausted from the meeting, so I decided not to speak with Mr. Martins about everything the same evening. Instead, I needed to go home and study for a test that I had the next day.

But as I was riding my bike down Main Street so that I could ride the rest of the way home, I was admiring all of the Christmas lights and decorations.

When I got to the vacant store space that I had spoken to Jeremy's dad about, I briefly stopped and looked at it in contemplation. I could imagine the sign that might say, "Christmas Town." And then I could imagine all of downtown *being* a 'Christmas town.' I knew that something magical was happening.

CHAPTER SEVEN
The Mogul

It was the last week of school before the Thanksgiving holiday. Despite not having anything to paint, sweep, wash, or any lights to install, I was still extremely busy every waking moment of my life. I didn't completely understand the gravity of everything that was happening, but I knew that I had to keep riding the wave.

I began using school recess as a time to sit on the bench on the playground and strategize about what I needed to be doing next. I had a lot of people I needed to meet with and talk with.

But before all of that, there was one person who sought me out and wanted to speak with me. It was Jeremy.

He came up to me during recess and sat down on the bench with me.

I said, "Hey, how's it going?"

He responded, "Much better, thanks to you."

I replied, "What do you mean?"

He responded, "I know what you did for me. I know that you talked to my dad and asked him to unground me. Actually, according to my dad, you CONVINCED him to unground me. So, he did. Thank you."

I replied, "No problem. Consider it an early Christmas present. Merry Christmas."

We both laughed.

After a pause, he said, "My dad and I are going to try and spend more time together and have a better relationship."

I replied, "You should. Your dad is pretty awesome, and you are kind of cool when you're not being rotten."

Jeremy laughed.

After a moment, I said, "You are lucky."

He responded, "Why is that?"

I replied, "Because you have a dad. Some of us don't."

He looked down at the ground solemnly.

After a moment, he said, "I'm sorry you don't have a dad. And I'm not just saying that. I mean it."

I replied, "I know. I believe you. But it's okay. It is what it is."

After some silence, he responded, "Can I ask why you don't have a dad?"

After a pause, I replied, "I don't know. He left when I was very little. I can only guess that he didn't want me. So, at least you have a dad that wants you. I've never had that."

I could tell that my words were making Jeremy uncomfortable, so I decided not to say anything else about it.

However, Jeremy said, "I don't know about your *real* dad, but I know that there are tons of dads and people who want you."

I replied, "What do you mean?"

He responded, "My dad thinks you walk on water. And I know Sally's dad looks at you like a son, because Sally told me. And I heard that the owner of the hardware store has taken a liking to you. And dude, pretty much the entire town wants to adopt you as their son."

I started laughing, and that caused Jeremy to laugh.

He quipped, "I'm serious!"

I replied, "Yeah, okay, I don't know. But thanks for making me feel better."

He responded, "That's what friends are for."

He got up from the bench, and said, "Hey, my dad said something about a new store and that you might let me work with you on it."

I replied, "I am not 'LETTING YOU' do anything. I am hoping that you will agree to help me with it sometimes when you can. It might be fun, but it will be a lot of work. You don't have to do it. I won't be mad."

He responded, "No, I want to do it! Please."

I replied, "Okay. I have a bunch of stuff to do in order for it to all happen, so it's not a sure thing yet, but I will assume you are on the team."

He responded, "Awesome! Just let me know what you need from me. But I can tell you that my dad said he's going to back you on it. I think at this point, my dad would back you on any business project in town. Just saying."

I smiled because that was nice to hear, and I said, "Okay, let's see what happens."

Jeremy responded, "Okay cool."

Just then, the bell rang and we went inside the school to resume classes.

That day after school, I rode my bike downtown to the hardware store. I went inside to speak with the owner.

Once I found him, I said, "I wanted to let you know a couple of things. Firstly, I got you that meeting with the bank president you wanted. All you have to do is call the bank and request the meeting. He will meet with you. And secondly, the bank is going to pay off my account balance with you. So, make sure you bring that information with you when you go in for your meeting."

He looked at me in shock, and didn't know what to say.

After a moment, he responded, "How did you manage all of that, young man?"

I replied, "I went to the bank and met with the bank president. We talked about a lot of things."

The man responded, "You mean you just marched into the bank, asked to see the bank president, and he met with you?"

I quipped, "Exactly, Sir."

The man shook his head and started chuckling.

He then responded, "And now you have the bank paying all of your account balances for you?"

I quipped, "Yes, correct."

He was laughing while being endlessly amused.

After a pause, I said, "I also might need your help, Sir. I am probably helping to open up a new store, and we will need help getting the store fixed up. We will have a line of credit with the bank to pay for everything, but I might need to use my account with you to buy what we need. Will that be okay?"

He exclaimed, "ABSOLUTELY! Your credit is good with me. Whatever I can help with, I would be happy to do it. Just give me a heads up if there are things I need to order."

I replied, "Great, thanks."

After a moment, I said, "Well, I have to get going. I have a lot to do. We'll be in touch."

The man chuckled, and responded, "YES, SIR!"

After I left the hardware store, I rode my bike up to Martins Gifts. I walked inside and saw Mr. Martins at the customer counter cashing out a customer. After he was done, he looked at me with a huge smile.

He exclaimed, "JUST THE MAN I WANTED TO SEE!"

I replied, "Oh? Why's that?"

He responded, "There is a rumor going around town that I'm opening up a huge new store on the other side of Main Street. As you can imagine, this is news to me! But when I asked someone about it, they suggested that I speak to YOU about it."

Mr. Martins was shaking his head and laughing.

I replied, "Sorry, I've been too busy to tell you. I came here as soon as I could. I had a Social Studies test I needed to study for, and then I had some business meetings downtown. But I'm here now."

Mr. Martins was still laughing and shaking his head with amusement.

After he settled down, he said, "So, what's this about?"

I replied, "I think we, I mean you, but I will help, should open up a

Christmas store, but it can sell other things the rest of the year. It will be located in that vacant space where the sporting goods store was. But we need to act fast because we want to catch the sales from this Christmas season."

Mr. Martins responded, "I'm not saying it's a bad idea, but that takes money, and money is not something I have right now."

I replied, "You don't need any money. I've secured a business line of credit for you at the bank."

He looked at me in a very perplexed way, and responded, "How in the world did you do that?"

I replied, "I worked everything out with the bank president at the bank up the street. It's all set. All you need to do is go meet with him. He wants to talk with you. But I've already lined up the money and the store space for you."

Mr. Martins seemed flummoxed by the entire thing, but he wasn't protesting, so I thought that was a good sign.

He was deep in thought, and then he said, "I think I know where I can buy a huge load of Christmas merchandise cheap, because there is a store that went out of business in the next state over."

I replied, "PERFECT! If you meet with Jeremy's dad, I mean the bank president, he will give you the funding to buy all of that stuff. We need it, and we need it fast. I will work to help you get the store set up, and my friend Jeremy wants to help also."

Mr. Martins was spinning his hamster wheels in high gear. I guess I had a bad habit of causing people to do that.

After some thought, he said, "My wife can run this store while I get the new store going. And I would appreciate your help if you are offering; and in fact, I might even require it if you are roping me into this adventure."

I replied, "Done deal. But you need to go meet with the bank president as soon as possible. Just call over there and he will get you right in. You can tell him that I already spoke with you."

Mr. Martins was grinning and nodding.

He responded, "Yeah, okay. Holy crap, I better get busy."

I waved and left him to his work.

A couple of days later, I stopped by to see Mr. Martins because Sally had told me at school that her dad needed to talk to me.

I went into Martins Gifts, and Mr. Martins seemed very busy on the phone. However, he saw me and excitedly motioned for me to wait for him.

When he was done with his call, he said, "Wow! You were not kidding. It looks like we have ourselves a new store, young man. I hope you know what you've got yourself into."

I replied, "Well, I know it's your store, Sir; but I will help you like I promised."

He shook his head in the negative, and responded, "Nope. It's your store, too. At least part of it is."

I replied, "What do you mean?"

He responded, "Part of the deal as outlined by the president of the bank is that YOU own 10% of the new store. That's how he wants it, and I agreed and signed off on it."

I was shocked, and quipped, "REALLY?"

Mr. Martins responded, "Yep. So, congratulations, and I'm sorry."

He laughed, but I was excited.

I replied, "So, what does this mean, exactly?"

He responded, "It means that you are going to get to see what running a business is all about; and I get to have the benefit of your brilliance, hard work, and public affection."

I replied, "Okay, what happens next?"

He responded, "I have just purchased all of that merchandise I spoke to you about. It will be here in a couple of days. But when I say 'here,' I mean the new store. I am getting the keys to that tomorrow morning. I'm sure it's a mess."

111

He continued, "Young man, this means that I will be celebrating my Thanksgiving by working on getting the new store set up. I might as well bring a cot for sleeping because I doubt I'll be leaving there for days."

He added, "Oh, and I've ordered a temporary banner sign for the store. The bank president told me you've named the store "Christmas Town." I love the name, but I'm not sure what you're going to do with that name during the rest of the year."

I replied, "People love Christmas, and Christmas Town can be year-round. But we can have different merchandise depending on the season. So, for example, people can still go to Christmas Town even in the summer when they're buying swimsuits and towels. We can keep the really nice Christmas feeling and smells, but sell what people need for whatever time of year it is. It will be like they can come into the store to get whatever they need no matter the time of year, but always get a taste of Christmas when they are doing it."

Mr. Martins was deep in thought, and he responded, "VERY INTERESTING! I think I am going to let you run with your vision, and I can tweak things from a practical point of view as needed."

I replied, "Sounds good."

After a pause, I said, "Mr. Martins, I can help you with the store over Thanksgiving."

He seemed appalled by my offer, and responded, "OH, NO! I don't want to interfere with your holiday. You can jump in and help the following Monday."

I replied, "No, it's okay. It's just me and my mom. We would be spending it alone anyway."

He responded, "Well, I don't want your mother to be alone. You should both be together for Thanksgiving. Even a small family of two is a family, and family is precious."

I thought about what he said, and replied, "Okay, but let me talk to my mother about this. She knows I have responsibilities now."

He chuckled, and responded, "Yeah, okay."

When we seemed to be done speaking, he said, "Alright young man, I need to make a bunch of phone calls before everyone goes home for the day."

I replied, "Yeah okay, I've got a bunch of stuff to do, also. I'll see you soon."

I waved and left the store.

My next stop was the bank. I needed to withdraw some money. After I did that, I rode my bike to a nice clothing store that I knew existed, but I had never even stepped foot inside it before. It wasn't on Main Street, but it wasn't too far from downtown.

When I arrived, I walked inside. Everything looked fancy. Even the name was fancy. Below their formal name on the sign, they identified themselves as a "clothier," which I guess was a snooty way of saying that they sold clothes.

There was a man and a woman inside acting like they were desperately waiting for any human soul that might walk into the store at any given moment. But it turned out that they were both really nice. It just took me a bit to get comfortable in there, is all.

The lady said, "What can we help you find, young man?"

I was feeling a little overwhelmed by the high caliber of the place, and I wondered if maybe it was the wrong store for me to be shopping in.

I hesitantly replied, "Umm, I'm not sure. I was sent down here by the president of the bank on Main Street. He told me to buy a couple of nice outfits so that I would be a presentable businessman."

The man and lady laughed in amusement, but in a friendly way.

The man piped up and said, "Would you by chance be the famous young gentleman who has transformed all of downtown?"

I replied, "Uh, maybe, that might be me, yes. I did some painting, cleaning up, and made sure it got decorated for Christmas. But there is so much more that is going to happen there."

My reply was enough to confirm for them that I was who they thought I was.

The man said, "We can definitely take care of you. What is your budget?"

I told them how much money I had with me, but that I could get more if needed.

He responded, "And you said that the president of the bank sent you here?"

I replied, "Yes. He's the one who is paying for it."

The man and lady looked at each other, and the man responded, "We can work with what you have. We can also give you a discount due to who you are and the circumstances involved."

I replied, "Okay, thanks."

I then just stood there, staring at them. I had NO CLUE how to shop for nice clothes.

They immediately realized that they were going to have to take the lead.

The man said, "Let's get you measured up."

I didn't know what that meant, so I continued standing there.

He got a fabric measuring tape thing, and came over to me and started taking all kinds of measurements, including a couple that seemed a bit close and personal. (Like I said, I had never done this before.)

After he was finished, he said some things to the lady which I didn't quite understand. I guess he was asking her to get some clothes of a certain type and size.

He then said to me, "Because of your age and size, we have limited choices, but we should have enough to put together one nice outfit, and then you can come back again after we place an order for more choices. Is that okay?"

I replied, "Sure."

A minute later, the lady came out carrying a bunch of clothes that looked more or less my size.

The lady said, "We might have to alter these, but they will work."

The man looked through the garments she brought out, and then asked me, "Do you want to go with a formal tie look, or do you want more of a 'I'm too successful to wear a tie' look?"

I replied, "That last one."

They both smiled in amusement.

The man very carefully put together an outfit. I could tell that he wasn't just throwing something together. He was putting a lot of thought and effort into it, so I knew not to dismiss it.

He handed me the outfit and said, "Go try these on. Don't worry if they don't fit right. We will fix that."

I nodded in acknowledgment, and the lady led me to a changing room. I went inside and changed into the outfit the man had chosen for me. The outfit consisted of some dark slacks with sort of invisible stripes on them. I say 'invisible' because the stripes were the same color as the slacks, but they were definitely stripes, and added texture or style, I guess they would say.

Then there was a cream-colored fancy shirt with some texture to it as well, with a collar that seemed bigger than normal, along with cuffs that were way too big. However, I quickly realized that the cuffs were meant to be folded over. Then to finish the outfit was a very sleek and rich looking formal jacket that was dark like the slacks, but had tiny little white or off-white pinstripes.

Once I had the entire outfit on, I looked at myself in the mirror. I noticed three things. First, was that the pants were too big; but they said they could fix that. The second thing was that I really needed a decent haircut. And the third thing I noticed was that I looked amazing in that outfit, and it made me FEEL absolutely amazing. I never said this until now, but looking at myself in the mirror on that day, at that moment, made me smile. And for the first time in my entire life, I was proud of how I looked.

I stood there staring at myself in the mirror because I didn't want it to end. I guess I stayed there doing that for too long, because the lady loudly asked if I was doing okay. I took that as my cue to quickly exit the dressing room.

As soon as I stepped out, they both looked at me from head to toe. I noticed that they both smiled.

The lady said, "How do you feel?"

I took notice of how the lady asked me how I felt, and not how I looked. It was interesting to me, because when I saw myself in the mirror, I thought more about how great I FELT than how great I looked, even though I loved how I looked, also.

I replied, "I feel great. I love everything about it. It's just that the pants are too big."

The man said, "Yeah, we'll fix that. But you like everything else?"

I quipped, "I LOVE IT!"

The man responded, "You can wear those shirt cuffs rolled up like you have them, or you can use cufflinks. We'll give you some cufflinks so you have them. So, all that is missing is some shoes."

The man and the lady looked at each other, and I knew there must be an issue with the shoes.

The lady said, "We will need to order you some shoes, but we can get them here overnight."

While she was saying that, the man was grabbing a pair of shoes that were clearly too big for me.

The man said, "This style of shoe would go well with your outfit. We will get these in your size, but do you like the style?"

I looked at them, and quipped, "Yeah, those are fine."

The man nodded, put the shoes down, and then asked me to take a seat so that he could get my shoe size, which he proceeded to do with his shoe size measuring device.

After that, he said, "Okay, you can get changed back into your regular clothes."

When he said that, I felt a tinge of disappointment and depression shoot through me, but hopefully they didn't notice. I went back into the dressing room and changed back into my old clothes. It wasn't until then that I realized how hideous my clothes really were. I knew I also had to get new school clothes right away.

I walked out of the dressing room and handed the lady all of the new clothes. She told me to come back the next day or when it was convenient for me.

Just as I was about to leave the store, I said, "Excuse me, I know this is a dumb question, but I really need a haircut. Can you recommend some place where I should go?"

The lady and man looked at each other, and I got the feeling that they may have discussed my hair when I was not present.

The lady responded, "Absolutely! Let me make a phone call, and then I will let you know what I came up with when you come back in."

I replied, "Okay, thanks."

I waved and left the store.

I desperately and immediately wanted to go to the clothing store where I had the gift voucher so that I could buy some new school clothes. However, it was getting late, and I needed to go home.

I went home, and I had a bunch of homework to do, and a test to study for. I couldn't believe that I was still in sixth grade. What a waste of time! I really needed to just jump into high school and get on with it so that I could start my real life, which had already started. My focus in life had shifted to making the new store and all of downtown a huge success. That's all I cared about at that point. But with that said, I knew I still had to get good grades in school.

The next day, I went to school, and then after school I went downtown, and directly to the clothing store to get some school clothes.

I walked up to the first person I saw who was working there, and I told them my name and that I had a gift voucher to get some outfits for school. The lady acted like she knew who I was and that she had been waiting for me to show up.

She explained to me that I could choose five outfits, and not to worry about the money limit on the voucher. I was very polite, but I told her that I didn't have much time, and I asked her if it would be okay if I only chose two outfits that day, and then I would come back another time to choose the others.

She indicated that my plan would work fine, and that they would make a note of this so that I could come back for more.

Unlike the other clothing place, I knew I could pick out my own clothes for school, and I knew my sizes already. I chose some jeans that all of the cool kids wore, and I picked out a couple of shirts that I really liked.

I brought them up to the lady, and she told me that I could get one pair of sneakers as well. I really wanted new sneakers, so I left the clothes on the counter, and then went over to where the sneakers were. I tried on a few pairs, and chose the pair that felt the best. They were very similar to the kind that Jeremy wore, so I knew they were good.

The lady bagged up all of my stuff, and I made sure to thank her and tell her how much I loved the clothes I picked out. She reminded me to come back for the remaining outfits, and I said that I would.

I then rushed off to go to the fancy clothier place. I arrived, and when I walked in the door, the lady was there, and she started smiling. It was nice to have someone smiling at me when I walked into a room. I spent almost my entire life with that never happening. Usually, I was invisible.

I had my shopping bag from the other store with me because I couldn't leave it outside with my bike.

The lady said, "You've already been doing some shopping."

I replied, "Yeah, but these are just school clothes. You guys have my really nice clothes."

She smiled because she could see that I was really excited about my new outfit that they had for me.

She gathered her thoughts, and said, "Okay, so here's the deal. We have your outfit and shoes ready for you today. You can take them. But we spoke with the president of the bank who sent you here, because he gets all of his clothes from us. We speak with him often about various things. So anyway, we told him that you came in, and what you picked out. He has instructed us to put your outfit on his account that he has with us. Thus, I don't need any money from you. Furthermore, he would like us to fit you with two more outfits, and he is paying for those on his account as well."

I was a bit stunned, so I didn't say anything at first. I wasn't expecting any of that.

Before I could think of what to say, she went on, "The thing is though, we need to order some things for you. We just don't have enough in your size to do it right. So, if it's okay with you, give us a chance to get some items in, and then you can return, and we will get you into two more outfits. We already have all of your measurements, so it will be easier than last time. Will that work for you, Sir?"

(She just called me 'Sir.')

I replied, "Yeah, that's great! I wasn't expecting that, but I would love more outfits like this one I am picking up now. Anything similar to that I will be happy with."

The lady responded, "Yes, we feel we understand your preferred style, so it will be similar, but we will vary it enough so that it's a totally different outfit and look. Okay?"

I replied, "Yeah okay, thanks."

I was about to grab my new outfit and rush out the door, but then the lady said, "OH! Your hair!"

I quipped, "OH, YEAH!"

She responded, "My friend works at one of the nicer hair salons in town. She isn't really taking new clients right now, but she will take *you*. She will be able to fix you up good; and if you like what she does, you can go back to her again. Will that be okay?"

I replied, "That sounds great. But how much will it cost?"

The lady told me, and I almost fainted, it was so much. I'm sure the lady saw the look on my face. However, I then had a thought.

I said, "Oh, wait, that's fine. I can pay that because I didn't have to pay for this outfit."

The lady nodded, as if she had already thought of that.

After a moment, she said, "Would you like me to set up an appointment for you for some time after school, like around this time of day?"

I replied, "Yes, please."

I then gave her my home phone number, and told her if that didn't work, to call Martins Gifts and leave a message for me there.

We finished up our business, and I left the store. I had too many things to carry, and it was a bit of a struggle to ride my bike home, but I made it.

Once I got home, I wanted to change into my new fancy outfit and show my mother. Yes, I had some really cool brand-new school clothes also, but I was most excited about my one really nice outfit.

I changed into it, and everything fit perfectly. I walked out into the kitchen where my mother was.

I said, "What do you think?"

She turned around, and when she saw me, her mouth dropped open.

She exclaimed, "HOLY SMOKES! Where did you get that, and what is it for?"

I replied, "I got it at that really nice clothier place up beyond downtown; and it's for me to wear when I'm conducting business."

She responded, "It looks like it's been specially tailored just for you! It must have cost a fortune! Where in the world did you get the money for that?"

I replied, "Yes, it *was* specially tailored for me. And there is more where this came from; but I didn't need to pay for it."

She was looking at me in a stunned and confused way.

She responded, "Well, they didn't just give it to you. So, how did you pay for it?"

I replied, "The president of the bank on Main Street bought it for me."

My mother couldn't believe what she was hearing, and the look on her face was so priceless that I started laughing. It made my day.

After a few moments, my mom said, "What business are you 'conducting?' And what does the bank president have to do with anything?"

I replied, "The bank president is funding some of my improvements downtown, and is also funding my new store."

My mom's mouth dropped open even more, and she was totally flummoxed and without words or a clue.

She responded, "*WHAT STORE?*"

I replied, "Well, I only own 10% of the store. But it's a good start. Me and Mr. Martins are opening a new store where the old sporting goods store used to be."

I was still laughing, because watching my mom's reactions were the best.

She responded, "How are you doing this?"

I replied, "I proposed it to the bank president, and he liked my idea, so he made it happen. But Mr. Martins is in charge and he will be running it."

After a few moments, she responded, "When are you doing all of this? Are you still going to school, or did you graduate already and I missed it?"

I started laughing really hard, and then so did she.

When we calmed down, I replied, "I've been working on all of this for months now, Mom. That's why I'm gone every day after school and every weekend."

She responded, "I thought you were doing painting jobs?"

I just looked down at the floor while laughing and shaking my head. I decided to give up explaining it all to her.

I replied, "I've done a lot more than just painting, Mom. But yeah, okay. You read the newspaper articles, didn't you? You saw all of the stuff people gave me, right?"

She started nodding, and responded, "Yeah, yeah, I got it. I know. I guess I just haven't fully processed and grasped the full extent of what you have been up to. I've heard stories about you at work, but because you're my son, it's hard for me to accept everything I hear. I guess I assumed it was exaggerated; I don't know."

I wasn't sure that I liked what she said, but that was how a typical conversation went between me and my mom. She was always caring in her own way; but at the same time, she always underestimated me as being less than what I was. I don't mean that in a bad way. I'm just saying that my mom and I weren't always on the same page, but maybe it's like that with many kids and their moms. Who knows. I think my mom always thought of me as a five-year-old. Maybe that's a better way to put it.

When she settled down, I said, "I'm expecting a call from the hair salon for an appointment. So, if you get that call, please find out what date and time my hair appointment is."

Shocked again, she responded, "Which hair salon?"

I told her the name.

She responded, "THAT'S THE MOST EXPENSIVE SALON IN TOWN! ARE YOU CRAZY?"

I replied, "It's fine, Mom. I've got it covered."

After a couple of moments, she responded, "Well if you are that much of a Mr. Big Bucks flying around on your private jet, then maybe you can help me out with all of *my* bills, because I'm drowning."

I replied, "I WILL, MOM! Just give me a chance to get the store open. Once the store is going smoothly, I should have some regular money. But I'll be busy working there every day."

She looked at me as if she didn't believe me.

I said, "Really! I'll help you with money from the store!"

She responded, "What is this store again?"

I replied, "I told you. It's going in where the sporting goods store used to be. I've named it Christmas Town. I'll get paid a regular amount for working there, plus I get 10% of the profit."

She nodded, as if she finally understood what was going on.

And then she said the magic words.

She said, "Well, I'm proud of you. All of this sounds amazing."

And those were words I didn't hear often from my mother. It's not like she wasn't proud of me. It was more like she was too busy to notice or say anything.

She then said, "Well, go change so we can eat."

I replied, "Yeah, okay."

And I did. I reluctantly changed out of my new outfit that I loved. But I changed into one of my new school outfits so that I could have more fun messing with my mom.

She noticed my new outfit and was pleasantly surprised, but she seemed more able to mentally comprehend the school outfit.

Still the same, it was fun. I know they were just clothes, but to people who can't have them, they are more than 'just clothes.' But with that said, I knew what was important was what I was doing for everyone downtown. I knew to keep my eye on the ball, and I did. Things were about to get even more interesting.

CHAPTER EIGHT
The Thanksgiving

Thanksgiving was bearing down on us, and I still hadn't spoken to my mother about me skipping Thanksgiving to work on setting up the store with Mr. Martins. As luck would have it, I saw my opportunity, and I took it.

When I got back home from working downtown, my mother had some news for me.

She said, "Did you order a huge family-sized turkey for Thanksgiving?"

I replied, "No. Why would I do that?"

She responded, "Well, a gigantic turkey was delivered to us today. I asked the woman delivering it if she was sure that she had the right address, because I didn't order a turkey. She then mentioned your name, and said the turkey was to be delivered to you and your family, which I guess is me. So, I accepted it. But what am I supposed to do with it? It's way too big for us, and I already bought a small one at the store a week ago, for you and I to have on Thanksgiving."

My mom then stared at me as if I was supposed to have all of the answers. I had absolutely no idea about any gigantic turkey. I wasn't even sure who would have my home address, because that was something I was not in the habit of giving out.

After some thought, I replied, "Well, it's obviously a gift from someone. But I don't know who has our address. I've been careful to not give it out to the news people or anyone work related.

My mother responded, "Well, people have been giving you all kinds of things, so why not a turkey, I guess.

And that is when I hatched my plan.

I said, "Mom, I have a complication regarding Thanksgiving, as well as an idea, and a solution."

She responded, "You seem to be full of all those items lately."

I replied, "Mr. Martins and I are trying to get the new store open. He's going to be working at the store for the entire long weekend. He won't be having Thanksgiving. I told him that I would try to help. He didn't want me to miss Thanksgiving, but I am part owner of the store, and I feel it's my responsibility to help him get it open. So, I was going to talk to you about me spending Thanksgiving, and the entire weekend, working at the store."

My mother stared at me, and I could tell that she wasn't very pleased. She had a certain look that she would give me when she was annoyed by what I was saying, but at the same time knew I was right. I got that look a lot from her.

After a pause, she responded, "So, I'm supposed to have two turkeys all by myself for Thanksgiving?"

I started laughing, and replied, "No. I have an idea."

I continued, "What if you cooked up the giant turkey, and then brought it over to the store. We could all have Thanksgiving together at the store. Plus, that solves the problem of the turkey being too big."

My mom responded, "Who is everyone at the store you are talking about?"

I replied, "You and I, and Mr. Martins; but probably his wife and their daughter Sally as well."

I could tell that my mother was slightly uncomfortable with the idea, but she was also intrigued by it.

After a long pause, my mother responded, "Can I ask you a personal question?"

I replied, "*Yeah?*"

She responded, "Is Sally your girlfriend?"

I quipped in a horrified way, "MOM!!"

She responded, "*WHAT?* It's a reasonable question. What's the problem? You don't like her?"

I wasn't expecting to be accosted by this subject, and I was huffing and puffing.

I replied, "It's not that. I like Sally. She's probably my best friend at school. She's been the only one I could trust for a long time. Jeremy and I only became friends recently."

My mom responded, "So, you trust Sally, like Sally, and she is your best friend at school?"

I was processing all of that, and then replied, "Umm, yeah, I guess so."

My mom responded, "Do you think she's pretty?"

I was irritated by her question and shaking my head, but I answered, "Yeah, she's pretty."

My mother was giving me a mischievous look which was annoying me.

I said, "Why are you asking me this?"

She responded, "Because I met Sally's mother at the school on Parent's Night. She made a point of introducing herself to me. She's a very nice woman. But she mentioned to me that Sally talks about you at home all of the time. So that's why I asked."

This of course was news to me.

I replied, "I don't think Sally likes me in that way, Mom."

My mom responded, "Does she do nice things for you?"

I thought for a moment, and replied, "I guess so. She sometimes buys me donuts."

My mother got a smug look on her face, and responded, "And when she gives you the donuts, does she just hand them over and walk away, or does she stand there and watch you eat them?"

I paused, and replied, "She stands there and watches me eat them."

My mother's smug look got even more smug, and she responded, "She likes you."

I let out a big sigh.

My mother knew she was testing my patience, and she said, "It doesn't matter. But yes, under all of the circumstances, I think your suggestion is a good one. But let me call Mrs. Martins to confer with her on it first."

I replied, "Yeah, okay. But you can assume that I'm working at the store for the entire weekend."

My mother nodded in acknowledgment, and responded, "What am I supposed to do with the smaller turkey that I bought for us?"

I thought for a moment, and replied, "Why don't we give it to the neighbors?"

I should first explain that we had some neighbors we communicated with who lived in an apartment house on our street. They were in a similar situation to us, meaning that they were barely surviving. I guess having that in common sort of made us friends.

My mother seemed to love my idea, and she responded, "Yes, good idea. Let me confirm things with Mrs. Martins first, and then I'll have you bring the smaller turkey over to the neighbors. Even if they've already bought one, they can certainly use another."

I quipped, "Okay."

I spent the rest of the evening in my bedroom doing homework, and then I went to bed early. My life was exhausting.

The next day, I went to school. At recess, I went to sit on the bench, and Sally followed.

After we both sat down, she said, "My mom says that your mom called her and that we are all having Thanksgiving together at the new store. My mom said that *your* mom said it was your idea. I think it's sweet that you made it so that we are spending Thanksgiving together."

My mind was twisting into knots trying to fully process what she had said, but I was careful not to flinch or react in any way.

After an awkward silence, I replied, "It's okay if you don't want to. It was just an idea since we'll be working on the store all weekend."

She responded, "I love the idea. I'm excited for Thanksgiving now."

I chuckled within myself, and replied, "Well, it's not just Thanksgiving. I'm going to be working with your dad all weekend. So, you can be there also. But if you're busy, I understand, and that's fine. The store isn't your responsibility. It's mine and your dad's. We both have to be there."

There was another awkward silence, and she responded, "Well, do you want me there, or would you rather it just be you and my dad?"

I paused, and replied, "I guess it would be nice if you wanted to help, also. But only if you want to."

She quipped, "You guess? You mean you're not sure? Or you don't care?"

I had an internal eye roll within my mind, and a sigh. I knew that I was starting to get tangled up in a mess.

I replied, "I mean it would be nice if you were there."

She responded, "Okay. Then I will be there."

Right after she said that, Jeremy walked over to the bench.

He said, "I hope I'm not interrupting anything."

I quipped, "Nope! Not interrupting! What's going on?"

He responded, "I was serious about helping you with the new store. When are you going to start working on it?"

I replied, "I'll be working there over the entire Thanksgiving weekend."

He looked a bit disappointed, or even ashamed, and responded, "Well, I can't be there on Thanksgiving because we're having a big family thing. And then on Friday we're doing a big shopping thing. But I can be there on Saturday and Sunday! Is that okay?"

I replied, "Yeah, that's fine. I don't expect anyone to work there over the Thanksgiving holiday. Me and Mr. Martins have to because it's our store. You can show up anytime you want, Jeremy; it's all good."

He responded, "Okay, I'll see you there this weekend then."

I replied, "Great, thanks."

Jeremy walked away, because he could sense that Sally and I were having some kind of weird interaction, which we were. Furthermore, I could sense great relief from Sally that Jeremy wasn't going to be crashing our "family Thanksgiving."

Fortunately, the bell rang to end recess. Sally and I got up from the bench and walked back into the building.

But on the way inside, Sally said, "By the way, I like your new school outfit. You look cool. Actually, now you look more cool than the others."

I quipped, "Thanks."

Mercifully, classes began, and the rest of the day was "academic," as they say.

Before I knew it, it was Thanksgiving Day. I left for the store early, and my mom had already been up dealing with the huge turkey.

When I got down to the store, Mr. Martins was already there. It looked like he had already been cleaning and putting shelving and display racks where he wanted them. He spent some time explaining to me how the store was going to be laid out so that I would know where all of the merchandise needed to go. He told me that *his* job would be to get all of the infrastructure correct, and *my* job was going to be to deal with the merchandise. That meant that I needed to open up all of the boxes, and then stock the shelves. There were a ton of boxes piled up to the ceiling in the back 'receiving room' from the shipment of stuff that he had purchased from a store that went out of business in a neighboring state.

I was getting a quick education in all of the different types of display shelving, and how to stock merchandise. It was more complicated than it seems, because some merchandise needed to sit on a large shelf, some needed to sit on a small shelf, and some couldn't sit on a shelf at all and needed to be hung on hanger racks. And you have to know how your merchandise will be displayed before bringing it onto the retail floor, clogging up space.

Mr. Martins and I were in over our heads, and we were so busy that we didn't really speak to each other much. It was just all work. I was starting to understand why Mr. Martins felt so frantic about the store opening. I was beginning to wonder if we were going to be able to get it open that following week as we had wanted. I decided to just do the same as Mr. Martins, and remain focused straight ahead on what I needed to do, rather than panic about not being able to do it.

When it was getting to be later in the afternoon, Mrs. Martins and Sally arrived with all kinds of place settings and hot side dishes for our feast. I heard Mrs. Martins tell Mr. Martins that she had spoken to my mom, and that she would be arriving shortly.

Sure enough, ten minutes later, my mom arrived, carrying the huge turkey. I think Sally's parents were amused at how large it was. I'm not sure they knew that my mom didn't choose the turkey. That's just the size that was given to us by someone who we still had no idea who it was.

My mom seemed to be amused, fascinated, and intrigued by seeing how hard I had been working. It's like she didn't think I was capable of working, even though I had literally done nothing but work since the beginning of school in September.

My mom and Mrs. Martins worked together to set up a table for all of us to eat at. Sally watched me work. I was dragging boxes out into the retail space, and then putting the items on shelves. This store was huge, if I hadn't made that clear enough before.

The retail space we took over had been occupied by a large sporting goods store with many different departments such as clothing, fishing, hunting, baseball, basketball, and the list goes on. This was not a small undertaking. The new store was many times larger than Martins Gifts.

Anyway, I motioned for Sally to come over and help me. She did.

We made small talk as we worked, and it was nice to have the company. I was glad she was there.

When our feast was completely laid out and ready, we all took a seat at our make-shift table. Our chairs were those cheap folding chairs that are used for big meetings in places like school gyms. This was certainly not going to be a fancy Thanksgiving, but it was going to be a meaningful Thanksgiving; and those are the best kinds of Thanksgivings.

When we were all seated and ready to eat, Mr. Martins said a short prayer, and then he added, "I am blessed beyond imagination for the company of the best business partner a person could ever have. I can never thank you enough for the blessings you have bestowed upon our family, young man."

He said all of that while looking at me.

I think my mother was somewhat shaken by his serious and deep sentiments about me.

When he was finished, we passed the food around and filled our plates. When everyone had what they wanted, we started eating. As usual, my mother had done a fantastic job with cooking the turkey. I think Mr. and Mrs. Martins were very impressed. They didn't realize that cooking was a true talent of my mom's.

I will also say that I enjoyed the side dishes prepared by Mrs. Martins. She made the absolute best crispy macaroni and cheese. I also had some cranberry sauce and garlic bread.

At some point during dinner, Sally accidentally dropped her fork. After it fell onto the floor, I instinctually got up from my chair and went down onto the floor to retrieve it for her. I then took it over to the sink we had in the store, and washed it for her. When it was clean, I brought it back over to her.

When I did, I noticed my mom and Mrs. Martins watching me intently, and displaying subtle smiles. I pretended not to see them. I just gave the fork back to Sally, and she humbly thanked me with a sweet smile on her face.

We all resumed eating and enjoying sparse but pleasant conversation. After everyone seemed more comfortable with each other, my mother looked at Mr. Martins and said, "I want to thank you for including my son in on your store. He's been very excited to be a part of it. It's very generous of you."

Mr. Martins chuckled, and responded, "Thank you, but it's actually the other way around. This store was your son's idea, and he is the one who put the entire deal together with the president of the bank. I am the one who is grateful that your son was generous enough to include ME."

Mrs. Martins laughed, and I smirked. I think my mom was a combination of confused and embarrassed. Sally was looking at me in a smug and proud way, and I pretended not to notice.

After an awkward moment, my mother said, "You'll have to forgive me. It hasn't been easy for me to get used to hearing pretty much the entire town talk about my 12-year-old son as if he was a 40-year-old business mogul."

Everyone laughed.

I embarrassingly quipped, "I'm almost 13, Mom."

Mrs. Martins said, "You must be very proud of him."

My mother, always hesitant to express such things, replied, "I am. I hear all of the stories about him while at work. People talk about my son as if he isn't my son. It's like he is an entrepreneur who is taking the town by storm. It's hard for me to relate to everything I've heard about him. To me, he's still my little boy who eats all of our weekly snacks within two days of me buying them, and leaves his banana peels laying out."

Everyone laughed, and I looked down in embarrassment. This is why a kid can't bring their mother with them anywhere. It's nearly impossible to maintain one's dignity with their mother making comments like that.

Mercifully, my mother refrained from making any additional statements that might result in embarrassment for either her or myself. Mostly, my mother had benign discussions with Mrs. Martins. Mr. Martins and I started talking about what tasks needed to be completed on certain days. I guess you could say that we were talking business. Sally remained silent and just swiveled her head back and forth between me and her father. She seemed to be taking some kind of pleasure in watching me and her dad talking with each other the way we were.

When we were done with our feast, Mrs. Martins offered all of us some pumpkin pie. Everyone accepted. She and my mother got up from the table and worked together to serve it up.

As we were all enjoying our pumpkin pie, my mother said, "I have really and truly enjoyed this. Thank you so much, all of you; including my son, whose idea this was."

Mr. Martins quipped, "You will find that your son is full of endless great ideas."

My mother managed a happy nod in acknowledgment of that.

When we were finished with pie, Mr. Martins gave me a friendly but serious look, and said, "Young man, you and I should get back to work if we have any hopes of getting this store of ours open."

I smiled. It wasn't because I was anxious to get back to work, but it was because he referred to the store as 'ours.'

My mother helped Mrs. Martins pick up from our feast, and this left Sally not sure what to do, or which direction to go in. I answered that for her by motioning for her to continue helping me with the merchandise. She seemed happy with my suggestion and invitation.

Eventually, my mom said her goodbyes and left to go back home. But before she did, she asked when I would be coming home. I told her that I wouldn't be home until late. At that point, there was some discussion between my mom and Mr. Martins. Neither of them wanted me riding my bike back home in the dark late at night. Mr.

Martins said that he would take me home in his car, and then pick me up early the next morning. So, I guess I was leaving my bike at the store.

Not long after my mother left, Mrs. Martins left, and she took Sally with her. Mr. Martins and I worked into the late evening hours, mostly in silence. But at some point, Mr. Martins decided that it was time to quit for the day. We established a time when he would pick me up at my home the next morning, and then we left the store and he dropped me off at home. I was dead-tired and went to bed almost immediately.

The next morning, my alarm woke me up. I took a shower and got ready to leave. Mr. Martins picked me up right on time, and I was ready right on time. I think we were both surprised that both of us were right on time. There was a lot about each of us that was very similar, and I guess being prompt was one of those things.

Mr. Martins discussed in the car about what he hoped to achieve that day. When our short ride was over, we both went into the store and immediately got to work. Mrs. Martins and Sally stopped by not long after our arrival. They were only there to drop off some donuts that Sally insisted she wanted me to have. Mr. Martins and I shared them.

Mrs. Martins and Sally didn't stay because Mrs. Martins had to run Martins Gifts, and she wanted Sally's help. Their shop had been closed for Thanksgiving, but now that it was Friday and a big shopping day, Mrs. Martins had to open the shop and keep it going. The Martins's were now juggling two stores.

Mr. Martins and I got a lot of work done that day, and he brought me home again later at night. The next day, Saturday, Mr. Martins and I were back at it again, but this time we had a lot more help.

Sally convinced her mother to let her work with me at the store. But in addition to that, we had another helper arrive. Around mid-morning, Jeremy arrived.

I had come to really like Jeremy. He was definitely my second-best friend after Sally. But the problem was that Mr. Martins didn't even know him, and Sally was still not sure about Jeremy.

I very quickly introduced Jeremy to Mr. Martins, making it clear that Jeremy was the bank president's son. I didn't want Mr. Martins to say anything awkward about the bank president or the bank with Jeremy there.

Additionally, when Jeremy saw that Sally was there, I think he wondered whether he should be there or not. He probably didn't want to be a third wheel, or interfere with me "making moves" or "gaming" Sally, even though I wasn't trying to do any of that. But I had grown very aware of EVERYONE'S perceptions, where me and Sally were concerned.

And if that wasn't enough, I was worried about Sally saying horrible things about Jeremy to her father, Mr. Martins. Basically, Jeremy's arrival added endless complications. But I didn't care. I wanted Jeremy there as long as Jeremy wanted to be there.

Jeremy made it clear that his mother had dropped him off, and that she would be picking him up in the evening just before dinner. We all nodded in acknowledgment of that definitive and helpful proclamation and disclosure, for planning purposes.

Jeremy looked at Mr. Martins for direction. Mr. Martins responded to that by pointing to me and saying, "That gentleman right there is the man in charge."

I smiled, although slightly embarrassed, and I motioned for Jeremy to come with me. I explained to him that he, Sally, and myself would be stocking the shelves with merchandise, but we first had to clean all of the shelving before using it.

Jeremy offered to do all of the cleaning so that Sally could just focus on stocking shelves with me. This was Jeremy's way of extending an olive branch to Sally. I think he knew that Sally didn't like him much, and he knew that she probably wasn't that excited about him being there.

We all worked in a pretty serious fashion, with Jeremy mostly on his own, and Sally and I making small talk while stocking shelves together. But before long, Jeremy had finished cleaning the shelves, and he came over to me and said, "What's next, Captain?"

I laughed at his reference toward me. I'm still not sure why he started calling me that, but it became a 'thing.' I believe it may have been his way of showing respect toward me, perhaps to make up for his lack of respect in the past. But what this also did was cause Sally to lighten up toward him a bit. Here was the wealthy and privileged son of the bank president calling *me* 'Captain.' Sally liked that.

I didn't know what else to do with him, therefore I suggested that Jeremy stock the shelves with me and Sally. So, that's what happened. And you know what?

It wasn't long before the three of us were joking and laughing together. Sally and I were both very reserved introverts. But Jeremy was an extrovert full of confidence and personality. Throwing Jeremy in the mix made things more fun for all of us.

I don't know how Jeremy did it, but at a certain point, he said the exact right thing at the exact right moment, and Sally laughed harder than I had ever seen her laugh. It was that moment when Jeremy had finally won her over. And it was not lost upon me that Jeremy had purposely expended an extreme amount of effort to do so. That was Jeremy caring enough to put forth the effort to fit into our tight group that perhaps had no space for him at first.

Jeremy may have had his own emotional issues and baggage, but when it came to social skills and charisma, he was the best.

At some point during the day when Jeremy and I were alone, I said to him, "I wish I was more like you and had your outgoing personality. Girls think you're funny and charming, and you have the charisma of a leader."

Without hesitation, Jeremy responded, "I wish I was more like you and had your deep character and wisdom. Every adult in this entire town admires you, and you *ARE* a true leader."

We both glanced at each other and laughed. I guess we had formed a 'mutual appreciation society' of sorts. And it was Jeremy's unabashed, insightful, and blunt honesty that I always loved. Whenever I thought I was being smart and clever, Jeremy could give me back something similar, but from a different angle. He and I came from opposite sides of the tracks, but we somehow met in the middle at the exact same destination.

After a short silence between that exchange between Jeremy and I, he said, "Hey, if I am interfering with something between you and Sally, I can leave. There will be no hard feelings, and I can help you some other time when you're alone. I don't want you or Sally to feel like I'm in the way."

Unbeknownst to us, Sally heard what Jeremy said because she had unexpectedly come back from wherever she was.

Sally responded, "I want you to stay, Jeremy. I like the three of us here together. It's fun."

That statement from Sally put a smile on both mine and Jeremy's faces. That was validation that Jeremy needed.

After that, the three of us were 100% relaxed with each other, and we started having even more fun than before.

Mr. Martins even remarked about it at one point, saying, "I've never in my life seen three kids having so much fun while working."

The three of us just smirked.

Around dinner time, Jeremy's mom came to pick him up, and we agreed that he would come back the next morning. He wasn't doing it to be nice or because he had to. He was doing it because he wanted to.

Right after Jeremy left, Mrs. Martins stopped by with dinner that she had picked up at a restaurant after she closed Martins Gifts for the day. She reported that sales had been good for both Friday and Saturday. I was happy to hear that.

After we ate dinner, Mrs. Martins and Sally went home. Mr. Martins and I continued working. We decided that much of Sunday needed to be devoted to decorating the store. After all, the store was called "Christmas Town," so it needed to look the part.

When it was getting late, Mr. Martins brought me home.

The next morning, Sunday morning, he picked me up early, and we started work at the store. Just like the previous day, Mrs. Martins and Sally brought us donuts. Sally stayed working with us while Mrs. Martins went to run Martins Gifts.

Jeremy showed up earlier than the previous morning. I was in charge of installing Christmas lights all over the store, while Jeremy and Sally helped me. Mr. Martins was working on getting the customer service area totally functional. He was getting the cash register working, along with the credit card processor, and all of that. It was a good sign that we were getting closer to being able to open. Everything was definitely looking like a real store, finally.

Around lunchtime, Mr. Martins received a special delivery. He was expecting it, but it was a surprise for me. Mr. Martins had bought an old but restored full-sized sled that looked like Santa's sleigh. It had been restored to look exactly like it was Santa's real sleigh. For me, it was love at first sight.

Mr. Martins was clearly very proud of himself for procuring such a wonderful and perfect piece. It answered for me why Mr. Martins had left an area of the retail floor empty. The sleigh, Santa's sleigh, would serve as the centerpiece for the entire store. It was perfect!

After the sleigh was put into place, I worked on decorating it, as well as the area around it. It was going to be the perfect spot for people to take holiday photos. We could even have Santa visit our store and do photos with customers. It was a reminder that I had plenty to learn from Mr. Martins. I had considered myself to be the 'Christmas decorating king,' but Mr. Martins put that in doubt. I was excited about the addition of Santa's sleigh to the store.

Later in the afternoon, Jeremy's mom came to pick him up. He had to get back home to do homework, and for some "family time." Every family has their own traditions, and at Jeremy's house they would all watch TV or a movie together on Sunday nights.

Shortly after Jeremy left, Sally needed to do the same. She had a couple of errands to run with her mother as soon as they closed up Martins Gifts. Therefore, she walked over to Martins Gifts to help her mother close up, and then to go do their shopping or whatever.

That left me and Mr. Martins alone at the store. Mr. Martins told me that he was going to have me go home before dark so that I could bring my bike back home in case I needed it for the upcoming week. It was a good idea.

He and I did some touchup work here and there, and then we took some time to admire our work. The store wasn't completely ready to open yet, but it was close. It certainly looked done and ready to an untrained eye. The shelves were stocked, and the interior looked like a Christmas store should look. But I guess Mr. Martins still needed the banner sign installed on the building, and he needed to correct a few issues with the electronics of the financial sales equipment. But the store itself looked great!

He and I were looking all around, contemplating what we had accomplished. It was hard to believe that we did it. It had seemed impossible a week earlier. But I guess when you work intently at something long enough, it gets done. That was a big life lesson for me. The work I had done to the entire downtown, and then the Christmas Town store, had taught me a lot about hard work and persistence. I truly believed that I could move a mountain as long as I shoveled pieces of it every day for a long enough period of time. So, yes, I had learned that very important lesson at that very young age.

As Mr. Martins and I were standing in silence appreciating the results of our hard work, he eventually looked over at me, and said, "I can't express how proud I am of you. You are an extraordinary young man, and part of my joy over this store is because of my pride in you and what you have accomplished."

I don't know why, but something about what he had said, or how he said it, affected me very deeply inside. I looked down at the floor, as my eyes were turning red. I may have wiped my face just in case a stray tear decided to fall.

Mr. Martins must have noticed this, and he came over to me and embraced me. How I didn't start sobbing right then, I don't know. There was just something about it.

It wasn't often that an older man, or mentor, or father figure, or whatever you want to call it, said something like that to me. And him saying that he was proud of me in that way was much more powerful than my mother's half-hearted polite gestures of *her* being proud of me. I think I needed to hear it from an older man whom I looked up to; and finally, I did. His words were like a completion of something desperately needed by me for years, but never received.

After I felt that I wasn't going to cry, I broke my embrace with Mr. Martins. He asked me if I was okay, and I nodded in silence that I was. He then gave me a pat on the back and suggested that I head home.

I got my bike, and after a few moments of composing myself, I let Mr. Martins know that I had a haircut appointment the next day, thus I wasn't sure if I was going to make it to the store. He told me that was fine, but that he wanted me at the store for the opening; and that we should have a "soft opening" later in the week so that we would be operating smoothly for the weekend. I nodded in acknowledgment and agreement to all of that.

I left the store and rode my bike home. As I was leaving the store, I noticed how beautiful Main Street had become. Downtown had turned into a Christmas village of epic proportions. What I didn't fully realize was that it was about to get much more so. Things were still only just beginning.

CHAPTER NINE

The Haircut

After a very meaningful and long Thanksgiving weekend full of hard work, I went to school the next morning. However, I took the bus instead of riding my bike. I did this because I needed to get to the hair salon, which was a bit out of range for an easy bike ride.

My day at school went by quickly. School felt so much easier than my life outside of school. At school, I just needed to sit at my desk and listen. That's it. How hard is that? It's not. I don't think most of the other kids realized how easy their lives were compared to what "we adults" did in the real world. Even though I wasn't an adult, I sure felt like one.

After school, I went out to the school bus area and got onto the bus that I knew went past the hair salon. I asked the bus driver to stop at the hair salon for me. He gave me a very strange look that had a hint of uncooperativeness to it. I explained to him that I was getting my haircut there; and I pointed to my hair as strong definitive proof that if anyone needed a haircut, it was most certainly me.

Fortunately, the bus driver knew me, and he knew that I was the kind of kid who would simply get off the bus and walk, if he refused to oblige my special request. For this reason, he nodded and motioned for me to continue all of the way onto the bus. I sat up front just in case I needed to prompt him to stop later on.

It didn't take long for the bus to get to the hair salon. I think the driver felt me breathing down his neck, so he had no problems remembering to stop and let me off. I could hear other kids on the bus wondering why I was getting off at the hair salon. I really didn't care about their whispering, and it was none of their business anyway. They were just children being children.

Once off the bus, I walked into the hair salon. My first impression was that it seemed a bit fancy. It also seemed to be geared mostly toward women. I started to feel weird about it, but it was too late to do anything about it by then. I needed my haircut, and there I was. Thus, it was happening.

Everyone in there seemed to immediately recognize me, and I got the feeling that they had definitely been expecting me, and were waiting for my arrival.

I was greeted warmly, and the lady who was going to cut my hair came over to me and introduced herself.

She said, "It's an honor to meet the 'downtown Christmas boy.'"

I laughed because I had not heard *that one* before. I had earned all kinds of nicknames, but that one was new.

She asked me to have a seat in the haircutting chair. Is that a real name for it, or did I just make that up?

She was looking at me and my hair carefully. I was watching her every expression in the mirror, and I could tell that she was experiencing a bundle of varied thoughts and feelings about what she was dealing with in regard to my hair.

She said, "May I ask when the last time was that you had a haircut?"

I didn't know how to answer that, and I replied, "You mean a haircut from my mother, or a real haircut, or any haircut, or what?"

She lowered her head and chuckled. Then she said, "That answers it for me."

After a pause, she said, "So, what are we trying to do here?"

I replied, "We are trying to make me not look like an idiot anymore."

Everyone in the entire salon erupted in laughter, including the other customers. I guess everyone had been listening to the exchange. Note to self: While in a hair salon, everyone is listening to what everyone else is saying. Duly noted.

After she and everyone else stopped laughing, she said, "How about you tell me what sort of mood or image you are hoping to convey by how you look."

THAT was a question I could answer. I replied, "I want to look like a professional store owner. I am part owner of the new store opening up called Christmas Town, and I want to look like *that*."

The lady nodded as if she fully understood what I wanted. I was relieved.

She then had me go over to a sink, and she washed my hair. But she didn't just wash my hair. She also massaged my head while doing it. And she didn't do it just once. She did it twice.

That was the moment when I understood why people paid extra for a haircut at a salon. I was already happier, and she hadn't even picked up her scissors yet.

When she was finished washing my hair, she brought me over to her "hair cutting chair". *Is that what we've decided it's called?* I settled in, and she put the big poncho thing over me, or whatever it's called. I'm pretty sure a person had to learn an entirely new language just to go inside a hair salon.

Anyway, she began cutting my hair. But I noticed that she wasn't doing it like my mother. My mother would just kind of cut here and cut there, while trying not to draw blood or cut out chunks by accident. However, this hair salon stylist obviously had an organized system, and it was mostly based upon cutting in layers.

As she was doing my hair, I heard other customers and *their* hair stylists talking about how much downtown had changed. They were not directing any comments at me, and their comments were not meant as compliments for my benefit. In fact, they all talked as if I couldn't hear anything they were saying. Thus, I pretended that I couldn't hear anything they were saying, even though I heard every word that everyone in the entire salon was saying.

I heard a lady say that downtown had turned into a Christmas wonderland, and the only thing it was missing was Christmas music and carolers. That was the one thing that I reacted to in the form of a silent smile. I knew then that I had my next idea.

After my hair stylist had been working on my hair for a while, she said, "I know you said you want to look like a store owner; but do you want to look like a 40-year-old store owner, or a 12 – 13 year old store owner?"

I replied, "Let's make me look like a 16-year-old store owner."

She and some others in the salon laughed. But that was me signaling that I wanted to look like a store owner, but I also wanted to look cool like the older teenagers in high school. Some of the kids in high school always seemed to have the best clothes and best hair.

She resumed her work, and before long, she did the razor thing on the back of my neck, followed by the hair dryer. I could already see that I loved how it looked. But when she was officially done, she asked me to tell her what I thought.

Quite honestly, my first impression was that my hair looked similar to Jeremy's. I even wondered if she was the one who cut Jeremy's hair, but I decided not to ask. Instead, I told her that I liked it a lot.

She hadn't just cut my hair. She had created something that I never thought possible. I had always assumed that kids like Jeremy and others just had really nice hair, and I had crappy hair. But for the first time, I could see that my hair was perfectly fine. It just needed to be done right.

She took off the poncho thing, and I walked over to the reception area where the register was. On my way over, one of the ladies in the salon said, "Now you look as famous as you are."

I thanked her for her remark in a stoic way, but deep down I was ecstatic over her comment because what she said was sort of what I was going after. I guess I had achieved it; or rather the hair stylist who did my hair had.

Once at the register, the lady quietly told me how much I owed. I already knew what I would owe, so there was no surprise. I handed the lady the money, along with some extra. My mother told me that I needed to give her a tip, so I made sure that I got additional money from my bank account to pay the extra.

The lady thanked me, and then I guess expected me to leave. But I couldn't leave. I had no way to get anywhere. I knew this was going to happen, but I had enough backup plans in place, where I was not concerned about it beforehand. I knew that in the worst-case scenario, my mother could pick me up after work in a couple of hours.

The lady figured it out, and said, "You don't have a fancy sports car sitting out in the parking lot with which to drive yourself home, do you?"

I laughed, and replied, "No, Ma'am."

She responded, "Can I call someone for you?"

I replied, "My mom can pick me up after work, but that's in two hours. I am wondering if maybe Mr. Martins will come get me if we can reach him. His store is Martins Gifts, but he might be working at our new store now. However, I don't know the number for the new store yet."

After a pause, I said, "Maybe if you call Martins Gifts and ask his wife if Mr. Martins can come get me at the hair salon? And if she says he can't, we can just call my mom and I'll wait."

The lady nodded in agreement. She found the number for Martins Gifts and called. She must have reached Mrs. Martins, because I listened to her explain who I was, and the situation. The call wasn't long. When she finished, she looked at me and said, "Mrs. Martins is calling her husband now at the new store, and he will come over to get you."

I smiled, and replied, "Okay, thank you."

I went over to the waiting area and sat down in a place where I could see outside onto the street and the parking lot.

I mused over how I felt like I had another parent now, in addition to my mother. It felt good.

When I saw Mr. Martins's car pull into the lot, I ran out the door and over to his car so that he wouldn't have to get out.

I jumped into his car, and said, "Thanks for getting me. My mom couldn't do it until after work."

He responded, "No problem. I need to give you the number to the new store so you have it."

I replied, "Yeah, that would be great."

I knew he had noticed my hair right away, and I could tell that he was dying to say something.

After a few moments, he said, "Wow, look at you! Now you look as famous as you are!"

I quipped, "That's the same thing that a lady in the salon said!"

He responded, "Because it's true."

After a few moments, he said, "Am I bringing you home now, or what?"

I replied, "No, I have something I have to do downtown first. But it would be great if you could bring me home when you are done for the day and ready to leave the store? But if you can't, we can call my mom and she will pick me up at the store."

He responded, "That's fine. I can take you home. I wanted to get home at a reasonable hour today, anyway."

He added, "Where do you want me to drop you off?"

I replied, "I need to go to the music store. So, anywhere near there. I'm not shopping. I have to meet with them about some downtown stuff. Even though my focus is *our* store, I still need to finish all of my work regarding downtown."

He chuckled and responded, "I thought your work downtown was done? It looks done to me. Everything is fantastic, and I've heard people comment about how it looks like a Christmas village."

I replied, "Oh, no. I've still got more stuff to do, but nothing time consuming."

He nodded in amusement.

After a few moments, he said, "I'm probably going to keep the doors to the store unlocked for the next couple of days so that customers can come in and shop. But we'll do our official opening on Saturday. I would like you to be there for that."

I replied, "Yes, Sir, I can do that. I have a couple more things I need to take care of, and I will do them this week. Starting Saturday, I plan to always be at the store."

He nodded, and responded, "Sounds good. I'll count on it."

I quipped, "Yes, Sir, you can."

Mr. Martins pulled over in front of the music store so that I could jump out. He told me to come over to the store when I was done. I nodded and waved while getting out.

I went into the music store and looked for the guy who I knew was in charge, or maybe he was the owner. I found him messing with the stereo equipment they had for sale. They didn't just sell music. They sold stereo equipment and speakers as well. I also saw electric guitars on the wall, so I guess they sold those also. It was one of those good old-fashioned music stores which everyone loved to browse through.

The guy knew who I was because I had painted his door and installed Christmas lights in his window.

I interrupted what he was doing, and said, "Hi, Sir. It's me again."

He turned around, and responded, "Oh, hi. How are you doing?"

I replied, "I'm fine. I was hoping to ask you about something."

He smiled and responded, "What are you up to now? Please tell me that you're going to make magical fairies fall from the sky and drop money on all of us so that we may have a chance of surviving the rest of the year in business."

I smirked, and replied, "The magical fairies thing is a good idea, Sir. I will work on that."

He laughed, and responded, "Please do. But what can I do for you today?"

I replied, "I had another idea that might help downtown, but I need your help to do it."

He got a very intrigued look on his face, and responded, "Okay, shoot. I'm willing to try anything. A few more slow months like this, and we'll no longer be in business, and I'll be standing on the corner with a tin cup."

I replied, "I know, Sir. I'm trying. I'm doing the best I can."

He responded, "I know you are. We all do. That's why you have our complete cooperation."

I replied, "Okay, well I heard some ladies talking, and they mentioned that it might make downtown more magical if there was Christmas music playing. So, my idea was to see if you could put some speakers out your upper windows, or even on your roof, and then play Christmas music. Like, don't make it overbearing, but make it so that it blends into the background and drowns out the traffic noise. You know what I mean?"

The man had a contemplative expression on his face, and was deep in thought off in space somewhere. I knew to remain silent and wait.

After a few moments, he responded, "Well, on any other day, with any other music, if we blared music out the windows or on the roof, we would have the police showing up and giving us a hard time."

I replied, "Well, first of all, this is Christmastime, and it's Christmas music we are talking about. So, that makes this different. And secondly, if the police ask any questions, just tell them that it was *my* idea, and I asked you to do it. You can blame me. The police know who I am, and they even gave me a special badge."

The man was highly amused by this. He was smiling and laughing, but in a good way. He wasn't making fun of me.

He responded, "I believe you. And I believe your plan will work. You seem to have some kind of magical touch about you, and I would assume that extends into immunity from the police."

I just smirked.

He then said, "I'll do it. I will work on it tomorrow. I have some old display speakers I can use. I just need to run the wire. I'll put a couple out the upper windows, and then a couple up on the roof. We'll just have to try it out and see what works and what doesn't."

I replied, "PERFECT! And just play soft and pleasant Christmas music, as if it was background noise. It should blend in."

The man laughed, and said, "Yeah, I'll stay away from the heavy metal Christmas albums."

We both laughed.

After we settled down, he said, "How can I reach you if needed?"

I quipped, "You mean if the police come knocking?"

He laughed, and nodded, as if that was his reason. I suppose it may have been.

I replied, "Starting on Saturday, I will be working at my new store that I have with Mr. Martins. It's located down in the old sporting goods store space."

He responded, "Oh, yeah. Christmas Town."

I replied, "Yeah, that's it. I even named it that."

He responded, "So, I assume you will be selling all Christmas stuff?"

I replied, "For right now, yeah. But after Christmas, we will be selling all kinds of other stuff, also."

After a thought, I added, "But if someone asks for music stuff, I'll send them to *your* store."

The man thought for a moment, and responded, "I've got an even better idea."

After a pause, he continued, "I've got a lot of Christmas music in the backroom. People tend not to come to my store for Christmas music. How about I give you all of my Christmas music stuff on consignment? Meaning, you sell all of my merchandise in your store, and we split the markup. I can produce invoices to prove the base cost. And then anything you don't sell, you can just bring back here after Christmas. What do you say?"

Believe it or not, I understood everything he said.

I replied, "Yeah, I like that. Let me just ask Mr. Martins, and then I can come over and get the merchandise."

The man responded, "There's too much for you to carry. I can load it up in my van and drop it off at your store."

I replied, "Great. Let me come back in a day or two after I check with Mr. Martins, and we'll do it. THANKS! I really like your idea!"

I gave him a wave and left the store. I then went right over to the Christmas Town store. I went around through the back since the main front door was still locked.

I found Mr. Martins, and said, "I have a question."

He quipped, "Yeah? What's that?"

I replied, "The music store up across the street wants us to sell all of his Christmas music merchandise on consignment. He said we can split the markup, and that he can prove the original cost. He said we can return all of the unsold stuff after Christmas. I told him it sounded good but that I had to check with you first."

Mr. Martins was thinking, and his hamster wheels were spinning quickly.

He responded, "Okay, well listen. Normally, if you have a small store that doesn't work because you are losing half of your markup, and you only have so much retail space available. But in our present situation, we have a huge store with lots of floor space and not very much merchandise, because we are trying to open a store in a week, which is crazy and never done, yet here we are. SO, under those circumstances, this is a great arrangement for us. I say we do it. I know the guy, and he's honest and easy to deal with."

I replied, "Okay, I'll tell him that it's a go, and he'll drop everything off over here. You don't have to do anything. I'll even stock the merchandise once it's in our backroom."

Mr. Martins nodded, and responded, "Deal. But just so you understand, since you're learning, part of doing a deal like this is that you have to do an inventory count and consignment sheet so that everyone knows what there is and how much there is. So, there is work involved. But I agree this is good for us."

I replied, "Okay. But what if I can find other arrangements like this?"

He responded, "What do you mean?"

I replied, "What if I talk to other stores on Main Street and ask them if they have any Christmas related overstock, like candles and things like that? You said we don't have enough merchandise. Maybe this is a way of getting more quickly."

Mr. Martins thought for a moment, and responded, "Yes, I like that. But just check with me first before doing it. But I like it. It will expand our line of merchandise, and give us more depth in case we have heavier than expected sales. But I need you to take care of the consignment sheets. So, that means you will need to inventory all of the items we take in, have a total count of each type of item, and have the other store owner sign it."

I replied, "Yes, okay, I can do that."

After a moment, Mr. Martins said, "Let me take you home now. I assume you have homework? You *ARE* still going to school, right?"

We both laughed, and I nodded in the affirmative.

The next day after school, I rode my bike downtown. I had a busy afternoon and evening planned. I first stopped at the music store. I told the man that our deal was on, but that I was responsible for the consignment inventory sheet. He then agreed to drop everything off at the store the next day after school so that I would be available at the store to receive the goods from him.

Not only that, but I saw that he was working on running wires to speakers for the public Christmas music. I told him that I was excited to hear it in operation.

I left the music store, and went to the fancy clothier place. When I walked in, I saw the lady. The man was either busy or not working that day. I explained to her that I was ready to get my additional outfits. She went to the backroom and brought out some choices that they had ordered for me in my size. I liked all of them.

I looked at her, shrugged, and said, "They all look awesome. How many things am I allowed to choose?"

She shrugged, sighed, and responded, "Honestly, I think you can just take whatever you want. When it comes to *you*, there always seems to be someone willing to pay for what you need. That's not to say that you should take over-advantage of that, but I'm just being straight up with you."

Her response didn't really answer my question. She was basically saying that I could take as much as I wanted. But the truth was that I wanted to be very careful not to do anything that would upset anyone.

She saw that I was conflicted, and said, "Let's do this. Why don't you take two outfits home with you today; see if you like them; and then you still have one more you can get for sure, but you can get more if there are others you absolutely have to have. Will that work?"

I replied, "Perfect, thank you."

She responded, "These are all your size. But if for some reason, there is an issue, or you decide you don't like something, just bring it back here within the next week or so, and you can switch it out for something else. Okay?"

I replied, "Yes, thank you."

I then looked at my choices again, and chose two outfits that I knew I loved for sure.

The lady took them, bagged them up, and gave them to me. She then said, "Your hair looks fantastic, by the way."

I smiled, and quipped, "Thank you."

I then told the lady that I'd be back at some point, and I left.

Next, I went down to the regular clothing store where I got my school clothes. I walked in and tried to find the same lady as before. She wasn't there, but I went up to a man who was working, and I told him who I was and that I was hoping to get more school clothes from a gift voucher I had.

He knew who I was, but needed to check with the manager about the gift voucher. When he came back out, he told me that I could choose three more outfits. I told him that I didn't have much time, and asked if I could just choose the outfits and then try them on at home. He told me that I could do that, and just bring anything back that didn't fit, but make sure the tags were still on the clothes.

I picked out my outfits and brought them to the man at the cash register. He took care of everything, put my clothes in a bag, and I was off. I guess that was the end of my gift voucher for *that* store. I thought to myself how I really needed to start earning an income from the Christmas Town store so that I could keep getting everything I needed, but pay for it with my own money.

The good news was that I was well clothed, had a fresh new haircut, and was ready to conquer the world.

CHAPTER TEN
The Opening

It was the day before our official opening of our new store, Christmas Town. Mr. Martins had managed to get the temporary banner sign installed on the front of the building, and we were already unofficially open for business. He left the front doors unlocked, and the lights on. However, not many people walked inside. Hopefully, business was going to pick up after our official opening on the next day, Saturday.

As promised, the owner of the music store brought his merchandise over in his van. I helped him unload it, and then I looked through all of his boxes. He already had an inventory sheet with him, which made things so much easier. I only had to verify what was on the sheet. Once I saw it was correct, he asked me to sign the sheet, and he kept a copy, and I kept a copy. I guess that's how business was done. Even though I was just a kid, he seemed to have no problems accepting my signature, nor did anyone else for that matter.

After I was done with that, I went to speak with Mr. Martins. I knew he had some things that he wanted to go over with me.

I said, "We have all of the Christmas music stuff. I'll put it on the shelves when I get time."

He nodded, and said, "Here, these are keys to the front door and the back door. You should have a set of keys since it's also your store."

I took the keys from him and looked at them. I knew they were "just keys," and many workers would get keys to stores which they work at; but for some reason, those keys seemed very significant to me. I carefully slid them into my front pocket as if they were precious diamonds.

He then said, "When this store is open, your job is to be wherever

I am not. This means that if I am at the customer counter ringing someone up, you need to be on the retail floor helping customers and making sure that nobody steals us blind. And if *I'm* on the retail floor with a customer, *you* need to be at the customer counter guarding the cash register. And finally, most important of all, is that if one of us is working in the backroom, the other one needs to be out front. Got it?"

I nodded in the affirmative, and replied, "Got it."

After a pause, he said, "Would you feel comfortable ringing up sales at the cash register?"

I replied, "Yes, Sir; if you show me how."

He then proceeded to show me how to ring up a sale using the cash register, and how to ring up a sale using the credit card machine. We did a few practice runs. He literally gave me an item in the store, and had me ring it up; first with cash, and then again with him paying by credit card. He also showed me how to reverse a transaction, and do a return. He made it clear that I could call him over for help if I ever got confused serving a customer.

After it seemed that we had a clear plan in place, and we each knew what we would be doing and how to do it, Mr. Martins said, "I want you to know that there is nobody else on this Earth that I would rather be doing this with than you. You've been an amazing business partner, good company, and you have awoken an inspiration within me that I thought was gone. I look forward to seeing where it all leads."

I was very humbled by his words, and I hung my head down because I didn't know what to say in return. It was another one of those moments when I felt things that I didn't think existed, or that I never felt I would feel in regard to a mentor, or father figure. Up to that point, I didn't really know what it was like to have a dad, and I wondered if this was what it was like.

I think Mr. Martins knew that I felt awkward and didn't know what to say, but I hope he knew that it was in a good way, and not in a bad way. I think he did.

When I lifted my head back up to look at him, he smiled proudly at me, and said, "You should probably go home and get some rest. Do you need a ride?"

I replied, "No, I have my bike, so I need to ride it home. But tomorrow I'm going to wear my nice business clothes, so would it be possible for you to pick me up in the morning?"

He responded, "No problem at all."

He and I then worked out the correct time for him to get me, and then I left the store and rode my bike home.

That night at dinner, I let my mother know what the plans were so that she would know. She already knew that the store was opening, and nothing I said to her was a surprise.

Later in the evening, I laid out the outfit that I would be wearing the next day, and I went to bed earlier than usual.

The next morning, I got up early, showered, and got dressed. When I went out into the kitchen to get a quick bite to eat, my mother saw me, and said, "HOLY COW, LOOK AT YOU!"

She gave me one of her very rare proud smiles, and I could tell that she had an abundance of unspoken thoughts going on in her mind.

Eventually she said, "I am still not sure how all of this started, and I don't know where it's going; but what you have done so far is nothing short of extraordinary. Good luck with all of it, Son."

And that right there, folks, was probably the best, and the most, that I had ever gotten out of my mother for anything I had ever done. Her words were my validation that something amazing was happening, even if I didn't fully understand it yet.

I simply replied with, "Thanks, Mom."

After I had some toast for breakfast, Mr. Martins arrived to pick me up. I said goodbye to my mother and left the house. I got into Mr. Martins's car, and we drove the fairly short distance into downtown to our store.

We opened everything up, unlocked the front doors for the customers, and waited for shoppers to arrive. It was a very exciting moment for both of us. I was hoping that I would be able to keep up with everything when it got busy. All we had to do was wait for them to come. If you build it, they will come, right?

And so we waited. And waited. And waited. And waited.

It was mid-morning, and we hadn't had a single customer come inside the store. I asked Mr. Martins if I could prop the front doors open. I thought that maybe if the doors were open, it might coax people to come inside. But guess what?

There were no people walking up or down the sidewalk to coax inside. Downtown was dead. Here it was, the beginning of Christmas shopping season, and there wasn't anyone shopping.

For a while, I stood outside the door, almost hoping that my mere presence on the sidewalk might attract people to the store. But there was nobody to see me. The only people I saw out on Main Street were very busy looking people who were going into specific stores to buy a certain thing. There weren't any shoppers randomly shopping for random things.

Mr. Martins called his wife to ask how she was doing at Martins Gifts, and she reported that the only customer they had was a 'regular' who stopped in to buy some wrapping paper and a card. That's it. But that was still better than we were doing, so I guess Martins Gifts was outperforming our new store.

This "deadness" went on all day. Later in the afternoon, I started to become agitated and upset within myself. Mr. Martins detected this, and said, "Young man, starting a new business is not easy. It can take weeks or months before things kick into gear. I know you were hoping for better, but I guess you are not immune to the laws of the universe when it comes to new businesses. You have to keep the faith."

I replied, "But Sir, we have a very limited Christmas sales period. We can't afford to wait weeks or months. We need things to happen NOW."

Mr. Martins felt my frustration (anger), and he decided to not push the discussion any further.

When the day turned into early evening, we still had not had a single customer. Mr. Martins suggested that it was time to close for the day, and for him to take me home. But at the same time, he proclaimed that he would be by my home at the same time the next morning to take me to work again. I just nodded in the affirmative. We closed up and left the store.

I arrived back home, and my mom asked how it went.

I only quipped, "No customers."

I then went into my room to change out of my nice clothes.

At dinner that night, my mother didn't ask any further questions. It was a silent meal.

The next morning, I dressed up in another one of my nice outfits, and Mr. Martins came to pick me up. We opened up the store, and started to have a repeat of the previous day.

I once again stood outside the store for a while, and I noticed how nice and Christmasy downtown looked. The store windows were lit up with Christmas lights, and I could hear Christmas music coming from the music store. All of the doors, windows, light poles, wreaths, ribbons, Christmas lights, Christmas music, along with many other decorations, made all of Main Street, on both sides, look wonderful, and feel wonderful. But the sidewalks were empty.

I began to have a meltdown within myself. I felt like I had convinced everyone that following along with my plans would result in more business for all of the stores along Main Street. Pretty much the entire town was depending on it. But my plans were not working. Nobody wanted to go shopping downtown. I guess that's why all of downtown, and pretty much our entire city, was dying. Maybe it was already dead, but some of us hadn't realized it or accepted it yet. Maybe I was everyone's last hope in the darkness of hopelessness. All of the store owners wanted me to be right. That's why they went along with everything I wanted to do. But it didn't work. I had failed them. I failed everyone.

I went back inside the store, and then to the backroom, where I could be alone. I knew Mr. Martins would stay at the register if I was in the backroom.

My anger fully erupted. I started kicking boxes around. I couldn't understand how all of my hard work could have resulted in NOTHING. How was this even possible? How can a person work so hard at something for a long time, and then get NOTHING in return? NO RESULTS! NOTHING! HOW IS THAT EVEN POSSIBLE?

I hated life in that moment. I felt it was unfair. I knew that everything was stacked against me from birth, but I felt deep inside that if I worked hard enough, and used my wits, that maybe I could overcome my low position in life. I thought that I lived in 'the land of opportunity.' Well, where was *MY* opportunity? HUH? Where was it? And what about all of the other store owners up and down Main Street? The owner of the music store had already told me flat-out that if things didn't improve, he was going to close his store. The rumor was that many other store owners downtown were in the same position, and were going to do the same. Everything was dying. I tried to save it. But I guess I was too young, or too stupid, or too unlucky, or too 'something.' It didn't work.

When I was finished with my tantrum, I went back into the retail space and pretended that everything was fine. I saw Mr. Martins looking at me closely to determine what was going on with me, but I don't think I gave him much to go by.

Later that day shortly before we were scheduled to close, Mrs. Martins and Sally came into the store. They had closed up Martins Gifts for the weekend because nothing was happening there, either.

Mrs. Martins and Sally were literally the first and only people to walk into the store during the entire weekend. Mrs. Martins looked tired and depressed. Sally looked worried.

I didn't want to hear what horrible things Mr. and Mrs. Martins might say to each other, so I went to a different part of the store. I ended up at one of our many little Christmas trees that we had set up as displays to sell our tree ornaments.

Sally followed me over there. I was hoping she wouldn't, because I was in the worst mood, and I didn't want to subject her to that, nor did I have the energy to pretend to be nice to her.

I think she knew how upset I was, so she didn't say anything to me. She just stood next to me silently while we both looked at the display tree with the ornaments on it.

After staring at the tree for a very long and awkward amount of time, Sally said, "Everything in this store is so beautiful. You did such a great job with everything. Even these ornaments on the tree are so pretty."

That was Sally trying to be nice. I decided to be nice back by not snapping at her. I just remained silent. Saying nothing was the best I could do in regards to being nice.

There was more silence, and then Sally very gently began touching, almost caressing, one of the ornaments. It was a small crystal figurine of an angel that was meant to be hung on a tree as an ornament.

I started watching Sally and what she was doing. It was like she was in a trance.

After a while of watching this, I said, "Sally, what are you doing?"

She opened her eyes, looked over at me, and responded, "I'm praying for a miracle."

I could see in her face that she understood how dire the situation was. I think she knew that if something amazing didn't happen soon, this would be her last Christmas at her home in our town. She knew that her family would have to move and start over again elsewhere.

I was looking at her, and just replied, "Well, we definitely need a miracle."

I then looked away from her because I didn't want to see her facial response to that, nor did I want her to reply to it.

Right then, Mrs. Martins called out for Sally, and told her that they were leaving to go home.

After they left, Mr. Martins said to me, "We should go as well. You have school tomorrow. I will try again tomorrow morning, and you can show up as you are able. School comes first, young man."

I just nodded. I didn't have the strength to say anything.

We closed up the store, and Mr. Martins drove me home. I was too upset to even speak to him, so I just looked at him and waved before I got out of the car.

I went inside my home, and my mother was there to see me get home. She could tell by my expression that I was upset.

I went straight into my room, slammed the door shut, and finally had my FULL breakdown that I had been dying to have all day, and really, all weekend. I cried and cried and cried. I was totally broken and destroyed. I knew that everything was a failure. I knew that everyone had trusted me, and I let them all down. Worst of all, Mr. Martins had trusted me, and now he and his family were going to be ruined. Sally would have to move away, which had been her biggest fear ever since the school year started. I let *her* down, along with everyone else in town.

After I had cried my worst tears, I sat on my bed, sniveling and crying any leftover tears.

I then heard a knock at my door. Obviously, it was my mother.

I said, "WHAT?"

She responded, "Can I come in?"

I hesitated, and replied, "I guess. Whatever."

She opened the door and came inside my room to find me sitting on my bed, still wearing my nice clothes, with my face full of tears.

I could tell that she was trying to decide how to handle me and what to say.

After a few moments, she said, "I assume this is about the store?"

I replied, "It's about the store and everything else, Mom. Nothing is working. Downtown is dead. There is NOTHING. NO shoppers. And our new store hasn't had a single customer. It's over. Everything is a failure, and it's all my fault."

After a few moments, my mother responded, "None of this is your fault. You don't control the town. You don't control downtown. You can't make shoppers materialize out of nowhere. This town was dying before you even set foot downtown. You did what you could, and you tried your best. That's more than most others can say."

Her words sort of made sense and were of some comfort, but they didn't fix the situation.

I replied, "I needed to figure it out, Mom. I needed to make shoppers MATERIALIZE. THAT IS WHAT I NEEDED TO DO, AND I DIDN'T DO IT!"

She knew I was getting worked up again, so she didn't immediately respond.

After several moments of me trying to pull myself together, my mother said, "Listen to me. I know things have not been easy for you. You've had a difficult life pretty much since you were born. Most things have not gone well for you. But that has made you tough. It's turned you into a fighter. And that means you are NOT a quitter. DON'T QUIT! DON'T GIVE UP! Be the person that I know you can be. Be the person that I know you are."

After a pause, she continued, "I know you might think that this is your worst moment and things look hopeless. But this also might be your greatest moment ever. Whichever one of those it is will depend upon what you do next. So, choose wisely."

My mom then gave me a stern look, and I knew that she was speaking from the depths of her soul. I knew that she truly believed in everything she had just said.

She then broke her gaze on me, turned around, and walked out of my room while shutting the door behind her.

I didn't cry anymore that evening, but I also didn't leave my room, except to quickly grab some food. I was still very upset, but my mother had given me a lot to think about.

My mother was a complicated woman. In some ways, I never felt that I got everything from her that I wanted or needed. But in other ways, there were moments when my mother showed a wise depth of strength that you would be hard pressed to find in another woman. It was this depth that always reminded me that she was indeed my mother, because I felt that same depth within myself.

I was tired and went to bed early that night. When I woke up the next morning, I had to go to school. I got dressed in my new school clothes, and rode my bike to school in the cold. It was one of those soberingly cold mornings that are very uncomfortable, but at the same time, reminds you that you're alive because you're so uncomfortable. In that way, it is rejuvenating. Those who live in a colder climate will perhaps understand what I mean by this.

I should note that by this time of year, I usually had started taking the bus due to weather, but I guess I really wanted (needed) to ride my bike to school that day.

All day during school, I tried not to talk to anyone, or even make eye contact with anyone. I felt ashamed for letting the entire town down, and I figured everyone in my class knew this. Of course, I forgot that everyone in my class were children. I was the only child who was an adult.

After school, I rode my bike downtown. The first thing I noticed was that some of the stores had not turned on their Christmas lights, and the music store wasn't playing Christmas music. I guess everyone had given up.

I went inside the Christmas Town store, and Mr. Martins looked bored. He was the only one in the store. This was not a shocking surprise to me. Why would there be any shoppers inside the store? There wouldn't be.

I didn't say anything to him when I walked in, and I think he might have been slightly surprised that I even showed up.

He was standing behind the counter near the cash register, and I walked up to the counter and started straightening out some small merchandise items that were displayed on the counter. However, the truth was that I was just moping.

After a minute or so, Mr. Martins said, "Do you know the difference between a boy and a man?"

I looked up at him and sheepishly replied, "No."

He responded, "A man never gives up. A man will keep trying new angles and different strategies until he finds one that works. A man must carry the pain and burden of enduring through the most difficult times of struggle. Conversely, a boy remains a boy until he decides that he has the strength of character to become a man."

He stopped speaking, turned away from me, and started fiddling with something in the other direction. I guess he had said all he wanted to say to me, and he wasn't going to say anything else.

A few moments later, he told me that he needed to go out back to do something, and he asked me to remain at the customer counter. I just shrugged in acknowledgment and agreement. What did it matter anyway? I knew there wouldn't be any customers. But I guess someone still needed to be in the retail space watching the cash register in case a gang of mice tried to carry it off.

While standing there alone, in silence, with nobody else in the store,

I pondered what Mr. Martins had said. What he said was not that different from what my mother had said. If both my mother AND Mr. Martins said the same thing, it must have meant that it was correct.

For whatever reason, I thought about how far I had come in life. I thought about how all of this had started with me in my old clothes and horrible haircut painting doors. I thought about the progression of where things went from there. And then that is when I remembered something critically important.

I remembered the interviews I did for the reporters at the newspaper. I remembered how the story that came out about me in the newspaper had been a pretty big deal and had literally changed my life.

I started thinking. I was thinking very intently. I don't think my hamster wheels had spun that hard in my entire life. I just stood there in my own universe, thinking. And then I had an idea.

I needed to make a phone call. But I wanted to do it before Mr. Martins came back out. I frantically looked up the number for the local newspaper.

I picked up the store phone and called them. I asked the lady who answered if I could speak with the reporter who had done the original interview with me. I asked for the reporter by name. The lady asked who was calling, and I told her my name, plus I added that I was the kid who did all of the work downtown.

She put me on hold, and then the reporter answered.

He said, "Young man! Wonderful and surprising to hear from you! What can I do for you?"

I replied, "Sir, I was hoping you could help me out."

He responded, "Yeah? With what?"

I replied, "Things downtown are still slow. But everyone has done so much work on making things look amazing and turning Main Street into a Christmas wonderland. But nobody from outside our town seems to know; or nobody cares, I'm not sure which. But I need to try and do something about that."

The reporter quipped, "Yeah?"

I replied, "Do you think you would be willing to come down here and do another story? I've just opened up a new store with Mr. Martins, called Christmas Town. I am part owner. Maybe we could do a photo in front of the new store. But mostly, I am trying to get shoppers to come downtown. I don't even care if it's my store or someone else's store that they shop at."

I stopped talking, and there was silence. I could hear the reporter hemming and hawing, breathing, or groaning. I think he was considering what I had said and wasn't sure.

He finally responded, "I agree it's interesting that you have ownership of a store at your young age. And you've done a lot for downtown. I don't see the harm in running another story, especially since your store is called Christmas Town, and it's Christmas season. So, yeah. Okay."

I think the reporter was hoping that I would thank him profusely and then leave him alone. But I wasn't done yet. In fact, I had only begun.

I replied, "That's great, thank you. But I have one more favor to ask, and this is a big one."

He skeptically responded, "*Yeah?*"

I replied, "Do you know anyone over at the TV station that covers our area?"

He was silent for a moment, and then responded, "I do. I know a few people over at the TV station. But the TV station that covers our area is not even based within our city."

I replied, "I know. But they cover our city."

There was silence.

I suppose the reporter knew what I was going to ask next, and he was hoping that I wouldn't.

After the silence went on for too long, I said, "If we could get the

TV station to come to our downtown and do a story, I think that might help things. It looks amazing here, if you haven't seen it; especially in the evening."

The reporter responded, "I've seen it in the evening, and you're right. It's a special place."

I replied, "Then let's show *everyone* that it's a special place."

The reporter was making all of his noises again, while he was considering whether or not he wanted to be a part of my latest scheme.

Eventually, he responded, "I will make some phone calls. You are obviously not one to give up, so I can at least make a call or two on my end. Won't hurt to try."

I replied, "THANK YOU! And please let me know what you find out. Also, I need to know when you and them are coming so that I can be sure everything is the way it needs to be down here. I will tell the other stores to be ready. So, make sure you warn me so that I can have all of downtown looking its best."

The reporter chuckled in amusement, and responded, "Fair enough. I can't promise anything, but let me try. How do I get a hold of you?"

I replied, "Call me at Christmas Town. If I'm not here, you can leave me a message."

We wrapped up our call and ended it.

I was fully aware that nothing had really happened yet. I perhaps had a commitment for another newspaper article, but what I really needed was a TV interview. However, that was not something I had in the bag yet.

Still the same, I felt different. I felt an inner flame within me had reignited. I felt hopeful again.

CHAPTER ELEVEN
The Interview

After my call to the reporter at the newspaper on Monday, I didn't say anything about it to Mr. Martins. On Tuesday, I went to school as usual, and then I went downtown after school. But this time, I had taken the bus to school, and brought my nice business clothes with me to school.

Then after school, I was able to take the school bus into downtown. Once I arrived at the Christmas Town store, I changed into my nice clothes.

When I came out of the bathroom after changing, Mr. Martins said, "Come over here for a moment."

I went over to the customer counter where he was.

He said, "I have a message for you."

I replied, "Yeah?"

He responded, "It was a reporter from the local newspaper. He wanted me to tell you that the TV crew is coming on Thursday evening just after dark, and he will do the newspaper story at the same time."

I slapped my hands together loudly, and exclaimed, "YES!!"

Mr. Martins said, "What is this about?"

I replied, "I'm trying to make shoppers materialize."

He had a big grin on his face, and he responded, "Okay. Is there anything I should know?"

I replied, "Yes. I'm going to do a TV and newspaper interview here in front of Christmas Town. But it's not just for our store. I am doing it for all of downtown."

He looked shocked, but in a good way.

He responded, "How did you manage this?"

I replied, "I decided I wanted to be a man, and I figured it out."

He hesitated, and then started laughing.

I was deep in thought, and then I said, "Mr. Martins, do you know of some carolers or a singing group that can come down here on Thursday evening and do some caroling on Main Street when I am doing the interview?"

He smiled, and responded, "My wife is part of a group that does that once or twice during the holidays. I can ask her."

I quipped, "GREAT! PERFECT! We need that."

He responded, "Okay. I will make it happen. Anything else?"

I replied, "I don't think so. I will take care of the rest, but I will be too busy to be in the store tomorrow. I need to go around to all of the other stores and talk with everyone."

He responded, "Yeah, okay. That's fine."

And that's what I did. On Wednesday, I showed up at the store after school, changed into my nice clothes, and then started going from store to store up and down Main Street. I told everyone that the TV people were coming Thursday evening, and that I needed ALL of the Christmas lights on, and everything looking its best.

I made sure to go to the music store and explain the situation to the owner, and remind him that we definitely needed the Christmas music playing. He enthusiastically agreed to make sure that happened.

On Thursday, I went to school on the bus, and brought my best fancy outfit with me. After school, the bus dropped me off downtown; and I went into the Christmas Town store and changed into my nice outfit.

When I came out of the bathroom and went over to the customer counter to check in with Mr. Martins, I saw that Mrs. Martins was there with her choir group.

I knew they were generously doing this because I had asked them to do it, so I knew I had to crawl out of my introverted skin and be very friendly and grateful toward them. This would become a skill that

I developed out of necessity, but would eventually become a natural part of who I was. It's what must happen when a natural introvert tries to transform into a leader.

I smiled at all of the ladies, and said, "Thank you so much for coming and doing this. Your voices are going to make Christmas feel like Christmas. We need as much of that as possible tonight."

The women seemed delighted by my disposition and presentation. I also heard a couple of them comment on my professional appearance.

Mrs. Martins looked over at Mr. Martins and said, "What should we be doing, and when should we be doing it?"

Without saying a word, Mr. Martins looked over at me. This caused all of the ladies to look over at me.

I replied to the query by saying, "When the TV news people show up, it would be great if you would sing carols up and down Main Street. But just go where the camera can see you and hear you. So maybe walk up the street a short way, and then walk back down past us, and then turn around and do the same thing again. We need the reporter and camera to always be able to see you and hear you."

Mrs. Martins responded, "How long should we do this for?"

Mr. Martins interjected, and replied, "Until you see the TV news crew packing up and leaving."

Everyone nodded in agreement with that statement. I just smiled.

When it was clear that everything was settled, and everyone started talking amongst themselves (meaning, not with me), I went outside to see how all of downtown looked from my vantage point at the Christmas Town store.

What I HEARD was beautiful Christmas music coming from the music store. What I SAW were empty sidewalks with the most gorgeous Christmas display I had ever seen in my life. Every store had its Christmas lights on, and all of the decorations everywhere on Main Street created the sensation of being inside a Christmas wonderland.

It was weird seeing such a beautifully serene setting with no people in it. It was like a Christmas ghost town. If the situation hadn't been so financially dire for our entire town, I would have said that it was peaceful and magical. But being a business owner as I was, there was nothing magical about seeing empty sidewalks.

And yes, the question went through my mind as to what the TV news reporter might think of the fact that our downtown was an empty ghost town void of any shoppers. I decided that I would just deal with that question if and when it came, but that I needed to remain relaxed and focused in the meantime.

It turned out that I didn't have much time to get nervous, because I saw the TV news van driving up Main Street. Also, in a separate car leading the way, was the reporter from the newspaper.

I stepped out closer to the street so that the reporter would definitely see me. I wanted to make sure that everything was set up so that the interview would take place in front of the Christmas Town store.

The reporter pulled up alongside the road and rolled his window down. I walked up to his car, and he said, "Where are we going to do this shot, boy?"

I replied, "I want to do the interview in front of the store right here; but I want the camera to see up and down Main Street on both sides."

He nodded, as if he fully understood my very vague and cryptic explanation, which would have been impossible for most others to decipher.

He motioned for me to step back so that he could get out of his vehicle, which he kept running. He went over to the TV news van and explained to them more clearly what I was wanting.

Based upon that, the news van backed down the street a little bit so that it wouldn't be parked too close to the store where they knew we would be doing the interview.

Once the van was parked, and the reporter had moved his car as well, the TV news crew started to set up for their shot. But this was when something very unexpected happened. I saw the big antenna built into the news van go up as high as it would go. They were setting up for a live shot.

For some reason, I had assumed they would record the interview, and then it might appear on TV a day or two later. But nope. They were going to do a live shot to be shown on that evening's news. I guess that's why they wanted to show up in the early evening. I wish someone had warned me, but I suppose it didn't matter.

With that said, once I saw that huge news van antenna going up, I looked behind me into the store at Mr. Martins. Maybe I was looking for some sort of comfort or encouragement? Who knows. But Mr. Martins responded by giving me a smile and a nod as his way of telling me to focus on what I was doing and forge ahead.

Right after that, the choir ladies filed out of the store while singing. They began their march up and down that section of Main Street. I wondered if people might think it was silly, since essentially nobody was there to hear them singing. They were caroling up and down an empty street.

As the crew was setting up lighting equipment in front of the store, the TV reporter who would be interviewing me came walking up to me. I knew she was the TV reporter because I had seen her for many years on the TV news. You could say that she was famous in our area. It was surreal to see her in person. She looked slightly different in person, though. More, umm, 'normal' than I had imagined. Hard to explain. People like that always seem to be 'more' than they are, when on TV. I know that doesn't make sense, but it's the only way I can describe it.

She introduced herself to me with a handshake, and she was very kind. I had seen her be very aggressive at times while on TV, so I was relieved that she was being nice to me.

She then said, "Have you ever been on TV before?"

I replied, "No, Ma'am."

She responded, "That's fine. It's easy. Just focus on me. Don't worry about the camera, lights, and everyone else standing around. It's just you and me, okay?"

I nodded in acknowledgment.

She continued, "This is a live shot, so when it's time for our segment, that man over there (the producer), will give us a signal, and then I will start speaking. Just let me speak at first. I am going to introduce the scene of where we are, why I'm here, and then I will introduce you. At that point, I will start to ask you questions. There aren't any trick questions. If anything, you might think my questions are dumb or too easy. But just answer them anyway, okay?"

I nodded again.

She went on, "Because this is a live shot, there will come a point when I need to wrap up the segment. This might mean that I interrupt you as you're speaking. I will try to be subtle about it, but if I do this, that is your cue to quickly end your sentence, and then let me wrap things up so that we don't get cutoff mid-sentence on live air. Alright?"

I quipped, "Yes, Ma'am."

She then nodded, as if she was satisfied that I understood everything. At that point, she walked back to the van, where she waited with a hot beverage until the producer guy would call her back over for the live shot.

As for me, I kept standing in-place like an idiot, as if we were going live on TV any second. But in a way, I think I was being helpful, because I saw and heard the crew moving and changing the lights based upon how I looked in them. So, they were using me as a test dummy to get the lighting right.

About ten minutes later, the TV reporter lady came out of the van and walked back over to me. I could tell that she had freshened up her hair and makeup, and she looked more like how she looked on TV.

She was given a microphone, and then she stood in a certain spot, and I was asked to move over a little bit to a specific mark on the sidewalk. The producer guy then yelled, "SIXTY SECONDS!"

It was probably the longest 60 seconds I had ever experienced in my life. But I knew the 60 seconds were about up when the reporter lady's face all of a sudden lit up as if she was a different person. Her eyes got bigger, and she all of a sudden had a "TV smile" on her face. I tried to remind myself not to scowl the entire time, even though that was my normal and natural facial expression much of the time.

The producer gave his signal, and the reporter immediately launched into her introduction. She said what town she was in, and that our downtown had undergone a magical Christmas transformation, thanks to a young boy who she was standing with. (That would be me, I guess.)

She then turned her focus from the camera to me. She said my name, and then added, "But I think most people know you by different nicknames. I've heard "Downtown Boy," "Christmas Boy," and other names. How do you like to be referred to?"

I was thinking how she had warned me that some of her questions might seem dumb. This was one of those. I assumed I would be referred to by my actual name, yes?

But I was quick on my feet, and replied, "It doesn't really matter to me as long as people remember our Christmas Town that we have here."

She reacted in a very amused and positive way to my reply. It was hard to tell if it was real or an act. I guess it didn't matter.

She responded, "How about 'Christmas Town Boy?'"

My face lit up because I LOVED THAT.

I replied, "Yes, that'll work!"

She giggled, and responded, "This is the most beautifully decorated downtown I've ever seen in my life. Not only that, but I can hear Christmas carolers going up and down the street, and I think I hear some instrumental Christmas music playing somewhere off in the background. Every single store is adorned with holiday decorations, and everything is lit up with Christmas lights. How in the world did all of this start?"

I replied, "It started by me painting the doors to the stores red or green. Then I moved onto the light poles. And then I just kept going from there."

She responded, "But what inspired you to do this in the first place?"

I replied, "I wanted to help all of the stores on Main Street get more business. I thought that if I made our downtown a nicer place, that maybe more people would come shopping here."

She responded, "Well personally, I think you should be very proud of what you have done. How do you feel about your finished results?"

I hesitated ever so slightly, and replied, "Well, I'm not done yet. Everything you see here is something that is growing and evolving. It's magical. This downtown was not much before, but everyone here has worked together, and now it's a magical place. Just like the name of my store we are standing in front of, this entire downtown is now a Christmas Town. It's magical, and there is more magic to come."

Just after I said that, it started to snow. It caught all of us by surprise. Even the reporter lost her flow and hesitated before speaking again.

Then she said, "Right after you said that this place is magical, it started to snow, as everyone watching at home can see."

For some reason which I still can't explain, I felt an inner calmness within me, and it was as if my "higher self" took over.

I replied, "Yes, that's right. And that is because there is magic here at Christmas Town. And I don't just mean my store. I am talking about our entire downtown, and ALL of the stores on Main Street. Our downtown is where Christmas magic lives."

She looked perplexed and intrigued at the same time, and responded, "What do you mean by magic, exactly?"

I replied, "The magic I am talking about is when you do things for others that changes their lives for the better, even though the other person may have thought it was impossible at the time. And that's what we have done here in our downtown. We all have worked together to create a special place, which seemed impossible to create at first. We worked together to create magic, and that magic now lives here. Anyone who comes here will feel it. I don't care what store you go into; you will feel the love and appreciation of your presence here. We want everyone to come here, experience this, feel this, and see that it lives within all of our shops, as well as everyone who works within all of our shops. Yes, we have more Christmas lights and decorations than most downtowns, but our magic is also what is within the stores, and the cooperation we all shared in order to create all of this."

I knew I had spoken WAY TOO LONG, but she never tried to interrupt me, so I wasn't going to stop speaking. There were certain things I needed to say, and I was going to say them so that I wouldn't have any regrets about what I should have said later on.

When I finished, she responded, "Wow! I have never heard a downtown described in such a way before. And I also don't think I have ever experienced anything quite like this."

I decided to keep pushing, and I jumped in with, "I want EVERYONE to experience this. Please come to our downtown, or Christmas Town. We have amazing shops, restaurants, and a bakery that sells the best Christmas treats. We have lights, Christmas caroling, music in the street, and we will be adding more things on an ongoing basis. I won't stop until my town is the official Christmas Town."

I could tell that the reporter was genuinely taken in by everything I had said. I knew for certain that she wasn't putting on an act for TV anymore.

I think she felt that the segment had gone on for quite a while, and that it should be ending based upon her normal experiences. She glanced over at the producer, and he gave a signal that must have meant to keep going. I guess the TV station decided to extend our live segment.

The reporter refocused on me, and said, "Tell us about this store we are standing in front of. You referred to it as 'your store,' but surely you don't own a store at your age."

I replied, "I am part owner. I own it with Mr. Martins, who also owns a great gift shop called Martins Gifts here on Main Street. But he and I own and run *this* store together, which is called Christmas Town, as you can see. We have everything you need for making your Christmas magical, including some unique gifts. Plus, we have Santa's real sleigh inside our store. And I'm not joking. It's his full-sized sleigh. It's inside our store, and people can come and take pictures if they want."

The reporter was smiling from ear to ear.

She responded, "If I may ask, what grade are you in? You are still going to school, right?"

I replied, "Yes, of course. I'm in sixth grade."

She looked at the camera and said, "This is remarkable. This young man is absolutely remarkable."

She then got a signal from the producer to wrap it up.

The reporter looked at me, and said, "So, you work at this store when you are not at school?"

I replied, "Yes, Ma'am."

She responded, "So, if people come here to this 'Christmas Town,' and come into your store, which is called Christmas Town, they will be able to see you and maybe meet you?"

I replied, "Yes, Ma'am. I'm here when I'm not in school."

Right after I said that, I did something strange which broke protocol. I looked directly into the TV camera and said, "Please everyone, come see our Christmas Town. It's more magical with more people here. Let's all make Christmas special for each other, and I promise that we will do our best to make Christmas magical for you."

When I was finished with my direct appeal to the viewing audience, I quickly broke my fixation on the camera, and looked back over at the reporter.

The camera then focused on her, and she said, "I think this young man said it better than I or anyone else could; so, I will leave it at that."

She then said her name, and the city where she was reporting from. A moment later, the producer indicated we were off-air.

The crew immediately shut the lights off and started to pack up, as if leaving everything on for another five seconds was a sin.

The reporter said to me, "That was amazing! You did an incredible job. We might need to come back here and do this again. Would that be okay? Like if we did a follow up?"

I replied, "That would be great. You can come anytime. Just call the store here to let me know, so that I can make sure that I'm here when you need me."

We then exchanged pleasantries, and she went to the news van, and I went into the store.

Mr. Martins was busy talking on the phone, and I could tell that he was talking to someone about the TV interview. He seemed euphorically giddy over it. His face was red, and he was almost laughing and crying out of happiness. I don't know who he was talking to, though.

But after he was done with *that* call, the phone rang again, and then again. He had to stop answering the phone.

He came over to me and gave me a big hug. It was the biggest and most enthusiastic hug I had received, maybe ever.

He said, "THAT WAS UNBELIEVABLE!"

I meekly replied, "Thank you."

Then he just looked at me. Stared at me. I could tell that he was having all kinds of thoughts, but he didn't verbalize them. He just kept staring at me while his smile kept getting bigger and changing in complexion.

Just then, Mrs. Martins and her carolers walked into the store. They looked exhausted.

They had seen the interview taking place, but wouldn't have heard much of it.

Mrs. Martins looked at Mr. Martins and said, "How do you think it went?"

Mr. Martins exclaimed, "HE WAS BRILLIANT! A SUPERSTAR! HE SAID EVERYTHING THAT NEEDED TO BE SAID, AND THEN SOME!"

Mrs. Martins and all of the other ladies seemed pleasantly surprised by Mr. Martins's exuberance.

Mr. Martins interjected, "My phone has been ringing off the hook by people we know who watched it on the news. It didn't just air locally. It also aired in the TV channel's media market within the tristate area."

There was more chatter between Mr. Martins and his wife, along with the other ladies. When things settled down a bit, the caroler ladies left so that they could go back home. It was not lost upon me that this must have been very inconvenient for them to be called out with short notice to sing up and down a street with nobody listening, while it started to unexpectedly snow. I made sure to thank them again.

Mrs. Martins then said, "I should get home. Sally is alone at home. She had homework to do."

Mrs. Martins looked at me and said, "If Sally had homework to do, doesn't it mean that *you* have homework to do?"

I replied, "Yeah, but I always do it quickly before bed."

Mr. and Mrs. Martins looked at each other as if trying to determine if that was true or not, and then they just shrugged. I was telling the truth. I was able to do my homework very quickly, and I got very good grades. School was always easy for me. With that said, I will also point out that I eventually began doing my homework at the store.

But anyway, Mrs. Martins's comments caused Mr. Martins to look at me and say, "I better get you home, young man, Mr. Christmas Town Boy. I imagine your mother might have some words for you. I assume she was watching the interview?"

I replied, "I don't know. I forgot to tell her that I was going to be on TV."

Mr. and Mrs. Martins looked at each other and started laughing. My statement may have seemed unbelievable, but it was true. I couldn't remember telling my mother about the interview. Oops.

After Mrs. Martins left, Mr. Martins and I shut down the store for the night. He then drove me home.

When I got home and walked inside, my mother was talking on the phone. She seemed very excited.

When she saw me, she said to the person she was talking to, "OH, HE'S HOME! I should go."

As soon as she ended her call, she exclaimed, "HOLY CRAP! You didn't tell me that you were going to be on the TV news!"

I replied, "Sorry. I must have forgotten to tell you. Things have been so crazy, and emotional, and difficult. It's all been a blur."

She responded, "Yes, I know. But oh my goodness! Luckily, I saw it. I don't always catch the news. But I saw your interview. FANTASTIC JOB!"

I replied, "Thanks."

She responded, "Everyone's been calling. A lot of people saw it."

I nodded.

She started to just look at me in a similar way to how Mr. Martins had stared at me.

After a long pause, she said, "So, what happens next?"

I replied, "What happens next is that I hope business for downtown picks up at least a little bit. I don't expect much, but it needs to increase at least a tiny bit. I hope."

After a pause, she responded, "Well, one thing for sure is that you've done your part. Whatever happens now is out of your hands.

You did everything you could. Nobody will ever think differently."

I nodded.

She then said, "Why don't you get changed and I will fix you something to eat."

I nodded and went into my room to change.

When I came out, my mom and I chatted more about the interview, and she watched me eat my dinner.

Later that night, I was indeed doing homework before bed. I found it to be a very grounding experience. There's nothing like being on TV, and then having to do sixth grade homework before you are able to go to bed. Such is life.

CHAPTER TWELVE
The Mayhem

The next morning after my TV interview, I went to school. It was Friday, so at least I only had one more day of school before being off for the weekend, even though I would be working all weekend at the store.

I took the bus to school so that I could also take the bus downtown after school. I didn't want to ride my bike whenever I needed to dress up in my nice clothes, because I didn't want to get all sweaty and dirty from a bike ride.

When I arrived at school, everyone was looking at me, including the teacher. I think Mr. M was trying to decide how to handle the situation. I had become a huge elephant in the room, and Mr. M needed to maintain order and keep the focus on school. Additionally, Mr. M knew that I was a quiet and shy boy who probably didn't want to be embarrassed with too much attention from everyone staring at me and talking about me.

But on the other hand, I had just been overly confident and very outgoing in a live TV interview that was broadcast all over the tristate area. So, umm, was I really that shy? I'm guessing that question was what Mr. M was trying to wrap his mind around.

Eventually, a kid in my class known for his outbursts due to his need for attention, said loudly, "WE HAVE A FAMOUS CELEBRITY IN OUR CLASS!"

There was a wide variety of reactions, including some laughing. I was embarrassed and looked down at my desk. I think most of the kids in my class were dying for someone to say something, so this kid was just doing what everyone else was hoping someone would do.

However, Mr. M wasn't having it. He didn't like the outbursts from this kid, and he noticed that I was embarrassed by it, even though I really didn't care. I was so beyond being a sixth grader by that point that I reacted to comments and outbursts in a similar way to how an adult would. It simply didn't matter. I was doing what I was doing, and various people were going to have different reactions to it. That's just life.

Mr. M sniped back at the kid and demanded quiet in the classroom. He then used that as his springboard to launch into the normal school day. Soon enough, everyone was bored in first-period class, and I was forgotten about for the most part.

After school, I got onto the bus that went through downtown, and I asked the bus driver to drop me off at the Christmas Town store. He smiled and nodded.

The bus drove the short distance to downtown, but it was taking longer than usual. I noticed more traffic than usual.

Once we were on Main Street, I lowered the window and stuck my head out to get a good look around.

Usually, the bus could drive right through Main Street with minimal stops, if any. But on this day, we were getting stuck at every traffic light. There were definitely more cars than usual. I also noticed that all of the stores had their Christmas light on, even though it wasn't dark yet.

When we reached the Christmas Town store, the bus stopped, and I quickly got off so as not to cause an inconvenience or traffic problem for the bus driver, or anyone driving on Main Street.

I went into the store and saw Mr. Martins cashing someone out. I also saw two other customers browsing in the store. This was the first time I had ever seen a customer at the counter purchasing an item.

I quickly slipped into the bathroom and changed into one of my nice outfits which I had brought with me. When I came out of the bathroom, I went to see Mr. Martins. The customers who had been cashing out were gone.

I said, "We actually sold something?"

He laughed. My comment probably sounded cynical and obnoxious, but I was asking a genuine question.

Mr. Martins responded, "We've sold a few things today. It's been sparse but regular all day."

I replied, "That's better than nothing. I guess. Maybe."

He quipped, "It is."

After some thought, I said, "Sparse is not going to cut it, though."

After a pause, I continued, "So, after my TV interview, we are only going to get 'sparse?' That's all we get? Really? If so, we're screwed."

I got a look from Mr. Martins indicating that he wasn't used to dealing with a tween boy in a snide mood. But he didn't yell at me for my language or attitude.

Instead, he responded, "You need to lighten up. Life is not going to come to you at your beck and call. You need to invite life to come, persuade it if you can, and then show some gracious patience so that you don't scare it off when it knocks at your door."

I thought about what he said. I found it interesting. That was a wise, understanding, patient, and kind man telling me to shut up. I liked how he did that. I immediately shifted my attitude to a more patient and professional one.

The rest of the evening was similar to what Mr. Martins described. Customers were sparse but regular. Some people were just looking, and others were buying something. I started to subtly watch what people were looking at and not buying, vs. what people were actually buying. I didn't fully realize it then, but I was beginning to build a database in my mind of what people were intrigued by, what they didn't care about, and what they were actually buying.

When it was closing time, Mr. Martins and I shut everything down, and I asked him to pick me up in the morning for work. He agreed, and then we left so that he could bring me home.

At dinner, my mom asked, "How is it looking down there?"

I quipped, "Sparse but regular."

She could tell by my tone that I wasn't thrilled by that. The rest of dinner was fairly quiet. I then went to my room, read some of a book for my Literature class, and went to bed.

The next morning, I got up early, got ready, and Mr. Martins picked me up. We went to the store and opened up for the day.

I was really hoping to see more customers, but we didn't have any. Main Street was fairly dead, so I knew it wasn't just us with no customers on that Saturday morning. But I also noticed that many of the stores didn't have their Christmas lights on, and there was no Christmas music coming from the music store.

I told Mr. Martins that I needed to take care of a few things on Main Street, and he just nodded. He didn't need my help since there weren't any customers.

I left our store and started going from store to store, asking everyone to turn their lights on. Everyone was very pleasant about it, and a few of them complimented me on the TV interview. I also went to the music store and asked him to turn the music on. When I did, he replied, "I didn't think it mattered because nobody is here."

I replied, "What comes first? Customers showing up, or customers having a reason to show up?"

After a pause, he responded, "Customers having a reason to show up."

I replied, "Then we need to give customers a reason to show up. So even if nobody is here, we have to give the reason. Then maybe they will show up."

That right there was what we will call "tween boy logic." It may or may not have been valid logic, but it was *my* logic, and the owner of the music store didn't argue with me about it. I was trying the best I could, and everyone knew it. So even if some of my notions were hair-brained, I had earned enough goodwill to have some cooperation from them.

After I had done my rounds up and down Main Street, I went back into the Christmas Town store. As I did, I was noticing an increase in traffic on Main Street.

I would say that right around lunchtime, Main Street was 'busy,' and there were plenty of people walking up and down the sidewalks. We had plenty of people coming into our store, and we had made a good number of sales. I was still cynical though, because I knew that Saturday would be our busiest day; and if this was as good as it got as far as sales, we were still screwed. But I kept my thoughts to myself and my mouth shut.

But later in the afternoon, shortly before dusk, it started to get crowded. And it should be noted that I have not used the word "crowded" until this point, so I don't use that word lightly.

I had a thought, and I mentioned to Mr. Martins that we might need the carolers again. I knew that people might be showing up to see what they saw on TV. We needed to be prepared to deliver on that.

Mr. Martins didn't disagree, and he immediately called his wife. Mrs. Martins was busy running Martins Gifts, but I guess she made some phone calls to her caroling group.

Shortly after that, right as the sun was setting, we started getting snow flurries. It was looking and feeling very Christmasy out there. All of the stores had their Christmas lights on, and the Christmas music was playing out into the street.

And guess what else?

Main Street was PACKED! Traffic was JAMMED!

Then shortly after that, the sidewalks became crowded with shoppers. And these shoppers meant business. Everyone who came into the store bought something, and most of them bought numerous things. And that wasn't all.

Many of the shoppers were asking for me personally, and most of them wanted a photo with me in front of Santa's sleigh. At first it felt awkward to have my picture taken with complete strangers, but after a while I got used to it, and I even tried to make it more fun for people by trying out various expressions and poses in front of the sleigh. People seemed to love it. I didn't fully understand it all, but it didn't matter. A happy customer is a good customer.

As the evening went on, I would describe it as MAYHEM outside. The police had to come in and direct traffic so that it flowed more smoothly. The police were also directing people to available parking in the hidden side and back lots.

I could see that all stores appeared to have people going in and out on a constant basis. So, this was not just our store. ALL stores on Main Street were packed. I also saw lines out the doors to our Main Street restaurants.

I didn't have much time to look though, because Mr. Martins and I were absolutely swamped. Mr. Martins was unable to leave the customer counter at all. He couldn't even slip away to use the restroom. He had to ask me a couple of times to run the cash register for five minutes. That was code for, "I need to use the restroom." I never said anything. I just did as he asked.

As for me, I never had a moment to myself. I started to notice our display trees were becoming bare of ornaments, and some items on our shelves were getting low. I began to restock everything as quickly as I could. However, I kept getting interrupted by customers who wanted to meet me and get a picture in front of Santa's sleigh with me.

I always put the customers first, and then I did the best I could to keep up with the restocking, while Mr. Martins was permanently stationed at the checkout counter. Mr. Martins later told me that lots of people came into the store and asked him if I was working there, and where I was. They all referred to me as "Christmas Town Boy," because I guess that's what I was permanently named during my TV interview.

Later in the evening at the usual closing time, Main Street was still packed with people and cars. We obviously stayed open, and we weren't the only ones. Almost everyone stayed open.

At one point, Mr. Martins said, "I know you need to get home at some point. You'll just have to tell me when that is, and we'll close down for the night."

To that I replied, "We aren't closing until there are no more customers. I'll spend all night here if needed."

Mr. Martins was very amused by my statement, and didn't respond, nor protest.

It wasn't until after 10:00PM that we noticed it starting to slow down, although it was still busy. Mr. Martins said to me, "How about we close at midnight?"

I replied, "Yeah, okay. That should be fine."

At around 11:00PM, we noticed some retail shops closing for the night. The restaurants still had lines out the door. Mr. Martins guessed that most of *them* would be open until 2:00AM. Who in the world eats dinner after midnight? Don't answer that. Doesn't matter. We were loving it, and we were grateful for all of the people who came to our downtown for whatever reasons.

When it was coming up to midnight, we weren't getting too many customers anymore. The only places that seemed busy were the places that sold food and beverages. Mr. Martins and I closed the store, and then he took me home.

I had to use my key to get in because my mom had already gone to bed. She left me a note, telling me that there was food in the refrigerator, and I only had to put it in the microwave.

I quickly had a little bit to eat, and then I went to bed. I think I fell asleep immediately.

The next morning, my alarm woke me up. I will confess that I could have used another three hours of sleep. But I got up, showered, got dressed, and went out into the kitchen.

My mom and I discussed how traffic around downtown was totally nuts the previous day. I told her that sales at the store were off the charts, and that I might be home late again that evening. She reminded me that the next day (Monday) was a school day. I just shrugged. I really didn't give a crap about that. The store was foremost on my mind, although I knew not to verbalize this to anyone. I knew I would still manage to get to school Monday morning, so no harm done.

I had a quick bite to eat, and then Mr. Martins arrived to pick me up. We drove to the store, and opened everything up. Being early in the morning, Main Street was calm and quiet as it had been the previous morning. We knew not to let that fool us.

We immediately got to work. Mr. Martins had some financial stuff to deal with, and I had to make sure that everything was restocked. I told him that we were going to run out of certain things, and he placed emergency orders for many items.

Even though it was early Sunday morning, downtown was bustling with all of us store owners. Everyone was in the same boat as us, and they were trying to get caught up on everything, while bracing themselves for getting slammed with customers again. And indeed we were. Slammed with customers, that is.

Around lunchtime, things started to pick up, and traffic kept increasing into the afternoon. We knew for sure it was going to be crazy again.

In case you were wondering, Mrs. Martins was dealing with the same situation at Martins Gifts, and she had Sally over there helping her. That's why I never saw Sally at the Christmas Town store. Martins Gifts was a much smaller store, and as long as Mrs. Martins had Sally's help, they were able to keep up with things okay.

Mr. Martins and I were not faring as well. Our store was huge, and it was insane that only the two of us were running it. But help was about to arrive.

Shortly after lunch, Jeremy stopped in with his mom. His mom was there to shop, and she ended up buying some very expensive decorative items we had.

But while his mom was busy with that, Jeremy said to me, "How are you doing?"

I replied, "I'm good, but we're having trouble keeping up."

He responded, "What do you need help with?"

I replied, "So many customers want pictures with me in front of Santa's sleigh that I can't keep up with the restocking; and Mr. Martins can't do it because there is a constant line of people at the register needing to check out."

Jeremy thought for a moment, and responded, "I will help if you want. I can do the restocking. I know how to do it from when we were getting the store ready to open."

I replied, "That would be awesome if you can! I understand if you can't, but we could definitely use your help."

Jeremy walked over to his mom, who was getting ready to leave. He explained the situation to her, and she agreed to let him stay. The only problem was that she didn't know how he would get home because of all the traffic later at night. However, it was figured out that he could walk up to the bank, and then his dad could pick him up on a back side street. Thus, Jeremy's mom left, and Jeremy stayed.

Having Jeremy there was a game-changer. I was able to do pictures with the customers, and the shelves and ornament display trees were still getting restocked. I heard Mr. Martins thank Jeremy several times. I knew that Mr. Martins intended on paying Jeremy for his help, but I also knew that Jeremy didn't ask or expect to be paid.

As Sunday evening rolled around, downtown was a zoo again. The police were directing traffic, and the sidewalks were crowded with shoppers. I noticed a group of carolers I hadn't seen before going up and down Main Street. I guess there were two or three different singing groups in town, and they worked with each other to provide full coverage for downtown so that there would always be caroling in the late afternoons into the mid evening.

It seemed to me that Sunday evening was busier than Saturday had been. At least it was that way for *our* store. The only thing I noticed that was different was that the customer traffic for the restaurants was winding down a bit earlier because it was Sunday night.

But with that said, downtown was still packed at 10:00PM. Things didn't taper off until 11:00PM. I should mention that Jeremy had left our store earlier at 8:00PM. His help was truly appreciated by myself and Mr. Martins.

Later in the evening, Mr. Martins was very cognizant of Monday being a school day for me. Mrs. Martins had already closed down Martins Gifts in order to get Sally home by her bedtime.

When it hit 11:20PM and we didn't have any customers in the store, Mr. Martins abruptly locked the doors and shut most of the lights off. He told me it was time to go home. I knew he was nervous about keeping up too late on a Sunday night, even though it was too late for that, since it was already way after my regular 9:00PM bedtime for school nights. I would end up completely violating that on a constant basis, and my mother never said a word about it. I guess 9:00PM was no longer my bedtime. From then on, I was given the freedom and leeway that most high school kids get, even though I was only in sixth grade.

Monday morning, I managed to catch the bus on time and get to school. I will admit that I was very tired. During recess, I laid down on the bench and rested. The teachers and other kids knew what I was dealing with. I'm sure there were some teachers questioning whether I should be working an adult job with the hours I was working. Any responsible adult would have raised their eyebrows at this.

I totally understand and don't blame them, but people have to understand that I WANTED to do this. It was MY choice. It was my passion. And my passion was regenerating life back into our entire town. Some kids choose to stay up until midnight reading, listening to music, or playing video games. I chose to stay up until midnight working at my store. Now tell me the difference between those? Why is it okay for a kid to stay up late listening to music, but not okay for me to stay up late working at my store?

Fortunately, nobody caused an issue about this, or said much to me about it. Secretly, most of the adults in town wanted me to continue doing what I was doing. Nobody could afford for me to stop; and certainly Mr. Martins couldn't run the store without me.

But speaking of that, Mr. Martins was indeed stuck running the store himself during the school days. However, the store wasn't slammed with shoppers during that time. The busy times were the weekends and the weekday evenings. As luck would have it, I was always available to work at the store during those busy times.

In addition to all of the chaos that Mr. Martins and I were trying to navigate and survive through during those first couple of weeks after it got busy, there was also a lot going on behind the scenes at the town level. The first was that the town officials, or police, announced that Main Street would be shut down to vehicular traffic during the evenings.

Each day at 5:00PM, Main Street would be for pedestrians only. It ended up that this would be extended to begin at noon time on Saturdays and Sundays as well.

Having Main Street only open to pedestrians was another game-changer. It added to the Christmas ambiance, and it served as a major draw for more people to make the trip from out of town to visit our downtown, which was becoming known as "Christmas Town," the same name as my store.

To be fully transparent, there were some people who might have said that I named the store the same name as what people called our town. There has always been a "chicken or the egg" debate over all of this, and I have always claimed that both happened at the same time. If you saw, heard, or listened to my original interview, you can see that I used the term "Christmas Town" interchangeably within that same interview, although technically, I named the store "Christmas Town" before I did that interview. So, technically, there is a strong case for saying that the store had the name first. The president of the bank can testify to the fact that I named the store Christmas Town in his office, long before the TV interview. But I wish not to bicker over such details.

In addition to our downtown (Main Street) being closed off to traffic in the evenings, I also noticed that all of the store owners amped up their Christmas decorations big time. Many stores started putting Christmas trees up on their roofs. They also added more wreaths, ribbons, and lights. What started as me cajoling them into decorating at my own expense, ended up being an intense competition between stores, and many of them began investing a ton of money in additional decorations. I had created a monster. It was awesome!

But beyond all of that, there was about to be a new Christmas addition to downtown that would dwarf all of the others, quite literally. It would add to the draw and appeal of our downtown, and become a new permanent Christmas fixture.

CHAPTER THIRTEEN

The Tree

Unbeknownst to me, a group of business leaders within the city decided to make a major investment in what was going on downtown. It was actually one of those social clubs that businesspeople like to belong to, who did this.

Based upon the increasing crowds flocking to our downtown, and the fact that Main Street was 'pedestrians only' in the evenings and on weekends, this business social club managed to procure a GIANT Christmas tree to display near the top of Main Street, within an area located at a fork in the road.

The backstory rumors were that the business owners on that end of Main Street wanted to create a magnet to bring in more shoppers further up Main Street. Most of the shoppers seemed to remain in the lower and mid-part of Main Street. The Christmas Town store was located within the busy part of Main Street. But some of the stores further up wanted to see the same heavy shopper traffic that we were seeing. Thus, they used their influence within this social business club to get funding for a huge Christmas tree up on their end of Main Street.

I was all for it. I was never in this just for my own store. I wanted to see success for ALL stores within the downtown shopping district. I had even stated this on TV. But many stores located in the busy section like mine, saw this new development as an effort to thin out and spread out the crowds a bit. And it was. But even so, I felt there would be enough business to go around. I mention all of this to illustrate the reality that politics and business always play a role in everything. With that said, everyone was about to learn that they could settle down and rest easy, because there would indeed be plenty of business to go around. In fact, things were about to escalate far beyond what they had been.

It was Friday evening, and the new Christmas tree was going to have its official lighting on Saturday evening just after dark. I had already seen the tree completely lit, and it looked impressively stunning. But rather than just leaving it lit and moving on with life, the prestigious social group that sponsored the tree and made it happen, wanted to have a well-publicized lighting as a way of getting the TV media to return to our downtown. I was certainly all for that!

In addition to the tree lighting, Main Street was going to be blocked off to traffic at noon for the first time. Main Street had been blocked off in the evenings, but never starting at noon before. It would be "pedestrian only." I think the tree lighting was another way of making sure that we got a big crowd, so that Main Street wouldn't look empty in the afternoon, in case we got a lighter crowd than anticipated.

On my end of things, I had two phone messages waiting for me when I arrived at the store for my work shift. Mr. Martins had spoken at length to the people who called, and he had taken down the messages for my reference. However, instead of handing over pieces of paper with the messages, he felt he wanted to verbally give me the messages himself.

He was chuckling, and said, "I'm beginning to feel a bit like your agent, manager, and publicist."

I replied, "Why is that?"

He responded, "The first message was from the President of the business social club that sponsored the tree."

I replied, "Yeah?"

He responded, "He asked if you would do the honor of officially lighting the Christmas tree at the ceremony tomorrow night."

I was really surprised, and quipped, "*REALLY? ME?*"

Mr. Martins responded, "Yeah, why not? You are the obvious choice. These folks aren't idiots; and although this is an honor, you should also realize that they are doing it to guarantee publicity for the event."

I replied, "Yeah, okay. I'll do it."

Mr. Martins responded, "Good, because I already told him you would."

We both laughed.

After a pause, he said, "The second message was from the TV station. They are going to be out here doing a story on Saturday, including covering the Christmas tree lighting, and they asked if you would be available for another interview."

I replied, "Yeah, okay. I'll be here, so I can do that."

He responded, "Yes, and that's why I told them you would."

We both laughed again.

After the moment had passed, Mr. Martins got serious and said, "I hope I'm not overstepping my bounds. You know, maybe I should be getting permission from your mom on this stuff, or asking you first. I apologize if I'm being overly presumptuous or stepping on any toes."

I replied, "No-no, you can make these decisions for me. I trust you like a parent and I will go along with whatever you think is best for me."

Those words I said just kind of fell out of my mouth without any thought. But I meant them. And for the first time, I saw Mr. Martins become somewhat touched and slightly emotional from what I had said. I guess my words were meaningful to him. However, I pretended not to fully notice, so as to avoid any awkward moment. I got right to work restocking shelves and displays.

It very quickly got busy with customers and we had another huge sales night, the same as all of the previous nights.

The next morning, Mr. Martins picked me up for a full day's work at the store. It was Saturday, and it was going to be a big day for more reasons than one. I made sure to wear what I felt was my best outfit.

As we always did in the morning, Mr. Martins and I rushed to get as much done as we could. Once we started getting slammed with customers later in the day, it was always difficult to get anything done at all. I had increasingly become a photo prop for customers to take pictures with in front of Santa's sleigh, and it made it harder for me to keep the shelves stocked. Thus, I had learned to overstock the shelves in the morning when I had the chance. If you came into the store at noon, you would see the store with too much product on the shelves. But there was no other way, and Mr. Martins agreed with what I was doing.

Just before lunch, someone came into the store for the purposes of confirming my availability to perform the Christmas tree lighting. I was busy at the moment, but Mr. Martins confirmed that I would be there, and he pointed toward me to show that I was present and accounted for. The person then gave Mr. Martins the time that I needed to be at the tree.

At lunchtime, Mr. Martins had ordered lunch for us, which was delivered. I took my break time to call my mom and let her know that I was doing the Christmas tree lighting, and if she wanted to see it, what time she should show up.

It turned out that when I told my mom I was "doing" the Christmas tree lighting, she took that to mean that I was just "attending" it. I didn't speak to her for long because I didn't have much time. Even so, she said that she would come down and watch it since she had nothing else to do.

The afternoon was really busy. As we all had hoped, Main Street was jammed with people. No cars. Just people. It was the most beautiful sight for us store owners to behold. But it was also very frantic, and I was going all-out for the entire afternoon.

Later in the day, we got word that the TV news people had been downtown for quite a while already. We were told that they were interviewing various store owners, as well as speaking with random members of the public.

Unlike last time, this was not going to be on live TV. It was obvious that they were filming tons of stuff, and then would put some of it onto the news later on. I wondered when I was supposed to do my interview. They hadn't stepped foot into the store; and believe me, I had been watching closely for this and wouldn't have missed it if they had.

I began to come to the conclusion that maybe they decided not to interview me, since I would be conducting the Christmas tree lighting, and they would have me on TV for that.

Well, soon enough, Mr. Martins prompted me that it was time for me to head up to the Christmas tree for the lighting, which was at the top of Main Street. It was going to take me a few minutes to get there, so I needed to get going.

After a thought, I said to Mr. Martins, "But aren't you coming with me?"

He smiled at me, and responded, "Who is going to keep the store open?"

I realized my stupidity, and quipped, "*Oh, yeah*" in a very sheepish way, after seeing how ridiculous my suggestion was. I guess in my own mind I was wanting Mr. Martins to see me do the lighting. But obviously, he couldn't come. None of the store owners could.

I used the restroom and got cleaned up a bit, and then waved to Mr. Martins as I left the store. Fortunately, things had slowed down a bit, and it looked like Mr. Martins would be able to handle things without me for an hour or so.

But as I was walking up Main Street, I quickly saw why business had slowed for us. It was because almost all of the shoppers had gone up Main Street to see the tree lighting. TONS of people!

I started to struggle my way up through the crowd toward the tree.

As I got closer and could see the tree more clearly, I noticed that they had set up an elevated platform in front of the giant tree. I guess that platform is where I needed to go. However, I was beginning to wonder how I was going to get there.

The entire area was COMPLETELY crowded with people, and as I tried to gently push my way through the crowd, I think some of them thought I was trying to butt in front of them to get closer than they were.

Fortunately, there was a man up on the platform who was nervously awaiting my arrival. He saw me fighting my way through the crowd to get to him.

He turned on the microphone, and said loudly for the entire crowd to hear, "There is a very well-dressed young man struggling to get up here to the microphone. Please all of you over there (he pointed to where I was), open up a hole for him to get through. That's Christmas Town Boy, and we need him up here."

All of a sudden, everyone around me was shocked to realize that they were standing near me. The crowd immediately began opening up a narrow pathway for me to get through.

Life got much easier at that point. I quickly made it up to the tree, while some people were applauding as I went by. It was one of those moments when I thought I had been transported to a different dimension on another planet. You have to remember that I had spent my entire life being nearly completely invisible without anyone giving a single crap about my existence, or lack thereof. So to me, what was happening at that moment was just plain weird.

Once I got through the crowd and walked behind a barricade that was encircling the tree, I was immediately met with a shocking surprise.

Some VERY BRIGHT lights suddenly snapped on and nearly blinded me. Once my eyes adjusted, I could see that the TV news crew was there wanting to speak with me. I guess this was the interview that I thought wasn't going to happen. Except it was happening.

The same lady reporter as before immediately launched into her "thing," as if we were on live TV. To be honest, I had no idea if we were live or not, and I realized that it didn't matter. I had to act as if we were live on air even if we weren't.

She said her name, where she was, and that we were about to do the Christmas tree lighting. Then she said who she was with (me), and made direct eye contact with me, and said, "It wasn't that long ago when we last spoke, but it feels like so much has changed since then. I've noticed there are three times more decorations than before, Christmas trees on many of the store roofs, a Main Street that is closed off due to it being packed with tourists and shoppers, and now right behind us is one of the largest Christmas trees I've ever seen. What do you think about all of this?"

I had to think quickly to catch that hot potato, and I replied, "I think all of this is magical, and maybe even a miracle. It's a Christmas miracle for our town and all of us who own shops along Main Street. I am very thankful for everything."

The reporter smiled in her certain way that I had come to realize was her genuinely loving my reply.

She responded, "I have been conducting interviews all afternoon with many of the store owners on Main Street, and every single one of them credit YOU with having created this so-called miracle as you described it. Some of them claim that you have saved this downtown from its gradual decay. People are saying that you saved their businesses. What is that like for you to have so many people in this town talking like that about you?"

Again, that was another hot potato that I wasn't expecting to catch.

After a brief pause, I replied, "Well, I didn't do all of this alone. I had a lot of help."

(I then rattled off a list of names including Mr. Martins of Martins Gifts and the Christmas Town store, the bank on Main Street, the hardware store, the social club that sponsored the big tree, the contracting company that painted the poles, and

the music store.)

I then said, "The truth is that every single store on Main Street contributed to everything you see here. I only started it."

The reporter responded, "Well, that is very modest of you, but without you taking the initiative to give of your own time and labor to kickstart things and inspire others, none of this would have happened. You should be very proud. I know everyone here in downtown is very proud of you."

When she said that I got embarrassed and started blushing.

She knew that I was at a loss for words, so she said, "I know you are here to light this fantastic Christmas tree, so I will let you do that now. Thank you for taking the time to talk with us, Christmas Town Boy, as everyone is now calling you."

I replied, "Thank you."

I waited a moment before turning my back to her, and then I went up the stairs to the platform, because the man up there was motioning for me to do this.

It should be noted that the crowd waited silently and patiently because they could see the very bright TV lights, and they knew I was being interviewed on TV.

Once I got all of the way up onto the platform, the crowd applauded because they knew the tree lighting ceremony was about to begin.

The man I was up there with (the president of the club sponsoring the tree), began his brief remarks. He said who he was, including which big company in town he owned; and the name of the club he was representing that had sponsored the tree. He welcomed everyone, and then he announced that I would be lighting the Christmas tree.

I literally had no idea what in the world I was supposed to do. Nobody told me a thing. I didn't even see how I was supposed to "light" the Christmas tree. There were no plugs, switches, levers, or anything up on the platform. Fortunately, I had seen a big Christmas tree lighting on TV before, and I knew that I probably just needed to do a countdown, and then a crew person would actually turn the lights on from wherever they did that.

When the man was finished speaking, he said to the crowd, "ARE YOU READY FOR THIS?"

The crowd yelled back, "YES," and some applauded.

The man then looked at me, and said, "Do you have anything you wanted to say, Christmas Town Boy; or do you just want to begin the countdown for us?"

I thought for a moment, as if his question was not a rhetorical one, even though it probably was, and I replied, "Yes, okay."

I don't think he knew what 'yes, okay' meant, so he just gave me the microphone.

After a pause, I said, "I want to dedicate our town's Christmas tree to every single person who drove here to enjoy our magical Christmas Town. Without you, there would have been no magic. Thank you!"

The crowd ROARED with cheers. I guess they really liked what I said. I was relieved and also shocked at how enthusiastically they reacted.

After the crowd calmed down, I said, "Let's do the countdown together! Ready?"

The crowd yelled, "YES!"

I was loving how tuned in to the crowd I felt, and how responsive they were. It was a magical moment for me, which has stayed with me ever since. Anyone who has done public speaking and interacted with a crowd in such a way, understands what I mean.

I took a breath, and then said, "TEN! NINE! EIGHT!.." And so on.

The crowd was counting down with me.

After I had exclaimed, "ONE," I prayed that something would happen and that the tree would actually light up. I say this while laughing, because I honestly had no idea at the time. I still wondered if I was supposed to push a button or something, and maybe I just didn't see it.

But that question was answered when the tree lit up in all of its glorious beauty. I turned around so that I could see it. The entire crowd cheered loudly.

After the moment was beginning to fade, the man I was with took the microphone from me, and he said to the crowd, "Thank you all for coming! Please enjoy the rest of your evening and all that our Christmas Town has to offer!"

The man then whispered to me, asking if I needed help leaving, and where I was going. I told him that I was going back to my store, Christmas Town.

He brought the microphone back up to his mouth, and said to the crowd, "I would once again ask that you allow this young man safe passage so that he may get back to his store, which also has the name of Christmas Town."

At that point, the man, who happened to be a very wealthy and important man in town, shook my hand, thanked me, and then motioned for me to leave the platform.

I walked down the stairs and through the opening that people had made for me to get through, even though the crowd was breaking up and it was much easier to get through than before.

As I was walking back down Main Street, I came to realize something.

There was a long line of people following me, and it felt like they were doing this purposely. I decided it was best for me to just pay attention to where I was going and keep walking.

I swiftly made my way down to my store, and went inside. I immediately turned around to see what the people following me were going to do, and they all started filing into the store.

Mr. Martins was shocked by this because things had been fairly calm during the tree lighting. Now all of a sudden, we were being slammed with hordes of shoppers.

I immediately went over to Santa's sleigh, because I knew that was where I would be needed. And indeed, that was where I was needed. People started asking for photos, and I cooperated. Other people were browsing through the store and picking out things to buy. Mr. Martins was bracing himself for a long line of customers at the checkout counter.

I took photos with the long line of people who wanted them, and Mr. Martins was handling the purchases of the customers who were buying things. All of the people were really nice to me. Most of them asked me simple things like my real name, my age, what grade I was in at school, and things like that. A lot of the older ladies liked to say that I looked similar to one of their grandsons and that kind of thing. I had gotten used to all of those questions and comments, and it became routine for me.

It turned out to be another late night for me and Mr. Martins. We stayed open until midnight. But even when we locked the doors, there were still people downtown. It was crazy! The restaurants and bakery probably stayed open until at least 2:00AM. I felt sorry for the bakery because they always opened up at 4:00AM to bake the things they needed to bake. So basically, those people were only going to get a 2-hour break. I learned later that they had brought in additional family members to make it all work.

After we closed up, Mr. Martins drove me home. I went inside, and my mom had already gone to bed because it was really late. But she left a note out on the table that said, "OH MY GOD, I SAW YOU!"

I know that might seem cryptic to some, but I knew it meant that she had gone to the tree lighting. Obviously, there was no way for me to see her there.

I immediately went to bed. I was exhausted.

The next morning, my alarm woke me up, and I stumbled into the shower, and then got ready for another busy day. While in the shower half asleep, I was thinking about how I couldn't believe that adults did this sort of work routine almost every day for the rest of their lives. Holy Crap!

Even so, I was loving my life and what I was doing. I wouldn't have had it any other way.

Sunday turned out to be much like Saturday, except no tree lighting and no TV interview. Thus, no drama. But what we *did have* were endless customers. It might have been our biggest sales day of the entire season, although I can't say that for sure. My point is that we were extremely busy the entire day, and most of the customers who came into the store left with something they bought.

Mr. Martins started doing something that always made me laugh. Whenever there was a brief moment when no customers were immediately present, he would exclaim, "CHA-CHING," as his way of indicating the enormous amounts of nonstop income flowing into the store. I laughed every time he did it. In some ways, he was a very serious man; but when he said that, it was like he was my age, and it made it funny. I could tell that he was genuinely excited by what was going on.

Later that evening after we had eaten dinner at the store from food Mr. Martins had delivered, we received word that the TV news had done a long segment on our Christmas Town (meaning downtown), and that they covered the tree lighting. As part of the segment, they aired some of their interviews with other store owners. All of the interviews had one thing in common. They were all very complimentary toward me for starting Christmas Town (downtown); and most of them said that I saved their store from closing for good.

The TV segment also aired *my* interview in its entirety, *and* the tree lighting. People said they thought I did a good job and handled everything well. I didn't get to watch my interview, since I was always working during the evening news.

I could see Mr. Martins beaming with pride. For me, this was all I wanted, and all I needed. The truth was that I think I had been seeking this kind of love and approval my entire life. So, I didn't need to watch myself on TV. I got everything I wanted just by watching Mr. Martins's eyes and face whenever people were telling him things about me or my interviews.

But one thing for sure was that I wasn't planning on stopping anytime soon. I would soon be having another one of my grand schemes to carry out. It wasn't Christmas yet, and my ideas just kept on coming.

CHAPTER FOURTEEN
The Parade

The tree lighting had been a huge success, and I was inspired and empowered by everything I had witnessed and experienced up to that point. I knew within myself that I possessed a lot of influence with both the public, and the local businesses. I decided to put that influence to good use. I came up with another hair-brained idea that would turn out to be a great idea, and a new tradition.

I wanted to start a charity fund that would benefit kids like me who grew up in disadvantaged situations. I realized that most kids were not as lucky as me. Most kids never escaped their challenging situation, as I did. Because yes, even at my young age, I had full awareness of the fact that most people would now consider me "privileged." In fact, there could have been a valid argument made that I was the most privileged kid in town. Thus, I was no longer "disadvantaged."

Of course, with that said, it should be noted that my mom and I were still living in the same small, old apartment that we always had been. My "home situation" wasn't any different. But everything else in my life was different, and it was all for the better.

But anyway, I knew there were lots of kids suffering in silence, just like I had for my entire childhood up to that point. They may have come from broken homes, dysfunctional homes, didn't have strong parental support, or didn't have adequate financial support.

I wanted to see if I could leverage my "situation" and help *those* kids just like I helped the store owners downtown.

My idea was to sell inexpensive raffle tickets to members of the public who were shopping downtown. The tickets would be available for sale at the checkout counters within most of the stores along Main

Street.

There were little signs that said, "Children's Christmas Fund, sponsored by Christmas Town Boy." Shoppers would know that this was me trying to do more positive things for others. This wasn't to benefit myself. The sign explained what the raffle was, and also mentioned that it was co-sponsored by our local bank on Main Street. Jeremy's dad (the bank president) was supporting me 100% on this, and the bank was providing ALL of the logistical support, in addition to maintaining the trust fund for the charity. The public could see that it was totally legit.

A shopper might decide to buy a ticket for $5. The tickets had serial numbers on them. The shopper would fill out their name and address on the ticket, which we kept. The shopper would keep the stub.

All of us store owners would sell as many tickets as possible through December 22nd. All of the tickets would be in the possession of the bank by the morning of December 23rd. Then at the end of the day, I would personally draw the winners randomly from a series of mixing drums. We did this drawing inside the customer lobby at the bank, where people could come and watch if they wanted. Then, the winners' names would be posted in the Christmas Eve edition of the local newspaper, in addition to being posted at the bank. Of course, notices would also be mailed to all winners.

The winners would then call the bank to claim their prize. The prizes consisted of gift certificates from the local stores on Main Street. I personally visited each store and asked for donations. And yes, they all gave. So, there would be gift certificates from clothing stores, restaurants, and various other retail shops.

Once a winner called the bank, they would be provided with a list of available prizes to choose from. It was first come, first served. Thus, it got to the point where everyone would check the newspaper first thing in the morning, and if they saw their name, they would immediately call the bank to claim their prize so that they could have the 'pick of the litter' in terms of the prizes available. Obviously, we had enough prizes for all winners, even if someone was the last person to claim their prize.

The prizes cost my charity nothing. Therefore, we got to keep 100% of the proceeds. We gave out the proceeds to recipients who were nominated or referred to us by teachers, the fire/police departments, and social workers.

I know this has been a giant rabbit hole I fell down into, but the charity lottery became a big part of our downtown culture, especially at Christmastime. I mention it because it was yet another reason as to why what happened to me next, happened.

It was creeping up on Christmas Day, and every day had been a busy shopping day for our downtown. Weekends were epic, but even weekday evenings were always busy. Mr. Martins had been in regular contact with the person at the bank who was in charge of running the ticket sales for my charity. Even though my mother was my mother, Mr. Martins came to be considered my "adult custodian," "legal custodian," "parental custodian," "manager," or whatever you want to call it, for all of my business matters. Not only was this how I wanted it, but my mom consented to the arrangement as well.

Mr. Martins kept me updated on how many tickets were selling, and it turned out that we were being successful in raising a ton of money. Because of that, there had been a lot of discussion amongst the adults involved about what to do with the funds. My only requirement was that it went to disadvantaged kids.

One evening at the store when we were closing up, Mr. Martins said, "There are a couple of upcoming events and items we need to discuss."

I replied, "Yes, okay."

He responded, "Well, they're both related, but I'll do this backwards because it makes more sense."

I started laughing because I thought that what he said was funny.

I said, "I don't understand any of that."

Mr. Martins was laughing because he fully realized what he had said, and how confusing it was.

He regathered his thoughts, and responded, "You know that the Christmas parade is soon, right?"

I quipped, "Yeah."

He responded, "I've been talking to the folks at the bank, including the bank president, and we all think it would be clever if we gave away some of your charity proceeds after the parade. But when I say 'we,' I mean 'you,' because we want you to do it. But we want you to do it with Santa Claus."

I was giving him a weird look of confusion and intrigue that made him chuckle.

After a pause, I replied, "Wait a minute. You want *me* to give away some of our charity funds with Santa Claus? Like as in me and Santa Claus together? *THE* Santa Claus?"

Mr. Martins was laughing. Now, mind you, I was old enough to fully understand the magic of Santa Claus. But this was me messing with Mr. Martins a little bit; because even though Mr. Martins assumed that he knew about my understanding of Santa Claus, he didn't ABSOLUTELY KNOW what my full understanding of Santa Claus was for certain, even though he did.

I could tell that he was hesitant to say more. I didn't want to take my private inside joke too far, so I said, "I'm okay working with Santa Claus. Tell me more."

Mr. Martins seemed relieved that I had let him off the hook, and that his assumption of my understanding of Santa Claus was correct, and that he hadn't ruined my entire childhood in that one moment.

After a pause, he responded, "We already have some recipients lined up. They are all kids younger than you, and I know you will approve of them. So, what we want to do, is at the end of the parade at the big Christmas tree, Santa Claus will give out several early Christmas presents to some very lucky and deserving kids, thanks to *your* charity. We all think it's a fun way to do this, and everyone will really enjoy watching it. What do you think?"

I thought for a moment, and replied, "It's magical. I love it."

Mr. Martins smiled, and responded, "I knew you would."

I knew he had more to say, so I remained silent. After a few moments, he continued, "And that leads me to the next item, which is related to the first."

He went on, "Because of how the parade ends, with you being with Santa Claus to give out the surprise gifts, the 'powers that be' would like to have you ride with Santa Claus up in the fire truck for the entire parade. What do you think of *THAT*?"

My expression must have been priceless, because Mr. Martins immediately erupted in laughter.

What he had just said to me was the last thing in the world I was expecting to hear. And yes, in our yearly Christmas parade, Santa always rode on a big fire truck. Some people might think that's weird, but that was our town tradition. Our parades weren't fancy like in big cities, but our parades were much-loved by everyone in our town.

After what he said sunk in a bit, I replied, "You want me to be IN THE PARADE, *and* ride on the fire truck with Santa? REALLY?"

Mr. Martins was still chuckling, and responded, "This is not me wanting anything. This is me telling you that our city officials and community leaders want you to be in the parade and ride with Santa Claus, yes. I'm just the messenger here."

I think Mr. Martins was watching me struggle to mentally grasp all of that.

After a few moments, he said, "I don't think you fully realize the impact you have had on this town, young man. Most people truly believe that you have lifted this entire town out of a death spiral. You have saved countless stores, businesses, jobs, and livelihoods, which many families depend upon to survive, including my own, by the way. Your impact on this town cannot be overstated. Everyone recognizes this, and they want to honor you for that."

For some reason, everything that Mr. Martins had said felt heavy to me. It made me feel humbled and solemn. I guess I had been hoping to accomplish everything that Mr. Martins said I accomplished, but perhaps part of me never thought that I would actually succeed at it in such a big way as I had.

Mr. Martins was staring at me as I was wrapping my mind around everything.

When he thought I could handle more, he said, "And to make everything official, you are going to be named the Grand Marshal of the parade. That's partly why they want you up in the fire truck with Santa Claus. I am telling you this now because it's going to be in the newspaper sooner rather than later."

After some thought, I replied, "Has a kid ever been a Grand Marshal of any of our town parades before?"

Mr. Martins laughed at my reply, because of all the things I could have said, I chose to ask something stupid like that.

Mr. Martin responded, "No, not to my knowledge. The Grand Marshal is usually reserved for a respected town elder. I believe you're the first minor."

Again, I was humbled, and I looked down at the floor.

Mr. Martins said, "I know I've dumped a lot on you at once; and I need to get you home because you have school tomorrow. But are you okay with everything I've said to you?"

I looked up at him and replied, "Yes, of course. I will do it. Just tell me where I need to be, and when, and if I'm supposed to say anything special."

I then added, "Are you going to be with me, or at least until I get onto the fire truck with Santa?"

Mr. Martins gave me a mischievous smile of amusement, and

responded, "I'm afraid not. But you'll do fine. I will tell you where to show up. Let me know if your mom can't get you there, and I will make other arrangements for you. But once there, the parade organizer will take care of you."

I replied, "Okay, but where will *you* be? I know the stores close for the parade, so you won't need to be at the store."

Mr. Martins responded, "Believe it or not, I'm on the parade committee. So, I have my own duties to fulfill that evening. But I'll see you the next day after the parade, for sure. I know you'll do great, and I'll be with you in spirit."

After he said that, I will confess that I was a bit disappointed that Mr. Martins couldn't be with me before or after the parade. But I knew that Mr. Martins had involvement in one of the social business clubs in town, so I wasn't surprised that he volunteered to help with the parade each year.

The next morning, I woke up and went to school. I hadn't seen my mother the night before because I got home late and she was sleeping. But then the next morning, I didn't have time to tell her everything that Mr. Martins told me, because she and I were always in a huge rush every morning.

I say this because my mom was in for a big surprise when she got to work that day. It turned out that Mr. Martins had told me everything he told me, when he told me, because the news of me being the Grand Marshal for the Christmas parade was in the newspaper that morning.

I found this out because after I got to school, my teacher, Mr. M, congratulated me on the big news. I asked him how he knew, and that is when he told me that it was in the newspaper. Fortunately, the other kids in my class didn't make a big deal about it because none of them read the newspaper.

I know my mom was shocked by the news, because after school when I got to the store, Mr. Martins told me that my mom had called him to confirm the news. My mother wasn't mad; she was just shocked. She knew that Mr. Martins would know for sure what was going on with anything regarding me. He filled my mom in on everything.

Mr. Martins asked me why I didn't tell my mother myself, and I explained to him that my mom was usually sleeping whenever I got home after work, and that we had little time to talk in the mornings. Mr. Martins accepted my explanation, since it was the truth. I think Mr. Martins wanted to be considerate of my mother, and be sure that he wasn't stepping on her toes.

That next Saturday, the last weekend before Christmas, was the day of the parade. Mr. Martins and I worked at the store all day, but then closed down early for the parade like all of the other stores. Mr. Martins seemed in a hurry, and he said he had lots to do. He quickly dropped me off at my house, reminded me to be looking my best, and to arrive at the start of the parade route on time.

I had already spoken to my mom about this, and she was going to bring me to where I needed to be; and then she was going to park the car and watch the parade from our traditional spot where she and I had always watched the parade together. This was a reminder to me of how crazy my life had become. I went from watching the parade as a child with wide eyes, to being IN the parade, AND riding with Santa Claus, no less. It was nuts.

I showered and got dressed up in my best outfit. I realized that I needed to get more "best outfits," because I was needing to wear my "best outfit" very often it seemed, and it might start to look weird with me always wearing the same "best outfit." It was then when I decided to get one or two more "best outfits" when I had the chance.

My mother must have been thinking similar thoughts, because she decided to dress-up my outfit a bit by adding something to my jacket. She pinned some holly berry leaf things onto my jacket to give it some color (green/red). I also wore a red tie instead of no tie at all.

By the time we were done, I looked much more Christmasy, and I agreed with my mom that her ideas were good ones.

When it was time to go, she drove me to where I needed to be. She let me out of the car, and then she proceeded on to where *she* needed to be in order to watch the parade.

I honestly had no clue where I was supposed to go, or who I was supposed to see. However, I let logic dictate my actions.

I saw the big red fire engine that was surely going to be the one which Santa Claus would be riding in. This meant that it would be the one that *I* would be riding in, also.

When I walked up to the fire truck, I was warmly greeted by several people, who all seemed to know who I was, and why I was there. They asked me if I needed anything to drink, and told me to wait nearby until they were ready.

I spent five minutes standing in place, looking all around me. I had never before seen what happens when a parade is starting, so it was interesting to witness the desperate chaos of everyone trying to get everything in perfect shape for the parade. Very stressful!

Eventually, I saw Santa Claus come out of nowhere and climb up onto the fire truck. He needed help because of his big and heavy outfit. Once they got Santa up there, they motioned for me to come over. They had to help *me* up onto the fire engine also, because I was a little too small to easily climb up on my own.

Once I was up on the fire truck with Santa, I wasn't sure what I was supposed to do, or say to him. Or maybe I was supposed to say nothing to him. Does anyone out there have experience hanging out with Santa Claus? What is one supposed to do or say?

I decided to just give him a little wave, but say nothing. He responded with, "HO! HO! HO!"

That's all he said.

I guess you could say that my initial few minutes with Santa Claus were awkward. I was trying not to scowl, because whenever I was "normal" and relaxed, my normal expression was a slight scowl, even though I wasn't meaning to scowl. I had done enough public appearances by then to be aware of this, and not scowl when I knew the public was watching me, or a camera was pointed at me. I needed to not scowl in front of Santa, either.

Very quickly, I saw the parade getting all lined up and ready for departure. Santa and I would be LAST, so I got to see the entire parade line up in front of us.

As we were about to start moving, I noticed that Santa was looking at me intently, or more like staring. It made me think that this was going to be a REALLY LONG ride with Santa. However, then something weird happened. Santa Claus started laughing, almost hysterically. He was laughing at ME.

And that's when I started to notice some very familiar things about Santa. I hadn't noticed them when I first got up onto the fire truck; but after he started laughing, and then looking at me more, I noticed things; and those things were very familiar to me. I am not going to say any more than that, because I am the keeper of Santa's secrets. But what I *will say* is that my realizations at that moment gave me so much joy and delight, that the flame still burns within me to this day.

After that, there was no more awkwardness between me and Santa. We felt perfectly comfortable with each other, and got along perfectly well.

My epiphanies also caused me to have a permanent genuine smile on my face, so that I didn't have to worry about faking it.

The parade was moving along, including me and Santa up on the fire engine. As we started to approach more people along the parade route, Santa said to me, "The kids are waving at me, but many of the adults are waving at you. Make sure you wave back."

I took his cue and started waving just as much as Santa was. I began having fun with it. Originally, I thought the whole thing was going to be really awkward, but something I needed to do as part of being "Christmas Town Boy." However, the more it all got going, the more fun I was having. I think Santa was enjoying it also. We were waving to everyone as a team.

Every once in a while, a fireman from within the truck would say through his loudspeaker, "Riding with Santa Claus in his sleigh is our Grand Marshal, Christmas Town Boy."

Whenever he said that, it would cause the crowd of people along the route to applaud and cheer. I always made sure to wave more enthusiastically to show my appreciation.

Eventually, we got to the part of the route where I knew my mother would be. I made sure to look very carefully for her. I wanted to see her and acknowledge her by pointing and waving at her, if possible.

Sure enough, I saw her. She was much closer to the street than usual, so I could see her clearly. She was standing up and waving at me like a crazy person. It made me laugh. I pointed right at her, and waved. I wanted to be sure that she knew for certain that I saw her.

However, me pointing at her caused people in the crowd to look at her, to see who or what I was pointing at. What they saw was a woman acting all crazy with her wild waving and yelling.

My mother saw everyone looking at her, and she reacted to this by yelling, "THAT'S MY SON!"

She added, "NOT SANTA! THE BOY!"

That caused everyone within earshot to erupt in laughter.

I guess my mother had decided to no longer continue her anonymity.

The parade continued, and I was enjoying everything so much that it went by quickly, and we were almost at our end-destination, which was the huge Christmas tree. And yes, even before the Christmas tree, the parade always ended at that spot. Having the Christmas tree there made for a much better ending for the parade, though.

But before we got there, we passed by the Christmas Town store, and Santa gave me a little nudge as we went by it. Then, when we went by Martins Gifts, I saw Mrs. Martins and Sally standing in front of the store. I made sure to wave wildly at Sally like I had done for my mother. Sally got a huge smile on her face, and she seemed to delight in the fact that I had made a point of singling her out and waving to her, specifically. Mrs. Martins just laughed with great amusement while watching me and Santa go by.

Quickly after that, we were passing by the bank, and I saw Jeremy and his parents standing along the street. I specifically pointed at Jeremy so that he would know I was acknowledging him, and he gave me a thumbs up. I also made sure to make eye contact with his dad while I waved at *him*.

Not far after that was the parade ending spot. The fire truck came to a stop right in front of the Christmas tree, which was glistening in all its glory.

After everyone saw that the truck had come to a full and permanent stop, people started coming toward the truck, and completely surrounded us on all sides. Santa was handed a microphone.

My understanding of the plan was that Santa would immediately start giving out the special gifts that were from my charity. But something else happened first.

There was a flurry of activity below us by some city officials. They passed something up to Santa, but I couldn't see what it was because it was wrapped in a towel. Santa set the object down behind him, away from me.

After that, we seemed to be waiting for all of the people who wanted to witness what was going on by the Christmas tree, to arrive at the area and settle into a spot. I assumed that we needed to wait for the kids and their parents who were going to be recipients of gifts, to be present and close to the truck.

Eventually, when it appeared that everyone who wanted to be there was there, Santa turned on the microphone, and exclaimed, "HO! HO!

HO! MERRY CHRISTMAS EVERYONE!"

The crowd cheered.

When the crowd settled down, Santa continued, "As you may have heard, we are going to do something a little bit different and special this year."

He went on, "Although I am still going to visit ALL OF YOUR HOMES tonight as you sleep, I wanted to wet your appetites by passing out a few gifts to some very lucky children, right here, and right now."

The crowd cheered loudly.

Santa said, "But first, I have been asked by our wonderful city leaders to make a presentation to a very exceptional young man who has affected the lives of everyone who lives in our town. None of the Christmas brilliance you see here surrounding us now, would be here if it was not for this young man taking his own initiative to begin something that would end up saving our downtown, and the stores and lives which depend upon this downtown."

After he said that, I obviously knew he was talking about me, but I was confused as to why he was saying all of that, and I didn't know what he was referring to when he said, "presentation."

It was then when Santa reached behind him and grabbed the item that was wrapped in the towel.

He unwrapped the item from the towel, looked out at the crowd, and said, "On behalf of a grateful city, and all of the citizens who call this place home, I hereby present to the young man known as Christmas Town Boy, an official 'key to the city.' These are rarely given out, but I think you will all agree that this is an appropriate recipient, and it is duly deserved."

The crowd cheered very loudly. I was in shock and still somewhat confused. Santa handed me the item, which was a see-through case that had inside it a large brass key that looked somewhat fancy. There was also a plaque inside the case that had my real name on it, as well as the current year.

My next thought was that I was probably going to have to say something, but I had no idea what to say. I was without words because I was so surprised by everything.

I could tell that Santa was looking at me closely to determine what I might do next. Santa seemed to know me really well, and he would be able to tell if I was going to say something, or if I was too blown away to know what to do.

After a temporary moment of being completely flummoxed, I looked at Santa with a certain determination, and he knew to hand me the microphone.

Once I had it, I looked out at the crowd, and said, "Thank you! All of you! I did all of this for you and our town because I wanted to help and make a difference. This is my home and I care about it. I guess everything that happened because of it, is my Christmas present to all of you."

I stopped speaking, handed the microphone to Santa, and the crowd ROARED with cheers. I could tell that Santa was ABSOLUTELY ECSTATIC over what I had just said, and he gave me a pat on the back.

After the crowd became mostly silent, Santa said, "Okay! Let us proceed with giving out a few gifts, shall we?"

The crowd applauded.

Santa said, "Now, I need to confess that I received a little bit of help with these gifts. Christmas Town Boy and the sponsors who have helped him, gave me some secret information about a few children who might appreciate some specific presents from me."

The crowd applauded. That was Santa giving a wink and a nod to the adults that these gifts were coming from my charity. However, I think the younger kids all thought that they were coming from Santa personally.

I should also say that all of the parents of the children involved were informed ahead of time as to what was going to happen. This way, they made sure to attend the event and stand close to the fire truck. The kids, however, had no idea that they were about to receive an early present from Santa. All of these presents were things which my charity bought and paid for. They were not additional donations from the stores. The stores had given enough already.

I knew about all of the gifts that were about to be given out, and I had approved and given my blessing for them. I should also say that I did not personally know any of the recipients.

Phew, enough of the disclosures.

Oh wait, I'm not done yet. Sorry. I should also explain that there was a box van parked discreetly nearby, and inside it were the gifts that we were giving away. Thus, there were a couple of people taking things out of the van so that they could immediately bring them to the recipients.

Okay, so anyway, when Santa saw that everyone and everything was ready, he got started. He said, "The first present I want to give away a little early tonight goes to a boy who apparently has wanted a new bicycle more than anything else in the world. So, luckily for him, he is now getting one."

Santa then called out the name of the boy. He and his mom were standing nearby. The mom raised her hand, and herded the boy closer to the truck. The boy seemed in shock, but with a wonderful grin on his face that made giving him the bike worth it.

One of our helpers walked the bike over to the boy, and the boy seemed surprised that the bike was as nice as it was. It wasn't just a bike. It was his dream bike, as described and requested to us in detail by his mother. The crowd was loving all of this.

Santa moved onto the next recipient, which was a little girl who dreamed of having one of those large doll houses. She was presented with her huge pink doll house, and she seemed to be overwhelmed by it, and it was fun watching her expressions.

Santa kept things moving along, and he gave away two additional gifts that were similar to the previous ones I just described. But then that brought us to the final gift. I knew what the final gift was, and I was excited to see how it would play out.

Santa took a little pause, almost as a way of signaling to the crowd that something different was about to happen. The crowd became very silent.

Santa said, "This next gift I am about to give is a very special one. In fact, it's the most special kind of gift that anyone can ever give or receive."

That statement by Santa really caught everyone's attention. People were very intrigued as to what the gift could be.

Santa continued, "Sometimes, the most precious gifts don't come in boxes, containers, or in wrapping paper. They come in the form of who we adore and miss."

After a pause, he continued, "It is my understanding that there is one very special young lady out there who has suffered a difficult loss. The word I got was that she had gone a couple of years without seeing her grandma and grandpa. And sadly, she recently lost her grandpa before she could see him again. I know it's been very difficult for her. And to make things even more difficult, distance and economic factors have made it impossible for her to see her grandma after the loss of her grandpa."

He continued, "Although I can't bring her grandpa back to her, I can most certainly bring her grandma to her; and that is exactly what is about to happen right now. And *that*, folks, is the magic of Christmas."

Santa looked away to a car where we had hidden the grandma, and the lady got out of the car and walked over to the fire truck. The mother of the little girl knew about all of this, and she was already in tears. I had noticed her crying during Santa's presentation, so I knew that she was the mom with the little girl to whom Santa was referring.

The young girl, who looked to be about 9 years old, seemed a bit dumbfounded, although she could see her mother was crying. I don't think the girl allowed herself to believe that Santa was talking about her and her grandma. It would have been too good to be true.

But once the grandma walked around the other side of the fire truck, the little girl saw her grandma and SHRIEKED with joy. She ran over to her grandma, and there was a very intense hug. That was followed by the mom going over and joining in the hug.

The mom had not seen her mother yet, because all of this needed to be kept a secret from the little girl. To do this, my charity had flown the grandma to the nearest airport, provided transportation from the airport to our town, and then put her up in a hotel.

Much of the crowd was able to see what was going on, and I noticed many people were in tears. Everyone could sense the intensity of emotions between the grandma, mom, and granddaughter.

When the emotional moment had passed, Santa piped up again, and said, "And to be sure that this little family has the best Christmas ever, they are being provided with a very generous gift voucher to our local grocer, as well as a few other gifts to brighten their Christmas."

The crowd cheered. They seemed to absolutely LOVE and approve of our last special gift presentation. It was the cherry on top of what was a fantastic parade.

Santa then exclaimed, "IT'S TIME FOR ME TO GET BACK TO THE NORTH POLE AND GET READY FOR CHRISTMAS EVE! MERRY CHRISTMAS EVERYONE!"

The crowd cheered as our local police began to clear the area around the fire engine so that we could depart.

Once the road was clear, we were escorted back from whence we came by a police cruiser with its lights flashing. Santa and I waved to everyone as we drove back down Main Street.

After we got through Main Street and were headed back to where the parade had started, Santa leaned in toward me and said, "And for you, Christmas Town Boy, I will be bringing you a very special Christmas gift, but not until Christmas Eve. You can open it Christmas morning."

I looked over at him in surprise and amusement. I wasn't sure what to think of what he had said, but I was definitely excited and intrigued.

We quickly arrived at our final destination, and the firemen helped both Santa and myself off of the fire truck. I knew that Mr. Martins would not be able to drive me home. But apparently, he had made prior arrangements with my mother to pick me up, and he had told her how to find me after the parade.

I was told by someone that my mother would be coming; and ten minutes later, she did. She and I drove home.

She looked over at me on the way home, and said, "What did you think of all of that?"

I replied, "It was the most magical experience of my life."

She smiled with a huge smug smile, and we drove the rest of the way home in silence while I held my 'key to the city,' as if it was a bar of gold. To me, it was worth more than gold. And guess what? It wasn't even Christmas yet. There was plenty more magic to come.

CHAPTER FIFTEEN
The Hug

After I got home from the parade and had settled into my room for the night, I set my 'key to the city' on a display shelf I had. But after staring at it for a while, I knew that it belonged elsewhere.

The next morning, Sunday morning, Mr. Martins picked me up for work. It was the last full shopping day for the downtown district. Monday was Christmas Eve, and most of the stores, including ours, would be closing early.

When I got into Mr. Martins's car, he immediately noticed that I was holding something. It was the case with the 'key to the city' in it.

He said, "You didn't like your key to the city, and you're bringing it back to do a return?"

I smirked, and replied, "If it's okay with you, I would like to display it at our store."

Mr. Martins got a grin on his face like he was very pleased with my suggestion.

He responded, "On behalf of the store and myself, it would be an honor. We'll find a good place for it where everyone can see it, but where it will be safe."

I replied, "Perfect."

We arrived for work, opened up the store, and then found a suitable place for my 'key to the city.'

Although the Christmas shopping season and tourist season for "Christmas Town" (downtown) had pretty much ended, we still had quite a few customers into the store that day. I once again had lots of pictures taken with me in front of Santa's sleigh; and we made plenty of sales. And in fact, one of those sales was from me as the customer.

I told Mr. Martins who I was buying a certain item for, but I didn't explain the full meaning of it to him. He was very approving of my purchase.

On Monday morning, Christmas Eve Day, Mr. Martins picked me up for work. We opened the store up, but to be honest, it was pretty slow. Downtown was looking as beautiful as ever, but it was mostly empty, except for some frantic last-minute shoppers.

We had several non-shoppers visit our store that day, though. Many of the store owners came inside to thank me for everything I had done. Many of them told me and Mr. Martins that they had made more money during that Christmas shopping season than they had made during the entire previous year. Others said that their monthly sales for both November and December had broken all of their sales records for those months since they had opened their stores, years or decades ago.

All of these owners indicated that they would be able to keep their stores open indefinitely, thanks to the very strong Christmas season sales.

I should also add that there were no longer any vacancies downtown. The remaining vacant storefronts had been snapped up by retailers who wanted a piece of the action, which our downtown offered.

Everyone hoped that the momentum started during the Christmas season would continue, at least to some degree. Plus, everyone knew that there would be next year, and that our town's 'Christmas Town' would be as vibrant as ever, if not more so.

Additionally, many of the business leaders in town were discussing ways to keep our downtown busy all year long. Everyone wanted to continue what I had started. It wasn't just going to be a 'Christmas thing,' although just a Christmas thing was enough, according to most store owners.

As it was nearing closing time, Mrs. Martins and Sally came into the store. They had just closed down Martins Gifts for the Christmas holiday, after having experienced record sales for both November and December.

It bears pointing out that the Martins family had gone from owning one store that was failing, to TWO stores that were raking in huge profits. It was a huge turn in fortunes for them.

While Mr. and Mrs. Martins talked privately with each other, Sally and I went to the other end of the store where it was quiet, and where we could have our own privacy. I had a special gift to give her, and I was embarrassed to give it to her in front of others.

I had stashed my gift for her down at the far-end of the store, because my plan all along was to give it to her there.

I think she saw that I was really nervous. Considering that I had done TV interviews, and had been with Santa Claus on a fire engine during a big parade, I still all of sudden felt very awkward and shy about giving Sally my present.

I picked up my wrapped gift for Sally, and said to her, "Umm, hey, I got this for you. It's no big deal, but I wanted you to have it. I guess it's your Christmas present."

I then handed it to her, although I was so awkward about it, I almost dropped it.

She took the wrapped box, and said, "So, this is a Christmas present FROM *YOU?*"

I replied, "I guess. If you want. It doesn't have to be. It can just be something I'm giving you, if you want. Or it can be whatever you want it to be. Or nothing at all. I don't know. I just wanted you to have it."

I was sweating bullets. *Why* was I sweating bullets? Ugh.

She seemed to enjoy watching my suffering, and she responded, "It can be a Christmas gift since that's what it is. But I don't have one for you. I didn't know we were exchanging gifts."

I replied, "We aren't. I don't need a gift. This is just for you. Go ahead. Open it."

She looked at the box with great intrigue, and she acted as if she didn't want to open it. It felt like she wanted to savor it and stare at it, as if opening it would ruin it for her.

I said, "Go ahead. I need you to open it because I might need to explain it to you."

She gave me another look of mystical intrigue, and she ever-so-slowing began unwrapping the box.

After way too long, she finally got the wrapping off, and she started opening up the box.

After she had one lid of the box open, she looked inside, and then carefully pulled out the contents.

She finally saw what it was. It was the crystal figurine angel ornament that she had said a prayer with when she told me that she was praying for a miracle, back when the new store had NO customers.

She looked at the ornament with a tiny sweet smile on her face, but she said nothing, and didn't react in any significant way.

I said, "Do you remember what it is? It's that same ornament.."

She interrupted me, and responded, "Of course I remember what it is, silly. I'm just surprised that *YOU* remembered what it is."

I replied, "Of course I remembered it. I thought we were screwed, and I had failed. But you prayed for a miracle with that angel, and then miracles happened. I think that angel is magical."

She responded, "If you think it's magical, then why didn't you keep it for yourself?"

I replied, "Because the magic seems to need you in order to work. So, I wanted you to have it. You should keep it. Don't give it away or get rid of it."

She seemed almost horrified and insulted by my statement, and responded, "Of course I won't get rid of it. But it's not because it's magical. It's because you gave it to me."

Her statement caused me to look down at the floor in awkward embarrassment. I didn't know what to say to that.

She sensed this, and decided to break the weirdness by speaking. She said, "My dad says that you are the hero of the town."

I glanced up at her and just shrugged.

Then she said, "But what matters more to me is that you're *my* hero."

I glanced down at the floor awkwardly, and I think Sally felt awkward about what had just fallen out of her mouth; but I could tell that she meant what she said.

We both looked up at each other at the same time and momentarily locked eyes, although neither of us knew what to say or do next.

After a moment, she said, "Because you are my hero, can I give you a hug?"

I once again just shrugged like an idiot, and replied, "Sure. Okay."

We were both jockeying for position, but no hug had happened yet.

I said, "How do you want to do this?"

She snickered at my stupid comment, and I was wondering how in the world someone so skilled at public speaking such as I had become, could be so dorky and say such a stupid thing.

But just then she went in for the hug.

We hugged each other in the most uncomfortable way that two kids of our age could possibly hug.

After it seemed like it had gone on long enough, we broke off from the embrace.

But I wasn't satisfied with that hug. It was lame.

I said, "Is it okay if we try again?"

She smiled and responded, "Yes."

This next time, I went in for the hug in a very gentle but smooth way. I didn't squeeze her tightly, but I hugged her like I meant it. And this hug felt like no other hug I had ever experienced before in my life. It made me feel weird and different, but in a good way. It was strange because I never thought that I would have wanted to hug a girl like that before. But I guess with Sally it was different for me, and I wanted to.

And because of that hug, everything changed in that moment. I was not the same person anymore, and I would never look at Sally the same way again.

We held that hug for longer than we should have. Eventually, we heard Mrs. Martins call out for Sally, and we immediately separated in less than a fraction of a second.

No further words were spoken, and we didn't even look at each other. Sally scuttled over to her parents, and I remained in the far end of the store trying to gather myself together again before reemerging.

I heard Sally telling her mom about the ornament gift that I had just given her. Mr. Martins said nothing because he already knew about the gift, although he didn't know why I gave it to Sally.

When I felt I was ready, I walked over to where they were all standing.

Mrs. Martins said to me, "We'll see you and your mom tomorrow for dinner?"

I replied, "Yes, Ma'am."

Because yes, my mom and I were going over to the Martins' house for Christmas dinner. Mrs. Martins had contacted my mother directly to invite us. My mom knew that I would want to go, so she accepted the invitation.

The plan was for my mom and I to spend Christmas morning at our home with each other; and then around lunchtime, head over to Mr. and Mrs. Martins's house, where we would spend the rest of Christmas Day.

Mrs. Martins and Sally left. After they did, Mr. Martins said, "What do you think, Mr. Christmas Town Boy? Should we call it a season and close up, Sir? You call it."

I smirked, and replied, "Yes, Sir."

He and I then shut the store down. We left our Christmas lights on, as did all of the other stores.

Mr. Martins drove me home. We wished each other a Merry Christmas, and said how we would see each other again the next day for Christmas dinner. I got out of his car and walked to my front door.

When I went inside, my mom was bustling with activity. She had all of the Christmas lights on, and our Christmas tree was glistening with magic. Yes, I know I hadn't mentioned anything about a Christmas tree for us in our little apartment, but that is not because we didn't have one. It's just that I had been so busy working, I didn't get a chance to participate in the home decorating that year. My mom had to do all of the Christmas decorating herself, including doing up the tree.

The good news was that we had an especially nice tree that year that had been dropped off at our home anonymously. My mom and I could tell by looking at it that it came from the expensive tree lot across town, but that's all we could figure out. It was very full, vibrant, and bigger than what we normally got. There were no "holes" in this tree. That was a first for us, because we usually had two or three holes we needed to fill, and my mom had taught me how to be an expert at doing that. But none of those skills were needed with this tree.

Anyway, my mom had managed to make our modest apartment look like a very cozy and inviting Christmas wonderland. Plus, there were a multitude of Christmas treats out on the counter, which she had been baking over a two-week period.

She said, "Why don't you go get changed while I cook us some dinner. Do you still want our traditional Christmas Eve meal?"

I quipped, "Yes, please."

She was referring to our long-standing Christmas Eve dinner of French toast and bacon. And yes, I fully realize that there will be some who think that is weird, or they might even turn their nose up at it. But my mom and I loved having breakfast for dinner, and my favorite breakfast was French toast and bacon. Thus, that's what we had adopted as our Christmas Eve treat, beginning as far back as I could remember.

After I changed into some comfortable clothes, my mom and I enjoyed our breakfast for dinner. After that, my mom turned on our traditional Christmas music and started bringing serving dishes of treats out into the living room.

I immediately started gorging myself with my favorites, which consisted of her gingerbread men, frosted sugar cookies, and chocolate drops. I had to be careful not to make myself sick, because believe me, it had happened plenty of times in the past due to my inability to control my voracious desire for my mom's Christmas treats.

My mom and I visited with each other, ate goodies, and admired our tree while listening to our Christmas music. I don't think I had visited with my mother for this long in months. In fact, I hardly ever saw my mom ever since school started back in September. All of my free time had been consumed by me working downtown.

After a pause in our discussions, my mom said, "I have a confession to make, and I might as well say it now to get it out of the way."

I nervously replied, "*Yeah?*"

She sighed, and reluctantly said, "This has been a particularly rough year for me financially. You already know about the car problems and stuff like that, but you don't know about the utility bills that have nearly doubled, and I was unable to get extra hours at work, because they had to cut back. I'm lucky I still have a job at all, because quite a few people lost their jobs this past year."

She continued, "But anyway, all of this has meant that Christmas is kind of lean this year. I couldn't manage to do much, and I didn't want you to be expecting much."

After my mom said that, I felt bad. But it wasn't because of her warning to me about there not being many gifts. It was because I could sense a disappointment, and even shame, within my mother.

I will admit that when I was younger, I likely would have taken her announcement as a disappointment for myself that I wasn't getting much for Christmas. But this year, I didn't think of it that way. This year, my mother's announcement resulted in me feeling nothing but great empathy toward my mom, and the pain she was feeling from her struggles.

After a pause, I replied, "Mom, I don't need anything for Christmas. I don't even want anything for Christmas. You don't have to give me anything. Really. And I'm being serious."

I continued, "Mom, this entire Fall season has been nothing but amazing for me. My entire life has changed. There are numerous people who will give me whatever I need. I literally want for nothing anymore. And in fact, it is ME who needs to start giving. So don't worry about any of that stuff. And I will try to help out with things now that I can."

I stopped speaking, and I could tell that my mother was getting emotional. Whenever she got that way, I had learned to stop speaking, and just let the energy in the room calm.

After she pulled herself together, she said, "Okay, thank you, Son. But with that said, we have a tradition of opening one gift on Christmas Eve, and I have one for you."

She went over to the tree to retrieve a gift. While she was there, I said, "Grab one for yourself also, Mom. I put a few under there for you, as you can see. You should open one, also."

And indeed, the tree had a large number of gifts from me to my mom under it. Some of the gifts had been given to me for the purpose of me giving them to my mom; while others were gifts to my mom which I had purchased myself with my own money. My mother was going to be busy opening gifts this year, and I think she realized this, and perhaps it was making her feel bad.

She fished out a gift for me, and threw it at me. I managed to catch it, and could tell that it was something soft and light. Not only that, but it was safe to assume that it was not breakable.

She looked at me, shrugged, and said, "Open it."

I did as she asked and opened my gift. It was socks.

Before I could even react in any way, my mother said, "I'm sorry. I know socks are lame, but they're your favorite kind of socks."

I replied, "Mom, I told you not to worry about it."

She responded, "I know, but it's difficult for me to see everyone in town giving you this and that, and the best I can do for you, my own son, are some socks."

I thought for a moment, and replied, "Believe it or not, out of all of the things I have been given over the past few months, NOBODY has given me socks. And I needed socks. So now, not only do I have socks that I needed, but they are my favorite socks. That's what Mr. Martins would call a 'smart gift.' Good job, Mom!"

My mom laughed, and I think she genuinely felt better after my comment.

After a couple moments, I said, "Go ahead and open yours."

She looked at the decent sized box, and then shook it.

I quipped, "No cheating!"

She quipped back, "Kitchenware!"

We both laughed while she opened her gift. And she was right.

It should be noted for the record that my mom was psychic when it came to identifying wrapped gifts, and her talent carried down to me to a degree.

When she saw it was a cooking pot from a high-end cookware brand, she was delighted. I knew she really needed new cookware.

She excitedly exclaimed, "Now I can start collecting all of the pieces to this set!"

Little did my mother know, but the ENTIRE cookware set was individually wrapped and sitting under the tree.

The backstory was that the reporter at the newspaper knew that I wanted to give my mom cookware for Christmas. He had remembered me saying that. So, when he was interviewing the owner of the hardware store about me, the reporter noticed that the hardware store carried a very nice line of cookware. And yes, our local hardware stores often carried all kinds of home goods in addition to tools. Anyway, the reporter mentioned all of this to the owner of the hardware store. The hardware store then offered to give me the entire cookware set so that I could give it to my mother for Christmas. And that's how that happened.

Anyway, after my mom and I had each opened our one Christmas Eve gift, we continued to eat Christmas goodies and talk about random things like the parade. When it was starting to get late, we both agreed to go to bed, since we were both tired. I was 12 going on 32 at that point, so I acted more like an adult, because I worked like an adult.

That Christmas Eve remains as one of the most memorable and meaningful ones of my life. It was my first Christmas Eve as a man, instead of a boy.

CHAPTER SIXTEEN
The Gift

The next morning, Christmas morning, I woke up later than usual because my alarm never went off, since I didn't need to go to school or work. My mother was up way before me.

But when I was finally up and about, I went out into the kitchen and living room so that my mother would know that I was still alive. Although I had barely woken up, my mother had obviously been up for a while, and she had our home buzzing with Christmas cheer. All of the Christmas lights were on, Christmas music was playing, and everything smelled like freshly baked cinnamon buns.

My mom, with the excitement of a 5-year-old, exclaimed, "LOOK! SANTA CLAUS CAME!"

I grinned, and looked over toward what she was pointing at. First, she pointed at my Christmas stocking, which was filled to the brim with gifts; and then she pointed to a big box sitting next to the Christmas tree.

The filled Christmas stocking was nothing new to me and not a surprise, but the big box by the tree was. I was not expecting anything "big" from my mother, and that was certainly a good-sized box. I realized that it could have just been a big box filled with leaves, but I knew it wasn't.

I went over to inspect the box. There was a tag indicating that it was for me, and it was from "Santa Claus."

I looked at my mom with a mischievous smirk.

Since we were apparently being very "adult" and honest with each other about Christmas, my mom said, "Just so we are clear, I have no idea what that is, or where it came from."

I could tell that she was telling the truth, so I replied, "Then how did it get there?"

She responded, "Again, being honest, it was delivered a few days ago. There was a note instructing me to not put it out until Christmas morning. So, that's what I did. That's literally all I know."

She added, "OH! But the note said that it was fragile. So, you probably shouldn't try shaking it."

I thought for a moment, and said, "Actually, I should have been expecting this. I know who it's from."

My mom quipped, "WHO?"

I replied, "Santa."

My mom laughed and figured that I was messing with her.

She responded, "Well yes. The tag says it's from Santa Claus, so yeah."

I replied, "No, really. I'm being serious. I knew I was getting it from Santa."

She responded, "And how is that?"

I replied, "Because when I was up on the fire engine with Santa during the parade, he told me that he would be giving me something for Christmas morning."

My mom was looking at me carefully, trying to detect any hint of me pulling her leg. She detected nothing of the kind, because I was being completely honest with her. However, she didn't know what to think of that, or if to believe me.

And I should say at this point that my mother did not know the secret about Santa that I knew. In fact, very few people in our town knew the secret about Santa that I had figured out while interacting with him so closely. And by the way, I kept that secret. I never spoke about Santa to anyone, and that even included when I was alone with Mr. Martins, or anyone else. I never verbalized anything about what I knew about Santa. It was a precious treasure of joy that remained a silent one. Thus, my mother had no idea what I knew.

Well anyway, my mother suggested that I open my stocking, and she would bring out the cinnamon buns.

I did as she asked, and I found many small and interesting treasures within my stocking that provided me with some amusement.

After that was taken care of, we enjoyed our little traditional cinnamon bun breakfast, and then decided to dive into the presents. We didn't have time to lounge around, because we needed to get to the Martins house for the main event.

My mom stared at the gifts under the tree, and said, "They're all pretty much for me. I feel bad."

I replied, "Don't feel bad, but you better get busy."

My mom started tearing through her gifts, and she eventually realized that she was receiving the entire set of cookware that she wanted. She seemed very pleased.

There were some other gifts for her that I bought from a few of the stores downtown; and she also had a couple more small gifts for me.

After we had opened all of our gifts for each other, there remained only the one big box for me from Santa. I think my mother was dying to know what it was, but I felt the gift was shrouded in magic, and I was almost afraid to open it.

Have you ever had a Christmas present that was wrapped in so much significant mystery that you were afraid to open it? It's as if you're afraid it won't be what you think it could be, and you will be disappointed; Or, it will be as epic as your imagination is telling you, and it will be way more than your emotions can handle. This was just such a gift for me.

Therefore, I engaged in some kind of stare-down with the gift.

Eventually, my mother couldn't stand it anymore, and she said, "OPEN IT! We don't have all day, and you have to open it before we leave. So go for it! Let's see what it is!"

In a way, I think it was a gift for both me *and* my mom, because she seemed just as excited about it, even though it wasn't for her. I believe my mother sensed the significance of it as much as I did. I inherited that skill from her, after all.

I went over to the tree, and very carefully and gently dragged the box over to where I had been sitting. I started slowly removing the wrapping paper, while my mom was completely fixated on laying witness to the entire unveiling.

After I got the wrapping paper off, I was left with a plain brown box. Whatever was inside had been packed inside a box that did not originally come with whatever was inside. This just added to the mystery and intrigue.

My mother got me some scissors, and I carefully cut through the tape that was sealing the box up tight. After I broke through the tape, I opened up one of the box flaps. Then I opened up the other box flap. Then I lifted up the remaining lower flaps. I looked inside.

What I saw was something rolled up in so much bubble wrap that I still couldn't see what it was.

My mom said, "WHAT IS IT?"

I replied, "I don't know. It's all wrapped up. I can't see it yet."

I could tell that there were multiple pieces to whatever it was. I started carefully lifting out the pieces, which included one large piece.

Once I had the pieces out, I started to have a very deep feeling come over me and sink down into my soul. I believed that I had figured out what it was, even though I had cognitively not yet figured out what it was.

I rolled one of the smaller pieces out of the bubble wrap. Yep. It was a fine crystal reindeer with gold hooves.

Then I unwrapped another piece, and then another piece.

Eventually, I very carefully unwrapped the big piece, which was a crystal Santa's sleigh with gold leafing along its edges.

Yes, it was identical to the crystal and gold Santa's sleigh that I so loved and admired inside Martins Gifts.

My face became very solemn, and I felt very emotional inside. I knew my mother was watching everything intently; and she did not understand what she was looking at, or what it would have meant to me. But she knew that I was very deeply affected by whatever it was.

Eventually, my mom couldn't stand it anymore, and she said, "What is it?"

After a pause, I replied, "It's everything meaningful. It's everything to me."

She knew I was close to crying; and she decided to just let it be, and let me have my moment, even though she had no idea what was going on.

After I had all of the pieces unwrapped, and I inspected them to be sure that there was no damage, I noticed a folded up note inside the sleigh.

I grabbed the note, and opened it. It said, "I know you will continue the magic, because you ARE the magic."

After I read the note, I had some stray tears streaming down my face. I quickly wiped them away. My mom remained silent.

I stared at the sleigh as a way of pulling myself together. After my mom sensed that I had composed myself, she said, "Is that what it looks like? Is that real crystal?"

I gave out a little laugh at her question, and replied, "Not only is it real crystal, but that's real gold as well."

My mother gasped in shock, and said, "How? I don't know what any of this is about? Where did this come from?"

I paused, and then replied, "It is a gift from Santa that has been handed down from Santa to Santa over the years. I know it was in Switzerland at one point, but I don't know where it may have been before that."

My mother stared at me with her mouth open, not knowing what to think, or what to believe. At the same time, she felt to not ask too many questions.

But after a few moments, she couldn't help herself, and she said, "What do you do with it?"

I replied, "I continue the magic, and then someday pass it down to someone else who will do the same."

After I said that, I think the conversation was getting too weird for my mother, and she pulled herself back into her practical reality in which she spent her entire life living.

She said, "You better pack it back up so that it won't break. You can't leave that thing sitting in your room."

I replied, "Yes, I know. I'll roll it back up in the bubble wrap. And it's not going in my room, Mom."

She responded, "Where is it going?"

I quipped, "Christmas Town."

She didn't ask any further questions.

I carefully packed up the sleigh and set it someplace safe. My mom and I were now officially in a hurry. We only had one bathroom, so my mother showered first so that she could "get ready" during the time I was showering. While I was waiting for her to be done in the bathroom, I set out my clothes for the day. I didn't have to wear one of my nice outfits, but I was going to wear my nicest school clothes.

When my mom and I were ready, we left for the Martins house. I had never been there before, but my mother had the address from Mrs. Martins.

Once we arrived, I could see that they had a nice house in a typical family neighborhood. It was the kind of neighborhood that I wished I had grown up in. It wasn't considered a rich neighborhood, but it consisted of houses only, and everyone had a garage as well as a large private backyard.

We parked in the driveway, and I noticed lots of Christmas lights on the exterior, as well as a large and glorious Christmas tree shining and sparkling through the huge picture window of what I assumed was the living room.

My mom and I went to the front door, with me leading. I rang the doorbell, and Sally answered. I immediately felt more at ease. She was wearing a Christmas dress, and she looked beautiful.

My mother was delighted by her, and complimented her outfit. Sally thanked my mom, and then invited us inside. Once inside, Mrs. Martins was right there to greet us. I think it was then when my mother felt more at ease. I knew that going over to "stranger's houses" for Christmas was not my mother's thing, but we had enjoyed Thanksgiving with them, and they weren't "strangers." I believe my mother was warming up to this fact.

After we were all the way inside the house, and my mother was talking with Mrs. Martins, I started looking all around at my surroundings. To be honest, I was surprised at how nice their house was. If I didn't know better, I would have said they were quite well-off. But I knew they struggled to make ends meet from time to time. But they were clearly on a much different financial level than my mother and I; although according to Sally, they were struggling to stay at that level. Everything is relative, right?

After a minute or so, Mrs. Martins invited my mom to take the tray of Christmas goodies she brought with us, and carry them into the kitchen. Sally then motioned for me to follow her out into the living room.

Once in the living room, I got a good look at their beautiful Christmas tree, along with their nice furniture and huge TV. It was eye-opening for me, because it showed me the possibilities of what my personal circumstances could be if I worked at something long enough as Mr. Martins had done.

Sally could see that I was distracted by everything around me, so she said, "HEY! Come over here."

I walked over to her by the tree. She proceeded to show me that she had hung on the Christmas tree the crystal angel that I had given her.

She said, "After Christmas, I'm not going to pack it away with the rest of the Christmas stuff. I'm going to keep it in my room so that I can look at it all year long."

I smiled, and replied, "I'm glad you like it."

She responded, "I love it!"

Sally and I then started looking at each other in that weird and awkward way again, like we had done in the store. I started to reach out to her with the intention of just lightly touching her arm. But just then, Mr. Martins walked into the room, and it caused my reflexes to snap my arm back to my side.

He exclaimed, "YOUNG MAN!"

For a split-second I wondered if he was yelling at me for almost touching Sally in that personal way. But he wasn't. I could tell from his expression that he was just excited to see me.

He came over to me and gave me some friendly and fatherly-like pats on my shoulder.

I lightened up a bit, and grew a smile on my face. I noticed Sally watching the interaction between me and her dad intently. I think Sally was fascinated by, and loved the dynamics between, me and her dad. I had come to figure out that Sally spent much more time with her mother, but she seemed to idolize her father, and her father's approval and opinions meant everything to her.

However, much to Sally's dismay, her mother called her into the kitchen. I saw Sally sigh in frustration when this happened, but she left the living room to go help her mother (and my mother) in the kitchen.

That left me and Mr. Martins alone in the living room.

He said, "How was your Christmas morning?"

After he said that, he had a smug grin on his face.

I smirked with amusement and slight embarrassment, and replied, "It was special. It turned out that I received a magical gift from Santa Claus."

He pretended to act surprised, and responded, "Oh yeah? What was that?"

With a smirk still firmly planted on my face, I replied, "Santa gave me a crystal and gold sleigh with a Santa and reindeer just like the one you had in Martins Gifts."

Mr. Martins responded, "SPLENDID! YOU DESERVE IT! That's one very smart Santa."

I snickered while Mr. Martins kept his smug amused grin.

After a moment, he said, "I'm glad to hear that you have one of those, so at least one of us does. I don't have mine anymore."

I smiled and replied, "Why is that?"

He responded, "It was time for it to move on to where it belongs on the next phase of its journey."

I looked down at the floor, still smiling.

After a couple moments, I said, "I would like to ask your permission, Sir, for me to display it inside our store, just like you used to display yours inside Martins Gifts."

Mr. Martins got a huge expression of delight and approval on his face as if I had just scored an A+ on a final exam.

He responded, "That sounds like the best idea I've heard all day."

I smiled and replied, "Awesome."

After the moment had passed, Mr. Martins offered to give me a full tour of their house. I found this invitation to be very intriguing; and there was something about him doing that which made me feel, umm, included, loved, and ACCEPTED.

I know that might seem weird to some, and others might not understand why I felt that way; but that's how I felt, and it was very meaningful to me that he did it the way he did it.

And so that's what happened. He showed me around the house, including the garage; and he did it in such a way that I would remember everything that he showed me, as if he needed and wanted me to remember everything.

After we were done with the tour and came back inside from being out in the garage and backyard, I could see curious looks on the faces of my mother and Sally. They would have thought that the full private tour was weird, maybe? I didn't think it was weird at all, and it was obvious that Mrs. Martins wasn't surprised by it in the least.

With all of us back together in the same room, Mrs. Martins announced that it was time for dinner. I guess my mom had been helping her get everything ready. I could tell from my mom's demeanor that she was very comfortable being there, and that her visit with Mrs. Martins (and Sally) had been going great. It put me further at ease knowing that my mom was not feeling uncomfortable or awkward about the visit.

Sally came over to me and wanted to guide me into the formal dining room herself, even though Mr. Martins had already shown me the formal dining room and I knew where it was. It was not that big, but it was really nice. Very quaint. I suppose that is a good descriptor for the entire house.

The dining room had plenty of room for a full family gathering, and its interior was mostly lined with beautiful dark wood decorative panels and trim. It looked like the fancy dining rooms in really nice family homes that I had seen on TV shows.

My mom and I were waiting to be shown where to sit. Mrs. Martins began pointing out everyone's seats. Mr. Martins was seated at the head of the table, with me and Sally adjacent to him on one side, and Mrs. Martins and my mom adjacent to him on the other side. Thus, I was essentially sitting in between Mr. Martins and Sally. Perfect!

After we were all seated and there was an anticipatory silence, Mr. Martins said, "We are informal here, but let me just say a quick 'grace,' if I may."

We all lowered our heads, and he offered a very simple blessing, which included being thankful for the presence of my mom and myself.

After that, we started passing food around. There were a couple of times when I held the heavier serving dishes for Sally so that she wouldn't have to. I began to notice the adults in the room paying attention to this, and smiling over it.

Once everyone had what they wanted, we dug in and enjoyed our amazing feast of Christmas roast beast with all of the fixings. It was really good. Mrs. Martins was a wonderful cook just like my mother.

Conversation was very light, and consisted mostly of Mrs. Martins and my mother speaking with each other about various things that had gone on with me over the previous few months. I think Mr. and Mrs. Martins were curious to hear my mother's perceptions of everything. Mr. Martins knew literally everything that had gone on downtown, while my mother had only heard bits and pieces and never fully grasped the full picture. Mr. Martins was silently amused by this, and Mrs. Martins spent a lot of time filling in some gaps for my mother. The dinner conversation was a good education for my mother, while the rest of us watched and listened with amusement.

After everyone had enjoyed their fill of our main feast, Mrs. Martins offered a variety of pies for dessert. I asked for cherry, since that was my favorite. I loved apple and pumpkin also, but it was always hard to pass up cherry pie if it was available.

We all ate our pie, and the adults had hot after-dinner beverages. When it appeared that everyone was substantially done, Mr. Martins said, "If you will all forgive me, I have some things to say, or announce, or suggest, or offer."

Mrs. Martins laughed at him in response to how he had phrased everything.

Mr. Martins regathered himself, and said, "I normally don't discuss business at the dinner table, but I would like to bring up some issues while all of us are here together. I want there to be full transparency, and for all of us to be on the same page with everything."

I could tell that Mrs. Martins already knew what he was going to say, but my mother was bracing herself for anything. It was the first time I had seen my mother get nervous while we were there.

Mr. Martins seemed to be trying to maintain direct eye contact with me and my mother, so whatever he had to say was meant for both of us.

He took a deep breath or two, paused, and then said, "With the Christmas season behind us, we are now at a crossroads as far as where we are headed with the new store, aptly named 'Christmas Town,' by our town hero, Christmas Town Boy."

There were some chuckles, and I looked down at the table in amused embarrassment.

He continued, "The current deal and understanding is that the young gentleman owns 10% of the store. He is owed a substantial payout from the Christmas season, and I am prepared to make that payout in the next couple of weeks. However, I would like to propose an offer for the young man to consider, and for his mother to ratify."

He went on, "If this store is to continue, and be a year-round enterprise, we need to transition it over to a new set of merchandise, and continue to shift merchandise according to the seasons. I am prepared to do that. However, that is going to require *me* reinvesting a good portion of my earnings back into the store."

He paused, and then continued, "I would like to offer the young gentleman a couple of options. First, he may take his full payout now, and also retain his 10% ownership. He is free to go to school as his only major responsibility, be a normal kid, engage in fun leisure activities which kids his age do, and live his life as he pleases with all of his free time at his disposal."

He went on, "OR, if it so pleases the young gentleman, he may continue working at the store as he has been doing, reinvest much of *his* portion of earnings back into the store as I am doing with mine, and work with me to transition this store to a year-round sustainable enterprise. I have found working with this young gentleman to be one of my greatest life pleasures, and he is the most dedicated and brilliant business partner anyone could possibly wish for."

He paused, and continued, "If the young man elects to accept this last option I have just outlined, I will increase his ownership stake from 10% to 25%."

He stopped speaking, and there was an audible gasp from my mother. As for me, my face lit up like a Christmas tree, and I had a smile stamped on my face that might not ever come off.

Before anyone could say anything or react further, I blurted out, "I WANT TO KEEP WORKING AT THE STORE AND GET THE 25%!"

I said it so quickly that everyone started laughing at my lightning-fast decision.

Mr. Martins was very amused by this, and said, "My next statement was going to be that the young man should take as much time as he needs to consider his options carefully, and only get back to me when he is ready."

I quipped, "I ALREADY DECIDED!"

Everyone laughed again.

Mr. Martins was snickering. He looked over at my mother and said, "Ma'am, is this arrangement your son has chosen acceptable to you?"

My mother responded, "As long as he does his school work and keeps his grades up, it sounds like a wonderful opportunity; and if he wants to do it, I'm all for it."

Mr. Martins glanced at me as a way of making sure that I understood my mother's conditions, which I did.

Mr. Martins then said, "Well okay then. That didn't take long to settle."

But right after he said that, I had a thought, and that thought was troubling me. I think Mr. Martins saw it on my face.

He said, "You look disturbed about something, young man. Better speak now than later."

There was a silence around the table while everyone was looking at me and waiting to see what my issue was.

After a couple of moments, I said, "I'm okay with everything that was said. And I understand my 10% share is supposed to be reinvested back into the store. I'm okay with that, but I was hoping to receive a little bit of that. But I don't want it for myself. I am wondering if I can have a small amount of my share, and have it given directly to my mother to help her with things at home."

When I said that, my mother became shocked, embarrassed, and touched, all at the same time. Mr. Martins was surprised by my request, but also seemed to be having an epiphany.

I just stared at Mr. Martins, waiting for his response.

He thought for a moment, and responded, "That is a reasonable and intelligent request from the most compassionate and generous young man I have ever had the pleasure of knowing."

Mr. Martins then went on to offer that a specific sum of money be released and transferred to my mother. The amount of money he suggested was quite sizable, and my mother's reaction was such that she felt it was an amazing sum of money beyond what she would have been hoping for. I guess my 10% share had earned a substantial payout.

We all looked at my mother, because at that point, we needed to know if that sum of money was adequate for her or not. I was obviously going to go along with whatever Mr. Martins was willing to do, and which was also helpful to my mother.

As we all looked at my mother, she started tearing up and couldn't speak. It was then when I think Mr. Martins realized how difficult my mother's financial situation truly was.

I knew that my mom consistently operated with almost no money in her bank account. I don't think that Mr. Martins fully knew that, and he probably couldn't relate to that.

As all of this was processing through Mr. Martins's mind, he seemed to have another epiphany.

He said, "You know what? Come to think of it, I may have

miscalculated the young man's share. I believe he can afford to reinvest almost his entire 10% share, and still be able to receive even more in an immediate payout to his mother."

Mr. Martins then suggested a sum of money that was TWICE what he had previously suggested.

This caused my mom to break down in tears even more. Mrs. Martins offered her some tissues. Mr. Martins remained silent and patient after that.

Eventually, my mom pulled herself together, looked at Mr. Martins, and said, "Thank you so much, Sir. This would be a godsend to the level of which I can't even fully express."

Mr. Martins responded, "Don't thank me, Ma'am. This is your son's money which he earned through his hard work and talents. You can thank *him*. But I'm happy to facilitate it; and I will agree to the payout, while leaving all of the other terms intact."

My mom then looked at me, because I think she felt that she needed my express permission or blessing to proceed. I suppose Mr. Martins felt the same.

I was uncomfortable with my mother crying, and me being in the superior position over her in regard to this matter. It caused me to have a very solemn mood. But I said, "Mom, I want to do this. You deserve it, and I want to help you. It's the right thing to do."

I then looked at Mr. Martins, and said, "I want to proceed with all of this, and I will work extra hours if I need to in order to make up for the additional payout to my mom."

My statement caused my mother to become more emotional again, and Mr. Martins responded, "You do enough as it is. I consider this a done deal and nothing more needs to be discussed."

I knew to keep my mouth shut and look down at the table. Whenever Mr. Martins said something in that way, I always respected it as the final law.

My mother once again pulled herself together, and said, "I just want to say that I am very grateful and blessed for my son, and for this wonderful family. Thank you."

Mrs. Martins then showed some comfort toward my mother, and that was the end of the entire discussion. As of that moment, I held 25% ownership in the store going forward. I felt that it was the greatest thing to ever happen to me in my life. That gesture and arrangement by Mr. Martins overshadowed every other wonderful thing that had happened to me. I was going to be able to continue working with Mr. Martins at the store indefinitely, and I was going to have a major share of ownership in the store that was my passion, and which I loved. All of my dreams were coming true.

It took a while for the mood of that big dramatic moment to fade, but my mom gradually returned to her normal self while she helped Mrs. Martins clear the table.

Mr. Martins and I didn't discuss business again that day. We both knew that it had been a heavy discussion, and everything that needed to be settled was settled. He knew for certain that I was going to live up to my end of the bargain; and I knew I just needed to keep doing everything that I had been doing. There was nothing more to discuss. I knew that Mr. Martins and I would be having additional discussions during work time when we were both at the store.

After everything was cleaned up from dinner, Sally made a general announcement and request that perhaps we all try out her new video game that she has received for Christmas. Mr. Martins agreed it was a good idea.

We all went out into the living room, and then took turns playing the game. Even my mom had her turn, and I saw her smiling, laughing, and having fun as if she was a teenager. It allowed me to see my mom in a different way.

We ended up having a tournament to see who was best at the game. After some eliminations, it got very competitive between me and Sally, but I finally beat her. *Was I supposed to let her win?*

The final match of the tournament was then between me and Mr. Martins. It was ferocious, and it was hard to tell who was going to win; but through some miracle, I ended up beating him. It turned into a bit of a ruckus at the end, and everyone could tell that Mr. Martins had really wanted to beat me, but he couldn't quite do it.

I saw Sally watching me and her father roughhouse with each other at the end after I had finally beat him. The look I saw on her face was one of more satisfaction than what she would have had if I had let her win earlier on.

With the fun of the gaming tournament behind us, Mrs. Martins suggested that we all settle down and watch a movie together. After some debate, we all decided on which Christmas movie to watch.

We chose our preferred seats, and got comfortable. Sally and I ended up sitting next to each other on a small couch they had. I guess some people call them "loveseats." Funny name.

As the movie was getting started, Mrs. Martins walked around the room, handing out little blankets for anybody who wanted one. Sally and I were given a bigger blanket to share. I draped the blanket over us, and we began watching the movie.

I heard some whispers amongst the adults about how cute Sally and I looked sitting together. I pretended not to hear anything that was said, even though I could hear everything that was said. I'm guessing that Sally was doing the same.

The movie was good, but I didn't pay much attention to the movie. Instead, I was thinking about everything that had happened to me from months ago, all the way up to my present circumstances of sitting in the Martins's home next to Sally.

The entire town kept calling me a Christmas miracle for downtown, and the town as a whole. But the truth was that *I* was the one who was experiencing all of the Christmas miracles.

And not only that, but I had received for Christmas everything I had ever wanted. Most of all, I had received the love of not only being part of a larger family, but the love of an entire town. Christmas Town. And as everyone knows I love to say; I was living a meaningful life.

If you enjoyed *Christmas Town*, you might consider checking out my very large book series, *Living A Meaningful Life*, as the main character in *Christmas Town* is loosely based upon the main character in the *Living A Meaningful Life* series. Book 1 of that series is called *The Bench*. Thank you all, and may you all have a Merry Christmas, regardless of the time of year you are enjoying this story. The spirit of Christmas lives within all of us and can thrive all year long if we so allow it.

Acknowledgments

Thank you Sarah Delamere Hurding for your editorial assistance, encouragement, and endless support.

Thank you to David Ferrari for your special support of the series.

Thanks to all of my clients and benefactors who have supported my mission of helping people become greater, stronger, more self-empowered, enlightened, and free of pain.

Thank you to all of the kind people in the world.

A special thanks to Janet Manley Atkins and others who have shown great support for my books.

ABOUT THE AUTHOR

Brian Hunter is an American author best known for his book series, *Living A Meaningful Life*, and his numerous self-help books, including his Best Sellers *Heal Me* and *Rising To Greatness*.

Brian had a rural upbringing, surrounded by small towns, farms, lakes, and the peace of nature. Eventually, he moved to Los Angeles, California, where he began a career in acting and modeling. Brian was in a wide range of TV and movie productions with small bit-parts. He then began spending his time mentoring and counseling young people and adults who suffered from depression and other struggles. Ultimately, he began his writing career. After writing several self-help books, Brian answered his magical calling to start writing the *Living A Meaningful Life* series. The series has turned out to be one of the largest family saga series ever to be written in recent history, and continues to grow and expand. The series has also become one of the largest audiobook sagas to ever be narrated, with all installments multi-voiced by Brian, himself.

Brian's goal is to use the successes from his works to fund philanthropic programs to benefit children, schools, and communities.

www.brianhunterauthor.com

ALSO, BY BRIAN HUNTER

Living A Meaningful Life is an epic book series, with numerous installments, that will change your life. We are all capable of doing extraordinary things. We must only decide within ourselves to BE extraordinary. The *Living A Meaning Life* book series is a powerful story, and journey, of one such 'family' who dared to be extraordinary. By looking past their own obstacles in life, and choosing to always 'do the right things,' they became extraordinary within themselves, and this resulted in them doing extraordinary things that changed the lives of everyone around them, and their community. The main characters must navigate life struggles, both personal, and community oriented. They do so by 'doing the right things,' through exhibiting integrity, decency, generosity, and compassion. Life is never easy, people make mistakes, but there is nothing that can't be overcome when we have the courage to do what we know is correct and true within our soul.

Surviving Life: Contemplations Of The Soul is a unique and powerful book full of compassion and empathy, which combines the issues of what hurts us the most, with thoughts and advice meant to empower us toward happiness and independence. *Surviving Life* is medicine for the soul. It guides us through our deepest pains and weaknesses, and leads us to a place of self-empowerment, inspiration, strength, and hope. The topics covered are raw, diverse, and very practical. *Surviving Life* includes many subjects, and answers many questions, such as, "What is your purpose on this planet," "When you think nobody loves you," "How can you feel good," as well as practical advice on battling depression, suicide, and figuring out who you truly are. *Surviving Life* is a practical and contemplative manual for people of all ages, and the perfect book for gifting to those who need guidance and love.

Heal Me is a powerful and touching book that will pull at your heartstrings, give you practical advice on overcoming a variety of life traumas, and will put you on the road to recovery and healing. *Heal*

Me examines such issues as the death of a loved one, loss of a pet, suicide, anxiety, addiction, life failures, major life mistakes, broken relationships, abuse, sexual assault, self-esteem, living in a toxic world surrounded by toxic people, loneliness, and many other issues. This is a self-care book written in a very loving, practical, and informative way that you can gift to yourself, family, young people, and friends, as a gesture of love, support, and hope.

Rising To Greatness is the companion book to *Heal Me*, and is a self-help book that takes you on a step-by-step transformation, from the ashes of being broken and lost, to the greatness of self-empowerment, accomplishment, and happiness. This book includes such topics as developing your sense of self, eliminating fear from your life, mastering your emotions, self-discipline and motivation, communication skills, and so much more.

EVOLVE is a cutting-edge, unique, powerful, and practical personal transformation self-help improvement book, which examines human life and all of its issues from a unique futuristic approach with a touch of humor. A selection of topics include: healing from personal losses and traumas, coping with sadness and depression, moving past fear that others use to control, manipulate, and abuse you, clarity in thinking, advanced communication skills, evolving your relationships, exploring the meaning of life, how everything in the Universe is connected, developing your psychic ability, and a little discussion about aliens possibly living among us. Yes, there is everything, which is all directly tied back to your own personal life.

LIVING A MEANINGFUL LIFE
BOOK SERIES INSTALLMENT SYNOPSIS

This is a series for adults, but has many themes, stories, and lessons, that would be enjoyed by a teen audience as well. Through its down-to-Earth, emotional, and touching storylines, the series shows the importance of developing self-empowerment, and a person's own deep character, through mentors, self-work, and 'soul-families.' The main theme is that of always 'doing the right things,' as a way of living a meaningful life. All installments within this series feature characters of all ages, from children to older adults. The series is neutral on religion and politics. There are tears of sadness, tears of joy, and lots of laughs. This is a series that changes lives.

Book #1, The Bench, is an important book that lays the foundation for the series. This installment provides the background for important mentors and characters featured in the series. This installment covers much of the main character's childhood, and provides important lessons learned, as well as a number of the back-stories referred to later on in the series.

Book #2, The Farm, is the more "juvenile" installment of the series but is a critical book that provides the background on the most important mentor of the series, as well as many of the back-stories for the series. In this installment, the main character is a young teen. This is also a "coming of age" installment, where the main character realizes the meaning of leadership, and the importance of having a mentor.

Book #3, The Lake, is the installment where the main character transforms from a teenage child to a highly dynamic teenage young adult. This installment is a major turning-point in his life. His destiny is decided in this installment, but he doesn't know it yet.

Book #4, The Favor, is the most pivotal installment of the series. Everything changes, and the main character's future is laid out before him. Highly emotional and intense installment. The main character is now a young adult, and a new future star of the series is introduced.

Book #5, The Promise, is the 'relief' installment after the intensity of Book #4. The main character must accept his new life, and live up to his promises and obligations. The new rising star of the series begins to become very prominent.

Book #6, The Sacrifice, reminds us that things can always change in an instant. This installment tests the resolve of the main character, as he must draw upon the lessons taught to him by his mentors, as he faces his greatest challenge yet.

Book #7, The Challenge, is the next most pivotal installment, where the previously rising star of the series solidifies his prominence as THE star of the series. This installment exhibits the power that people can have if they dare to rise up and soar like an Eagle.

Book #8, The Wedding, gives us what we have been wanting and waiting for. But in addition to that, this is the "coming of age" installment for the young star of the series, who all of a sudden, blossoms into a young man with his own independence and ideas, as most older teenagers do. The young star continues to surpass all expectations.

Book #9, The Crew, gives us a closer look at Rudy's huge inner-circle of friends, and their antics. This installment is another high-point in the series, as it chronicles Rudy's growing success, but also a very emotional event which rocks his world. How Rudy handles this "event" will prove him worthy of his destiny. A highly emotional installment.

Books #10 and above: You will have to read them to find out. The journey continues to become even greater and more meaningful. The best is yet to come. The journey will never end.

Printed in Great Britain
by Amazon